# The Dead Woman Writing

# The Dead Woman Writing

Rajat Pillai

Srishti
PUBLISHERS & DISTRIBUTORS

**Srishti Publishers & Distributors**
N-16, C. R. Park
New Delhi 110 019
editorial@srishtipublishers.com

First published by
Srishti Publishers & Distributors in 2014



Printed and bound in India

*Dedicated to*
*the one who worked very hard*
*throughout his life and held*
*his head high, always...*
*My father, Muraleedharan Pillai.*

# Acknowledgements

I would like to start by thanking my wife Priya. She is life's gift for me. Thanks for being with me through all the turbulent ups and downs of our life. Aryan, our little bundle of joy for giving me a purpose in life. My mother Padmaja Pillai for making me whatever I am. From her I inherit my interest in history and crime thrillers. My brother Sumit Pillai for being my able partner to plan and execute the marketing and promotion strategy. My history teachers Ms. Alka Bhatia and Gopalakrishnan sir for being the greatest motivators of my life.

Sucharita Dutta-Asane my editor and literary consultant for giving brilliant suggestions on improving the manuscript. It was a very difficult story to tell and she pitched in with some great inputs. She is the best in her field and it is clearly evident from the way this book has evolved.

Suneetha Balakrishnan, Hardip Singh and Vinay Ullal for their friendship which I value a lot.

Special thanks to Wasim Helal for this brilliant book cover and for being patient through the multiple iterations till it emerged. Also to my photographer Salam Salih to make me look so much better in his photographs. Thanks to my creative designers Snehal Kale Puranik and Arun Anvekar for all the brilliant designs they have created for the promotion art.

Srishti Publishers and the entire team for their faith in the book and its potential.

# Author Notes

Writings in various domains have influenced me during the writing of this book. Especially, Plato and Dostoyevsky for their insights on life. Aleister Crowley and Anton LaVey for their alternate point of view on faith and their writings in those domains which have been an influence for segments in this book. Thomas Harris, Frederick Forsyth and Dan Brown for their endeavour to take the thriller genre to another tangent.

I have great respect for all the famous personalities, artists, writers, mathematicians, celebrities and scientists mentioned in the book. I am only suggesting that they probably believed in the existence of supernatural powers from evidence available in the public domain. No aspect other than this is either expressed or implied.

The details of many criminal cases, suspect names, terror attacks and judgement details mentioned in the book are true and can be verified from publically available information sources like books, magazine articles and internet.

All institutions mentioned in the book are also shown to be ideologically against the dark ideas of the Sarvanpur cult mentioned in the book. I have nothing against occult believers or worshipper of dark forces; the story is about only this particular cult and how its activities went out-of-control under manipulation. This book does not intend or suggest to pass any unfavourable judgment on occult believers and atheists. These are personal views, beliefs and opinions of the fictional characters in the book.

Also, I have great respect for all religions of the world and was careful to portray them in their full glory in this book. The intention of this book is not to portray any individual, group, profession, institution, personal choices or faith in bad light. It is just an honest creation for readers to introspect on the human condition and the state of the world.

*"Come hither; I will shew unto thee the judgment of the great whore that sitteth upon many waters: With whom the kings of the earth have committed fornication, and the inhabitants of the earth have been made drunk with the wine of her fornication. So he carried me away in the spirit into the wilderness: and I saw a woman sit upon a scarlet coloured beast, full of names of blasphemy, having seven heads and ten horns. ...And I saw the woman drunken with the blood of the saints, and with the blood of the martyrs of Jesus: and when I saw her, I wondered with great admiration. And the angel said unto me, Wherefore didst thou marvel? I will tell thee the mystery of the woman, and of the beast that carrieth her."*

*—Book of Revelation (Apocalypse) 17: 1 - 7*
*New Testament, The Holy Bible*

# Part - I

# Devika Decides to Write

# March:
# The Talk of the Town

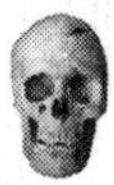

They sat on comfortable cane chairs with colourful cushions. There was a light-weight cane table between them. On the lawn, patches of green grass gave way in places to dry grass or bare brown mud. During the Raj, the administrative departments were clubbed together and called the Imperial Civil Service; with the coming of the MNCs and the software boom, civil services had lost some of its novelty among the urban population, but in the small towns and villages, it still carried an 'imperial' aura.

Shravan and Alpesh had to return to work soon but they did not compromise on these pleasant evenings spent in tranquil settings over tea and the newspaper, except when there were senior level meetings, ministers' visits or a pressing law and order situation. The two friends were engrossed in the *Dusk Star*, an evening newspaper that had flashed a news article on Sarvanpur's recurrent nightmare.

**Sarvanpur Cult Serial Murders:**
**Trial starts next week**

Sarvanpur: Today the case of the Sarvanpur cult serial murders moved a step forward with Magistrate Yashwardhan Shastri taking cognisance of the chargesheet. He stated that a case of various offences including murder and abduction are made out against the accused and co-accused. Magistrate Shastri issued warrants for production of the main accused on Monday. Meanwhile, student unions are conducting rallies and protests against the alleged excesses carried out by the police department in college campuses and hostels around town to track down suspected cult members. The students allege that this 'witch-hunt' is largely based on flimsy evidence…

"Sounds very unlikely, but there are rumours that some really influential people have links with this cult," said Shravan as Alpesh bent forward to keep the paper on the cane table.

Sipping his tea Alpesh said, "I am very surprised that educated, middle class and middle aged citizens of our sleepy town, known until now only for its medical colleges, were party to such a notorious institution."

Sarvanpur, with its three big medical colleges, one engineering college, an arts college and four major hospitals, was increasingly referred to as an educational hub, but of late, it had gained notoriety for a whole new reason – a dark one.

"*Educated* and *civilised* are terms we use for certain groups of people whom society wants to label as 'safer than the rest'. You manage the prisons in this region and I look after its law and order. We know how many educated and civilised people enter our lockups every other day," said Shravan as he took a bite of the multigrain biscuit.

The two friends inhaled the fresh air around them. The best thing about Sarvanpur was its refreshing air. Even in the evening, it had an almost therapeutic effect.

"I sometimes wonder as to what forces rational people to transform like this," Alpesh said.

"It's probably the same thing that turns some people into terrorists or religious fanatics. Nothing works like rigorous brainwashing by well trained minds," replied Shravan.

"*Nahin yaar*. Recruits in terror camps are mostly imbecile or impressionable young people. I am talking here about middle-aged, supposedly normal people losing their mind." Alpesh leaned forward again, his gaze intent on his friend.

"Alpesh Ji, there are four religious channels on cable TV, ever seen the followers of these 'godmen'? To me they appear like obsessed maniacs who have lost touch with reality. Are they normal people? What age group are they?"

A rat scurried across the lawn. "Remember the nerve gas attack inside the Tokyo subways in 1995? Who were behind that madness? Scientists and engineers – educated and civilised people. In western countries there are more examples of such people."

"*Correct*. I remember reading about a case of 1977 or 1979 when some college students from Pune went around on a serial killing rampage targeting old, retired couples. They were assumed to be harmless youngsters until then," added Alpesh.

As had been their routine in the past year, after tea the two friends stood up to walk around the lawn for a leisurely stroll before returning to work. Alpesh looked around him at the impressive lifestyle Shravan and his wife Devika were leading in their newly renovated villa.

"I like the shade of paint on the building. The place looks more vibrant. Seems like the government is taking good care of its ACP, Shravan Soni and family." He chuckled, then continued as an afterthought, "I envy you my friend, I really do."

"It would have been better for your career had you not tried to play super cop so frequently," commented Shravan.

"If I find vehicles plying on the wrong side of a one-way road, or being parked in the 'No Parking' zone, I will ensure that justice prevails and the vehicles are towed away. I don't care if it is the home minister's convoy. I don't care if they transfer me to manage some godforsaken set of jail as DIG-Prisons. I will ensure that the rule of law is respected by all," Alpesh retorted, his right hand clenched into a tight fist.

Shravan's response was a cold comment. "Alpesh Ji, every action will have a reaction."

"Sure, that is life. I am willing to live with that," said Alpesh.

Shravan's wife Devika could hear the two friends from her desk in their lawn-facing bedroom. Sitting in the dim light of her writing desk's table lamp, she wondered when her husband would mention her request.

She did not have to wait long.

Shravan took out a piece of paper from his pocket and handed it to Alpesh. "What is the process for Devika to meet the jail inmates on this list?"

"*Wah!* I am surprised you had to ask me for this. You are the Assistant Commissioner of Police of this town, my friend. Why does the all-powerful Shravan Soni need my help for something as trivial as this?"

"Devika and I steer clear of each other on the work front. She does not like getting any over-the-top special treatment by using my name or influence." Shravan looked at the lamps around the villa illuminating the lawn. "Minor help is fine but no out-of-the-way preferential treatment. Devika wants to know the procedure followed here by people if they want to meet these jail inmates."

"I can help her with that. The critical factor is that these inmates should agree to meet her. One more thing, if you don't mind my asking about it..."

Such hesitation was very unlike Alpesh, but the topic was sensitive and he was cautious.

"No! Go ahead Alpesh Ji."

"Well, we are all aware she's been in a state of emotional breakdown since her mother's death. You also told me some months back that she was detected with some, err, disorder."

"Yes, I remember."

"Shravan, are you sure you want her to venture into such work in her present state of mind?"

"She has recovered from that, Alpesh. She'll manage, I'm sure of that." Shravan replied.

Alpesh cleared his throat. "These types of ailments can be subdued but they don't vanish. If I were you, in the same situation, I would think ten times before encouraging her to pursue something like this." He looked at the setting sun and continued, "I have heard that some of the people on that list of yours made a joke out of some mentally tough officers of the department during their interrogation. Do you think it is prudent at this time to expose her to such demented minds?"

Shravan replied after an unusually long pause and a sigh, "What can I do? I have tried but she is stubborn. This is her passion; she is not willing to give up on that, no matter what anybody says."

"It's tricky, assuming that it is a psychiatric condition."

"No, not a psychiatric condition. She just has a complex hormonal condition found in some women that causes, among other things, depression and mood swings."

"You make it sound trivial, my friend."

Devika, overhearing the conversation from the bedroom window, smiled at how her husband dealt with the situation. *Shravan has a knack for saying a lot yet revealing little.* He was indeed making her disorder sound very trivial. She wished it was as trivial.

# March: Demons Inside her Mind

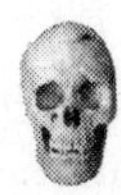

Acute Premenstrual Dysphoric Disorder (PMDD). The gynaecologist sitting across the table could finally give a name to Devika's condition.

The first symptoms surfaced during her college days and intensified as she approached her thirties. The disorder, observed in five to nine percent of women between 20 and 40 years of age commonly occurs in women like Devika who suffer from hypothyroidism, but in most cases it is in a mild form. PMDD is a fancy name for a disruptive condition—waking up on most mornings wanting to drown oneself; of laughing hysterically for an hour and then pulling one's hair in anger for the next; of spending sleepless nights, feeling miserable, crying without a pause; to be in a state of constant self-persecution, listing all the things that were wrong in one's life. During festivals, when other houses would happily celebrate Christmas, Diwali or Holi, year after year, Shravan and Devika's house would witness nervous breakdowns and depression. Shravan was confused, not knowing what triggered her violent mood swings, whether it was the anxiety of hosting dinners or missing her father during the festival season, or just plain panic caused by the din of celebration.

In her recurrent bouts of depression Devika would break mobile phones, china plates, crockery; slap herself obsessively, shout, scream, cry hysterically...incidents that rattled the household. They visited various doctors, most of whom were baffled by her condition.

And then, after years of tumult, unhappiness and desperation, they found the gynaecologist who finally figured out the core problem.

Sitting at her writing table and overhearing the conversation between Alpesh and Shravan, Devika tried to shrug off the memories of the past. She had her laptop, an old IBM which had been with her through the years. To her left was a book shelf which had more than 40 books on Criminal Psychology and some books on Criminal Investigation. There were also books on feminist leaders and activists like Mary Wollstonecraft, Emmeline Pankhurst and Wangaari Maathai. On the wall in front of her desk was her display board where she had pinned her favourite photographs and quotations. Devika's repository of her most private thoughts and memories. Some of them read,

*'We are all perishable items, live your life accordingly'*. Right next to it printed in bright blue was a quote, *'When God pushes you to the edge of difficulty, trust him fully because two things will happen. Either he will catch you when you fall or he will teach you how to fly'*. Another hand-painted one read, *'Keep you head up. God gives his hardest battles to his strongest soldiers'*.

The most prominent words on the board were from a quotation from an unknown source painted in fabric colours by her neighbour and close friend Jyoti. *'Success is like getting pregnant. Everybody congratulates you but nobody knows how many times you were screwed before you got there.'*

Right next to it was a laminated photograph of Devika and her friends on their last day of college at Delhi College of Arts and Commerce. The young faces in the photograph including Devika's were brimming with energy and enthusiasm. They held a placard, "One day we will light up the world!"

Devika smiled at her past image – smiling, confident, and carefree. Life had seemed full of possibilities. Infinite possibilities that were snatched away with the passage of time. The irony in life is that youth comes right in the middle, while the before and after are largely dull. She was still in touch with some of the other smiling faces in the photograph; they were busy with their jobs during the week and on weekends managed the tantrums of their spouses and kids. None of them 'illuminating the world'.

After college she joined NDTV as an apprentice. The media house offered a decent stipend and was slated to give her a confirmation after six months, depending on her competency. Devika was an assistant on their bi-weekly show on trends in the retail sector. At the same time she contributed regular articles to *Reader's Digest* and *Femina*. It was smooth sailing except for the occasional moodiness, but her superiors were used to her occasional unpredictability which was compensated by her remarkable creativity on the work front. Six months later, just as she was about to enter the big wild world of media, her parents compelled her to get married. Trusting her parent's choice, she took the plunge though half-heartedly. After marriage her life took a turn she had not expected. She travelled with her husband through the interiors of the country without a proper day job and no way to get one.

After all these years, she still felt overwhelmed by the way her life had metamorphosed. *Where is the real Devika? What is her purpose in life? Did she give herself up to make others around her happy? Was she playing it safe by deceiving herself? Life's reality and her inconsequential existence, was she taking it too seriously?*

Lost in thoughts, she forgot that it was time for her evening prayers. Shravan left for office again and it was eleven by the time he returned that night. At the dinner table their cook Radhemohan served cauliflower stuffed paranthas, potato stew and tamarind chutney. Even though the food was very tasty, Shravan ate absentmindedly. Devika waited patiently. She knew he was trying to organise his thoughts.

"I was wondering if this writing assignment is the right thing to do at this time, I mean, considering the present situation. I am not against the writing bit, but is this the right time for the research?"

"The opportune moment when everything is going to be perfect in our life will never come. Once we want to do something, we need to make a start at some point of time or the other," said Devika.

"Devika, to keep yourself occupied you can look into some other kind of work. You understand what I am saying? That will be a slow and steady beginning."

"There is nothing in this town or 20 kilometres in all directions. No media houses. No advertising firms. Nothing. Only hospitals and medical colleges."

"I understand, but I am sure we can figure out something, my dear."

"Figure out what? It has been the same since our marriage, this nomadic existence... first you were transferred to Beawar in Ajmer district where there were no opportunities that suited my skill set."

"Devika, I am in the police service. Transfers are a way of life for us!"

"Then we were outside Pune in some place where they have automobile manufacturing units. The only important landmark around our house was a river. No media houses. No advertising firms. No newspaper offices. Nothing. Only the river!" Devika's nervous energy gained momentum. Her left finger nails dug into the surface of the table.

"I am not coming in the way of your work, Devika, please understand that. Just felt that you are not mentally in a state to handle this kind of work. Only now, after a year of medication, we can safely say that you are more in control of yourself than you ever were."

Devika dropped her spoon on the table and reclined against the chair back. "Please Shravan! This boredom is killing me from within. I want to do something thrilling. This work excites me and I want to give it a try again."

This was going nowhere. Shravan kept quiet.

"Alright! Do what you want. If you ask me, I believe that the time has come for us to start a family. It's been five years since we got married...."

Devika's face was red. "It's not you, but your parents who believe we should start a family. They decide everything that takes place inside our house. We have been on this for quite some time now. It is not happening, Shravan! What am I expected to do? Sit for years doing nothing, praying that we are blessed with a child?"

Shravan drank a glass of water and said, "I think you know this is not what I meant."

"Since childhood we girls are taught by our own mothers that sacrifice and adjustment for the family are important virtues for a woman. I think that expectation is biased. Why don't men have such unspoken rules governing them?"

"Let me make this clear, I have nothing against you working. You don't need to sacrifice or adjust to anything. It's the nature of the work that worries me. An assignment like this requires a peaceful mind, not an already agitated one."

"I am sorry but this is it. Nothing else interests me, Shravan. I can't garner so much passion for anything else." Devika spoke with a sense of finality.

"I am saying this out of concern for you. Don't counter my love with rage. You will regret it once you don't have this love," he said.

"You don't understand me, Shravan. Nobody understands me." She pushed back the chair and left the dining room.

There was no further conversation that night. In bed, they turned their backs to each other and went to sleep. They would patch up the next day, they both knew. There were never two nights in a row when they slept with their backs to each other.

Next morning when Devika woke up, Shravan had already left for work. She rushed to the lawn outside her house where the newspaper man had placed the newspaper on top of the letter box. It was the day of her fortnightly column in the *Konkan Times*, a limited circulation English newspaper for the Konkan belt.

After shifting to Sarvanpur, Devika started visiting the newspaper office regularly for four months, trying her luck to get a job with the paper. *Konkan Times* was on a cost cutting mode and were not able to give her a day job matching her profile; the other newspaper with good circulation, Dusk Star, was published from Arvinwadi, twenty-five kilometres away. Her perseverance finally paid off, as did her previous experience with *Reader's Digest* and *Femina*. Devika got a fortnightly column with the *Konkan Times*:

LIFE AND TIMES IN OUR TOWN

*by Devika Soni*

What clinched the deal for her though, was the strong critique she presented in front of the chief editor of the existing editorial columns in the newspaper.

Her column today was titled

**'Time to Uncover the Real Truth'**

*The national media is pouncing on our small town and making headlines out of each gruesome detail of the infamous cult that operated from here. While everybody else seems overly interested in the graphic details of the cult's nefarious activities, there are some of us who want to look at these events from a different angle. How did this happen at Sarvanpur out of all the places in this country? What makes our town so vulnerable? The more I tried to find a rationale the more it eluded me. After pondering on it for days I could think of three big reasons, and there could be more – isolated existence, overly liberal multicultural background of people who dwell here, and abundance of impressionable minds. So here we had a group of people who knew each other very well because there is a very limited social scene in our town and people had nothing else exciting to do. Then they experimented with various things, got bored and became still more adventurous. The more naive ones followed the mature ones assuming that they would know what is good and they would know where to stop. They never stopped. They probably never realised how dangerous they had become for themselves and others too. The official version of the story is a simplistic one: 8-10 crazy people who got together and went on a serial killing rampage. The truth is deeper than that. The number of people involved is definitely higher. The social stature of these members if unmasked will be alarming. The cult had a bigger purpose than what we assume. They had an almost perfect strategy and were more organised than we would like to think. However, our entire legal machinery seems to be in a coordinated effort to sweep all the dirt under the carpet. I think we need to dwell on it a little longer to ensure it does not happen again. This is not a chain of events we should leave unanalysed. I think this whole set of events is inspiring me and will probably end up becoming a book one day. The whole and complete truth should be out there is what I believe in. This story as of now is incomplete.*

As always she cut the article from the newspaper column to paste it into her 'Archive Album'. She read the article again and her initial enthusiasm died out as usual. *It could have been better and more interestingly articulated*, she thought as she put the album back into the cupboard.

She oiled her hair and sat in the sun for some time. It was Tuesday. The 'whip family' called *Kadaklakshmi* in Konkan walked across the street – a weekly ritual – in search of money. The wife had a toddler strapped to her dress and was beating a small drum with a stick while her husband, clad in a bright red robe, whipped himself repeatedly. It was a self-flagellation ritual, all for some money. For Devika it looked like a manifestation of her dark past, when her self-whipping mind went out of control and marched out into the open to make an amusing spectacle for others. Nobody, not even your closest relatives see your pain and inner turmoil. You become a laughing stock. Just then she felt a slight touch against her body. It was the neighbourhood cat Zeenu, rubbing itself affectionately against her. Devika ran her fingers over its grey furry body. The cat purred affectionately. It was hungry and Devika realised that she was hungry too.

After a quick bath she had breakfast, and saw the postman enter the garden and drop the mail into the letter box. Devika knew what to expect. She made a quarterly contribution to the 'Women's Welfare Syndicate, Chennai', to 'Help Age India' and 'CRY'. The postman would have brought in her receipt from the Chennai NGO. She made the donations in Shravan's name. Devika was also actively involved in the local chapter of 'India Against Corruption'. She attended their fortnightly meetings in the hall adjacent to the Public Library and had become good friends with prominent journalists, lawyers, doctors and other intellectuals of the town.

She kept herself occupied with different activities as she waited for the subject matter for her second book. Now that it had revealed itself, it was time to plunge into research and begin writing.

"Madam Ji, this is my daughter Laali." Devika was disturbed from her thoughts by Radhemohan's voice as he introduced his adolescent daughter carrying a ragged shoulder bag with her clothes and belongings.

"Oh! So this is your beloved daughter," said Devika as she smiled and greeted the girl. The girl Laali just stared at Devika with just a faint smile on her face. Clad in an old brown coloured *salwar kameez*, her cat like eyes with a dazed look were kind of unsettling. Her built and nose-ring made her look older than her age which was around 16. She had a dusky complexion and neatly plaited jet black hair.

"My mother had looked after her since infancy after my wife died during childbirth. Now my mother is too old, so I decided that it was time Laali left our village in Satara and came here. She will be staying in the servant's quarter with me. If that is not a problem with you," said Radhemohan with a smile on his face.

"No! Not at all. You had mentioned this before and we both are fine with that. You father and daughter enjoy your time here. So Laali, will you continue your studies here?" said Devika.

"No! I don't like to study," she replied after a bit of hesitation.

"Radhemohan had mentioned that you are only sixteen years old. What else do you plan to do? Education is important, isn't it?" interrupted Devika.

"Not for everyone," replied Laali momentarily looking away from Devika's face.

As they both walked towards the servant's quarter, Laali momentarily glanced behind and looked at Devika. For some reason Devika found the gaze to be uncomfortable. Devika could not help but wonder why Laali came across as a detached and disinterested girl. Maybe it was just today. Probably it was her nature because her parents were not around when she was growing up. However, there was something strange about the girl. Something that was not normal.

The doorbell rang. She could hear Radhemohan at the door, talking to someone.

"Who is it?" She shouted out from the drawing room.

"Madam, courier! There is an envelope for you."

Woodpecker Publishers had sent her royalty cheque; a paltry sum of 2200 rupees. Writing had turned out to be a futile endeavour.

Devika's debut book was a work of non-fiction about a woman inmate of Tihar Jail who was on death row on charges of murdering her parents, siblings and their spouses over a property dispute. It's not every day that a woman is charged with the cold blooded murder of eight people of her own family. Devika did extensive research for over a year and unearthed all relevant aspects of the case including the conspiracy theories surrounding the case since the father of the accused was a known businessman with many rivals. She went to the jail to meet the rather aggressive woman and her husband, a co-accused in the case.

Satisfied with her own work and its potential, she sent the synopsis and sample chapter to the top ten publishers, nine of whom rejected her as she was a first time writer with no market value or potential. Woodpecker Publishers, an upcoming publishing house, took up the challenge and agreed to publish her book, '*What happened at the Farm House on Dusshera Night*'. The editor, commissioned by the publishing house, was a young inexperienced apprentice who had just passed out of college the previous year. The publishing house was trying to cut costs in an industry where the margins were already wafer thin.

Devika corresponded with the editor over phone and mail without having the slightest idea that the person at the other end was ill-equipped to handle this kind of a manuscript. While the book was being 'edited', the popular magazine *India Today* published a cover story on women inmates across the country awaiting Presidential pardon. The woman from Tihar who was the protagonist of Devika's book was featured prominently in this article, leading to immense public interest in the case.

Wanting to capitalise on this opportunity, Woodpecker Publishers immediately listed the book for pre-order on various e-commerce websites and received 1400 orders within the first five days, something unheard of for a first time writer in India. The company was under tremendous pressure from the e-commerce websites to print the book as soon as possible. When her editor called in, Devika was down with flu and migraine. The final draft of the book had been emailed to her and she had forty-eight hours to suggest any changes.

Devika managed to browse through the first few chapters and suggest the necessary changes; the proofreading happened in a flash and the draft was sent for print in one big hurry. Devika personally visited bookshops and college libraries in and around Sarvanpur to present the complementary copies as part of the promotions. *The Konkan Times* carried a big article along with a photograph on the launch event of the book at the Public Library hall. The final product however was utterly flawed. The book was full of grammatical mistakes along with over-the-top sensationalism and erroneous misinterpretation of certain aspects of the case. There was wide criticism of Devika's work across the internet. After the initial upswing, the sales of the book nosedived. Though Devika partially blamed herself for the debacle, it was evident that the publishing house had not done its job. In the hurry to make a quick buck its team had made careless moves. Cost cutting and the tearing hurry at the publishers' end came at a huge personal cost to Devika. Honest work had failed once again and she was left holding the consequences of someone else's mistake.

Devika opened the drawer of her desk and took out a copy of the book she had sent to her father, Rameshwar Soni, Professor of English at Deshbandhu College, Delhi. Like a doting father he had asked all his friends, acquaintances and students to buy his daughter's debut book; he had enthusiastically bought a copy from the nearest book store on the day of its release. Disheartened, he had marked in red the problematic areas in the first few chapters and sent it in a parcel to Devika with a note:

"I am glad you dedicated this book to me. I would have been happier if you had set some high standards with your first work.

There is much to be desired on the quality front. Hope you learn from this and do well next time."

Devika had made a laughing stock out of her father in his college. He had to face students and teachers who would giggle behind his back; if he couldn't teach his daughter how to write well, what would he teach his students?

Devika crumpled the cheque; her reward for the two years of hard work she had put in for the book. She sat back in her chair and stared out of the window. Her relatives and friends used to comment on the fairytale life she led – 'nice husband in a secure job, nice house, servants to help so that she didn't need to lift a finger – what else could she want in life?' What they could never understand was that everyone has to go through their share of trash in life. The ones who appear to be lucky are just good at concealing their problems. These people could not imagine all the commotion in her life and inside her head that she had to deal with on a day-to-day basis. In some people the tendency for happiness or grief has nothing to do with their surroundings or their life's situation. It is governed by only one thing, their mind. The poison was deep inside. Its release had no sense of timing, reason or warning. Today her mind had again started to whip itself.

*Wasted two years of my life after this futile nonsense. I am such a loser.* Her head was like a noisy metal dye-casting workshop, unbearably suffocating and unendingly noisy.

She walked to the table on the other side of the bed where the medical box was placed and took a strip of Serta capsules from it. The gynaecologist's words echoed in her head. "It has many side-effects. I am prescribing it but please don't have it until and unless you feel really low." The pill was harmful for her, she knew. In some countries the drug was issued with a warning due to the suicidal tendencies it created among users, especially among the under-25 group.

*This is not good for me. I should control my own mind.*

She returned to her desk. With the pill in one hand and the glass of water in the other hand, she sat motionless, trying to make up her mind. The medicine made her feel like a vegetable, without thoughts and without any emotions, but it was better than living with a jangle of noises inside her head.

The phone rang. She could hear Radhemohan from the other room. "Madam, your mother-in-law and father-in-law from Kolkata!"

*I know what they are calling me for*, she thought. Same old conversation. Same old topic. Beating around the bush till the important point is reached. 'When are we going to hear the good news? When will we have the first baby in our family?' The dreaded question to which Devika did not have an answer. She looked at the quotation in front of her.

"*Success* is like getting *pregnant*. Everybody congratulates you but nobody knows how many times you were *screwed* before you got there."

Her hands started to tremble, her palms were sweaty. The three prominent words from this quotation floated randomly in front of her eyes even though she was trying hard to avoid being sucked down the whirlpool.

Success - Devika wasn't sure why she wanted it but it was something to do with her sense of self worth.
Pregnant - The one big unresolved reason for tension in her house especially with Shravan's parents who thought that she was deliberately delaying it for the sake of her career. She was supposed to exist only to procreate.
Screwed - Her life seemed screwed up, more or less.

The three words were now ramming themselves against her head. Devika gulped down the pill. She tried to avoid it, but sometimes, this tablet was her only way to face the world.

# April:
# The First Letter

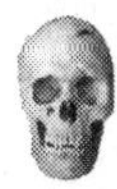

Shravan stood under the shower, his second in the day. Unlike the morning shower taken in a hurry, he enjoyed the after-work evening shower. He had come back from work earlier than usual; the evening was to be dedicated to friends and whiskey but would Devika attend the party? There was every possibility of her declining. It was the wrong time of the month; he could see it in her eyes when he walked into the house. Shravan knew that for the next three to four days he would have to be careful. A wrong sentence or even a word could send his wife into a vortex of chaos and desperation. In the initial years of his marriage, the drastic mood swings baffled him. In the beginning, before she was diagnosed, he would worry about returning home from work and would find excuses to be away and not face his domestic reality. However, the thyroxin tablets had a positive effect on Devika and life seemed to improve.

Wiping himself with his towel after the shower he wondered what awaited him on the other side of the bathroom door. When he stepped out with his towel wrapped around his waist, he saw Devika seated on the bed.

"Yes, Papa, what was the sugar reading today?"

Her father was a diabetic and had recently been losing too much weight.

"Did the doctor increase the insulin dosage?" Devika asked as she smiled at Shravan. Shravan was relieved. The phone conversation with her father had diverted her mind for the time being. He just hoped that she remained cheerful throughout the evening.

Shravan wore his kurta-pyjama while Devika ended her call. "Okay, bye Papa, take care."

She looked at her husband. "What's the hurry, Shravan sir? Booze and friends too tempting, I see. Can I wear my sari at least?"

"Today no limits, full relaxation. Bring on the booze, I am ready." Shravan replied with a smile.

"What can I say? In wine there is wisdom, in beer there is freedom, in water there is bacteria," Devika quoted Benjamin Franklin.

Devika wore her green silk sari and picked up the birthday gift, a mini football wrapped in gift paper, and another box which contained a dress. The couple crossed the road to the house adjacent to their villa. It belonged to Shravan's junior Anshuman, an inspector with the police department. Anshuman's wife Jyoti was one of Devika's few close friends in Sarvanpur. Her only other close friends were Asha Sagade, a college friend, and Revathy Pai, an advocate she knew from her IAC sessions.

"I forgot my mobile phone at home," Devika said as Shravan opened the gate.

"Tell me something new. You do that every other day. Now please don't go back to get it."

"Good evening, Sir! Welcome Madam!"

Anshuman was at the door looking elegant and handsome with his jet black straight hair combed backwards and a well-trimmed moustache. They had a modest two bedroom house. Today, it was decorated with balloons and ribbons and swarming with kids who had come to attend his son's third birthday celebrations.

After the boy cut the birthday cake, they settled down in their separate zones. Devika, Jyoti and Monica, Alpesh's wife, sat at the dining table near the kitchen, arranging the plates. The children continued to play in the hall. Shravan, Alpesh and Anshuman withdrew to the guest bedroom for their part of the celebration.

"Cheers ! The kids and women are away. There is whisky and ice in the glass. I hand over the proceedings to our dear Alpesh as usual," said Shravan, opting for Antiquity whisky on the rocks while Anshuman had it with soda.

Alpesh took up his whisky. "Here is a good one, a little long, but I couldn't resist the temptation."

"We don't mind either, go on, it's time for the first joke," said Shravan as he settled down on the bed, relaxed, ready for the evening.

"Young Julie was a naughty, sexy girl. She got married and had eight children. Then her husband died. Then Julie married for the second time. This time she had seven children. Her second husband also died. Julie married for the third time. This time she had nine children. Her third husband died."

"Alpesh sir, did the husband die of exhaustion?" Anshuman asked.

"Officer, mouth shut please! Let me complete. Then sexy Julie died. At her memorial service in the town hall, the priest said, 'Thank God ! Finally they are together.' Julie's brother asked, 'Who are together? Julie and her first husband or Julie and her second husband or Julie and her third husband?' The priest replied, 'I was talking about Julie's legs!'"

The three men burst into laughter.

"Good one Alpesh Ji! And this is the angelic man who is going to pioneer prison reforms in this region," said Shravan, laughing.

"Shravan sir, Alpesh sir, would you like to have the cake, gulab jamun and wafers now?" Anshuman asked.

"Cake. The rest of the stuff is for kids. By the way, Devika wanted to talk to you about the two things she wanted your help on," said Shravan.

"Yes sir. You mentioned it earlier; I will talk to her right away," Anshuman left the room with his glass of whisky. As he entered the dining area near the kitchen where the ladies were seated, he could hear Monica, nine years younger than her husband Alpesh, whining as usual. "Alpesh is on the path to becoming a legendary couch potato. It is worse now, either he's in office or on the sofa watching television or taking a nap. I wonder if these men realise that we sit all day at home waiting for the evening to have a decent conversation at least."

Anshuman was curious. He slowed down his pace; he wanted to overhear the whole conversation.

"There is a slight mismatch in your personalities. I think every couple faces that," remarked Devika.

Jyoti said, "Marital incompatibility is a tricky business. Either you get lucky in the first year itself when you have the regular fights and then you can do something about it, or else you get unlucky and take five, ten, fifteen, even twenty years to figure it out, by when you decide not to do anything about it."

"I am starting work on my second book," said Devika trying to underplay the excitement in her tone.

"Really! So finally you've got your subject matter!" Monica exclaimed and then suddenly paused at the sight of Anshuman appearing at the entrance.

"Devika madam, Shravan sir said you wanted to talk to me about something."

"Yes Anshuman. The two places I wanted to visit, Mehek's house and the farm house. Any luck there?"

"I can help you with that. We will be opening Mehek's house next week, Tuesday, specifically, to collect fresh evidence. Also, I will be going to the farm house on the 4th of May. Would you like to come along?"

Devika smiled happily. "That's so nice of you, Anshuman. By the way, now that your son is three years old and ready to go to play school, when is Jyoti planning to join work again?"

Jyoti was an air-hostess before her marriage.

"I think I have to look for jobs at a hotel or a nearby resort. There is no scope for an air-hostess in a town where the nearest airport is a hundred kilometres away," Jyoti said.

Anshuman smiled and added, "You won't believe that every now and then her past job still disturbs my sleep."

"What are you saying?" asked Devika.

"She turns into an air hostess in her sleep, instructing and serving passengers," said Anshuman.

"Please, he's kidding." Jyoti looked embarrassed.

"A week back, in the dead of night, when I was fast asleep, she scared me to death by announcing in her sleep, '*Dear Passengers we have started our descent towards Mumbai Chhatrapati Shivaji International Airport. You are requested to keep your seats in upright position, fasten your seat belts, your tray table closed and your window shades open....*"

Jyoti's mouth opened wide while Monica and Devika had a tough time trying to stop laughing.

Next morning, after Shravan left for work, Devika put some milk in a bowl for Zeenu the cat. At a distance she could see Radhemohan's daughter Laali sitting in the lawn staring into emptiness twirling a blade of grass around her fingers. This girl was very strange. Since the time she was here she had barely talked to Devika. Leave alone talking but not even a smile or an acknowledgement. Laali was always busy in her own world and lost in her own thoughts. It was not just that she was an introvert which bothered Devika, this girl was unpleasant and her stare was even more. Devika was about to put fish food into the bowl for the goldfish when she received a call. It was from the Courier Despatch section of the *Konkan Times*.

"Devika madam, there is a letter for you," said the voice on the other end of the line.

"I'll send Radhemohan. You know him, don't you?"

In the afternoon Radhemohan brought the letter along with his usual grocery items. It was a bright red envelope with various stamps – a solitary one rupee stamp, and a cluster of three one rupee stamps. The label was a cut out of a computer printout.

Devika Soni
*Konkan Times*
Sarvanpur- 01

She opened the envelope and found a white sheet of paper inside. It had random words cut from newspapers and magazines glued to the paper. Devika read the words carefully. Her eyebrows curved as she read the message, feeling baffled at what it seemed to convey.

Dear DeViKa,

Hope LIFE is treating YOU well.

Just DO what you were told to do. Use the gift. WHY Chase THINGS You don't understand? Why Uncover TRUTHS You cannot HANDLE?
MEHEK

*Mehek?* Puzzled, Devika turned the paper around. *There was only one famous Mehek in Sarvanpur and she was dead.* The letter was surely not from the person it claimed to be. After multiple rounds of autopsy, her body had been donated to the Sushrut Medical College at Sarvanpur. At the medical college, the body, used as a cadaver, was dissected as part of surgery lessons for the students of medicine and was later disposed and buried in some random burial place. 'The Dead Witch of Sarvanpur,' as she was now increasingly referred to by the people, deserved this kind of death. Everyone prayed for her to rot in hell. *Dead People don't send mails. Also, what has Devika done to make this sender so angry?* She could think of only one explanation. This letter was surely from some imposter trying to get attention. Devika re-read the message. *What gift was she talking about? Why is this sent to me of all the people?* One of the words attracted her attention – UNCOVER.

She opened the drawer of her cupboard and pulled out her 'Archive Album' of newspaper cut-outs of her columns. She frantically turned the pages till she reached the last one. She looked aghast. It looked like the imposter was answering to the title of her previous column in the newspaper- 'Time to uncover the truth?'

Whosoever was trying to communicate was reading her column in the *Konkan Times* for sure. *Why this kind of interest in her? What was the reason behind this communication?* The tone of the sentence was threatening and the reason for the communication unclear. As far as Devika could think of, she had not bothered anybody so much as to receive this kind of a letter. Now that she knew how to reach out to the sender of this letter, Devika thought for a while as to what she wanted to ask. She switched on her laptop and went through a word file, a rough draft of her next column about the Chief Minister of Goa asking the Supreme Court to lift its ban on mining in the state, a counter to the measure taken by the apex court after rampant illegal mining in the region. Devika decided to play along with the imposter and gave a title to her column – 'What is the Objective?'

She emailed the article to the editorial team after two rounds of editing and asked Radhemohan to make coffee while she stood near her bedroom window overlooking the lawn. The boundary wall faced a narrow lane. She was lost in thoughts when Radhemohan walked into the bedroom with her coffee. Just as Devika turned towards him, two loud shots echoed around the villa. The bedroom window's glass pane crashed on to the floor, shattering into fragments all over the bedroom. Devika fell on her knees. Radhemohan ducked sideways and fell along with the pot of coffee and mug.

"My God! What is going on?" Devika shouted as the blood drained from her face.

"Don't worry, Madam, just lie low," said Radhemohan.

Radhemohan got up and tip-toeing carefully over the shards of glass and chinaware on the floor, he went to the window. He could not see anybody. The guards outside the gate rushed to that side of the wall; there was no one. Devika went towards the bedroom wall in front of her and looked at the bullet holes. She touched the dents with trembling hands.

*What the hell is going on around me? First the letter, now the gunshot!* She was paralysed with fear.

Next day all the daily newspapers carried the news of bullets fired into the house of ACP Shravan Soni from a country-made revolver by unknown assailants. The articles stated that extensive interrogation was being carried out with suspects picked up from various places around Sarvanpur.

A week later an anonymous email from a dummy email account came to feedback@konkantimes.com. The editorial team forwarded the message to Devika.

Dear Devika Soni,

Follow the instructions. You have no choice.

Regards,

Friend

The Cyber Crime Cell of the police department traced the IP address from which the email was sent.

When Shravan returned that evening Devika was sorting out the magazines that were to be sold. He had information for her.

"We traced the origin of the email, Devika. It was sent from a flat in Sahyadri Hills residential complex belonging to a father and son."

"Mehek had a flat in the same residential complex," said a puzzled Devika, an eye on the windows.

"We are on the case. It is just a matter of time before we figure out who is behind this," Shravan assured her.

"Shravan, I don't know what this person wants from me."

"We can't figure it out either. This town is infested by some weirdoes. What instruction does the letter give? Why you out of all the people in this town?"

"I am not even related to anything. As usual I get myself into trouble for no contribution of my own," rambled Devika.

"Relax! The interrogation is starting tomorrow. Hopefully, we will have some answers."

"What is this gift the letter mentions? What is the instruction mentioned in the email? I am so lost."

"Relax, Devika, please. Don't make matters worse."

Devika slumped in the sofa, her head against the backrest, panic in her eyes.

"Just drink this glass of water and take a deep breath. Come on!" Shravan managed to calm her down this time.

Next day, the father and son from Sahyadri Hills residential complex were interrogated. The old man was a retired 'signals' officer from the India Army and the son had just completed his MBBS from AFMC, Pune. They were released after questioning. It was evident that someone had hacked into their wireless WiFi router to send the anonymous mail.

That night while Devika and Shravan were sleeping in their bedroom, a gust of cold breeze blew aside the curtains.

*Thud! Thud!*

Devika woke up because of a sound which looked like something was hitting against the bedroom window. She got up and looked at the window anxiously. There was nobody near the window. Devika slumped back onto her pillow.

*Thud! Thud!*

It was the faint sound again. She opened her eyes and still no one at the window. *It's just my imagination*, she thought and tried to close her eyes. This time she heard a clear scraping sound. She opened her eyes and thought she saw a dark shadow just floating past outside the window. Her heart stopped beating and her breath ceased. The faint sound of the scratching on the glass continued. The blood drained from her face as her ears tuned to locate the sound. It suddenly shifted from the window pane to the opposite side. The sound was now coming from the closed bedroom cupboard. Devika eyes darted all around in panic and droplets of sweat appeared on her forehead. Her body shrunk to the corner of the bed against the wall. Her ears followed the scratching which had shifted to the mirror of the dressing table.

"Shravan! Shravan!"

She tried to wake up her husband who was fast asleep. Then the bed shuddered but Shravan did not wake up. The scratching on the dressing table mirror intensified and Devika saw the faint image of a woman standing across the mirror staring down upon her.

Devika screamed loudly,

"*Shravan!*"

This time he jumped up from the bed and put on the table lamp.

"What happened, Devika? What happened?" he asked in panic.

"Nothing. Err, nothing!" Devika said as she got up and drank a glass of water.

"Did you have a nightmare, dear?"

Devika was in a confused state of mind. She was not sure if this was real or a figment of her imagination. The last thing she wanted was to discuss it with Shravan and reinforce his scepticism about Devika not being in a proper state of mind to handle the assignment.

"It's nothing!" she said. Devika got up from the bed, walked towards the window to bolt it and something caught her eye. Laali was walking in the lawn in the moonlight. At close to midnight it was strange that she was sitting alone in the lawn. She had a twig in her hand and to Devika it appeared as if she was marking something on the ground.

# April:
# The Dead Woman's House

The diary was recovered from Mehek's house after her death. It was a crucial piece of evidence for the police since it helped them track down the other members of the cult. Devika managed to get a photocopied version of the diary from Inspector Anshuman. The last page had the names of fellow cult members, addresses, numbers and written notes on them. The notes read like a character analyses of each member including their strengths, weaknesses, skills and their future utility. It was as if a teacher had evaluated the students in her class and given all of them rather poor grades. The evaluation about the members was mostly cynical and occasionally offensive. Two members in the list were crossed out for obvious reasons. One thing was clear; Mehek deserved credit for having brainwashed these educated people and to make them do unimaginable things. This capability put her in the same league as other famous cult leaders from around the world. There are few leaders in the history of this world who could coax their followers into mass-murder and mass-suicide for reasons other than religion, rebellion or patriotism. From this point of view, Mehek was in the league of cult leaders like Charles Manson, Adolfo Constanzo and Shoko Asahara. Her life had been short but nothing short of remarkable from that point of view. In the first few pages of her diary were random notes and thoughts. One of them read:

*I draw inspiration from the thousands of women who faced injustice and wrong throughout their lives and were not given their due respect even after death. I am not going to be a victim of the system. I see myself fighting against tyrant systems of unjust institutions.*

The more Devika read the diary, the more she was convinced that she had come across a mind different from that of normal people. It belonged to another world; part brilliant, part naive and largely evil. For Devika, the journey into Mehek's mind was fascinating, its novelty awe-inspiring. Had Mehek been captured alive, psychiatrists would have had a field-day trying to understand the functioning of her twisted mind. Mehek was indeed a special creation of nature.

Devika flipped the pages and glanced upon one particular paragraph which had multiple corrections, as if it were a rough draft of a portion of a letter or message that Mehek had been carefully drafting.

*The end of our world as we know it is here. Our planet and its natural resources – air, water and land, are overburdened by the billions of people thrust into it. These people have no respect for the air they breathe, the water they drink and the land where they dwell. They are in a mad chase running behind an elusive over-rated state they call 'progress'. Unlike the pagan world, nature is disrespected and disrobed in the world today. All these billions of resource hogging parasites of our planet deserve to die. For that, we need to trigger anarchy. The world needs a RESET, a fresh start. After Doomsday is over, we will have a new world. The future belongs to those who will respect nature, follow their own rules and make the earth a beautiful place. Before the end of this year, we will show you a small demonstration of the infinite possibilities which can be implemented if we use our mind. Infinite possibilities! If we work together and channelise our resources. Religions of the world will automatically help us get to our objective.*

It worried Devika; it was one of the last entries and mentioned an attack. However, the police claimed that all the cult members had been arrested and any attacks they would have planned for the end of year had been foiled. Devika flipped the pages again. There were other random thoughts which she might have read from somewhere and noted down.

*Men are like wine. It takes time for them to find their own self. Once they are there, they become interesting and attractive.*

*The propagation of light is low and its retention temporary. Dark propagates itself faster because it is forbidden, tempting and intriguing. Its retention is also more permanent. Darkness is the default state of the universe. Light can claim to be the fastest, but it will remain a glorified second behind darkness which is omnipresent.*

There were other random thoughts, including one written with a sketch pen:

*Government, religious institutions and the general public have historically persecuted forward thinking people at all times. However, even after death their fame remains while those who prosecuted them are forgotten. There has to be a price to be paid for free thinking. The world will oppose us but we all should stand united against it.*

Mehek's image of herself seemed to be that of a path-breaking revolutionary. Devika looked at the clock. It was time. She dressed up in her brown cotton kurta and jeans, tied her hair with a hair band while she looked at herself in the mirror. *Control your excitement Devika. I know you are going to the field after a long gap. Enjoy your day today since tomorrow is going to be a bad day at the hospital anyway,* she said to her image in the mirror.

When she walked out of the villa with her bag and her notepad, the two police constables stationed at the gate greeted her. One of them stopped an auto-rickshaw. As Devika settled down in the back seat, she realised what a rickety old thing she had got into.

"Tavern Shopping Centre," she instructed the rickshaw driver.

The auto-rickshaw dragged itself noisily towards Sarvanpur's town centre. Devika was amazed that the auto had been given an RTO permit. Finally, after what felt like hours, they reached their destination. On the opposite side of the road, facing the shopping centre stood the Sahyadri Hills residential complex. Anshuman was at the gate clad in his white shirt and khakhi trousers, "Devika Ji, they have opened the flat already. Come with me."

The regulatory yellow tape, 'Police Line – Do Not Cross', was placed outside the door. The sealed lock on the door was broken and was now hanging from the latch. Devika and Anshuman entered Mehek's flat.

"We believe there are more untraced members of the cult. With their leadership either dead or in prison, they may not be dangerous but still we need to be wary. The doc mentioned about them but even he has not seen their faces. Even the other captured cult members don't know anything about them," said Anshuman.

"So you people also believe that there is a *sleeper cell*. I am surprised that this was denied until now. Mehek's diary clearly mentions an attack at the end of the year. If the cult members in the jail were unaware of such an attack, then there are surely others out there who are part of this plan," said Devika.

"Devika madam, you see these people? They are staff members from the forensics department here to collect more evidence and possibly fingerprints that were missed out the first time. What makes this job difficult is that the unknown members of the cult in all probability have no previous criminal records."

"I believe we should try even if it is a dead lead," said Devika, "It is a better option than leaving everything to fate."

"Let's hope we get something substantial today. Once these people are nabbed, we could close the case," said Anshuman.

"Yes, case closed. I tell Shravan regularly at home that his department seems to be in one big hurry to close files without investigating anything on the periphery. By the way, did I tell you that some imposter sent me a letter posing as Mehek before the bullets were fired into our house?"

Anshuman was amused, "I came to know about the email, but didn't know about the letter. Shravan sir had put Inspector Karim in charge of the investigation. This town seems to be full of nutcases. Just took a group of mad people to unleash more insanity." He handed her a pair of rubber gloves. "Please wear these and don't touch anything."

As the team of three went around trying to get the fingerprints and other evidence, Devika went around the dusty flat. Mehek had obviously led a luxurious life. All the rooms were carpeted, the wallpaper in all the rooms had a pattern of jasmine flowers and the light fittings were of a medieval European style. The hall didn't have a TV, only a laptop table with a laptop and attached speakers. The sofa cushions were of genuine leather and the furniture was mostly made of teak. There were two big framed works of art in the hall. One of them was a portrait of a young Virginia Woolf; the mentally unstable but gifted feminist writer had somehow found an admirer in the now dead cult leader. Devika herself had read most of Woolf's novels, and had in fact read *Mrs Dalloway* four times, something she never usually did. She was particularly impressed while reading a biography about the sacrifices made by the writer's husband Leonard to keep her happy. The artwork in front of them was a counterfeit of Virginia's portrait by the artist Roger Fry.

The other framed artwork in the hall was a counterfeit of Maurycy Gottlieb's *Shylock* and *Jessica*. It was an uncommon painting to be displayed in the hall but surely meant something to the deceased.

*The absence of a guardian figure or anger against a villain-like guardian figure?* Devika wondered.

Perhaps unrelated, but while reading her diary, on multiple occasions Devika had felt that she had a thing for older mature men.

Mehek seemed to have hired local artists to draw this for her after probably providing them with the printouts of the original. Devika was particularly surprised by the framed sketch in the bedroom which was a counterfeit of Jacques-Louis David's 'Marie Antoinette on the way to the guillotine'.

"Who keeps such stuff framed in their bedroom? A woman being taken for her death, a gruesome beheading," she asked Anshuman. The bed was a king sized four poster one. The wardrobe was very neatly arranged and well stacked. One side was full of Mehek's work attire and the other side was a collection of silk saris.

Devika laughed as they looked at the well provided wardrobe. "If you would allow me, I would like to take some of these gorgeous beauties back home."

There was an elaborate make-up shelf stacked with expensive brands of hair gel, mascara, makeup base, cleansing liquid, eye liners, creams, nail polish, deodorants, perfumes and lip colour. Devika noticed a pattern to it. 13 shades of lip gloss, 13 types of eye liners, 6 deodorants, 6 perfumes and 13 bottles of nail polish. A while later, Devika went to the bookshelf in the bedroom and started to look. There were some biographies of feminist leaders. It was kind of creepy since most of the books were the same as those on Devika's bookshelf. The other books were from a wide range of topics from hypnotism, books on illusionists, to *The Book of the Law* and books on Shamanism among others. The only book which was out of the rack and placed on Mehek's reading table was Anton LaVey's *The Satanic Witch*.

"You must be wondering whether these books are in circulation in India. They are not! These are all international editions Mehek received as gifts from like-minded friends living abroad," said Anshuman.

He brought an album to her. Devika flipped the pages of the album which contained pictures of a mansion.

"Where is this place?"

"Devika Ji, this is the Portuguese Mansion situated on Vasco Road. For some strange reason Mehek had visited this place on multiple days and taken photographs of this building from various angles."

"Eccentric hobbies of weird people," Devika was visibly surprised.

Anshuman now handed her another fat album in which there were newspaper clips of interesting articles compiled by Mehek. In most of the articles Mehek had marked the important points with a fluorescent highlighter. All the articles had something to do with occult and black-magic. The first article was cut out of a magazine regarding the French seer Nostradamus and his tryst with occult. Many people considered Nostradamus as a slave of the evil or insane. It was highly debatable whether he was a follower of rituals to gain access to 'psychic' powers. Nostradamus feared prosecution and managed to save himself only by maintaining an excellent relationship with the Church.

The next article was on the Nobel Prize winning poet W.B. Yeats and his fascination for occult. Mehek had highlighted one of his quotes.

*"If I had not made magic my constant study I could not have written a single word of my Blake book, nor would The Countess Kathleen ever have come to exist. The mystical life is the centre of all that I do and all that I think and all that I write."*

This was followed by a magazine article on a legendary figure in the world of fiction .

> *Arthur Conan Doyle was a member of the supernatural organisation called 'The Ghost Club'. Its objective was to study the truth behind supernatural activities. Conan Doyle's good friend, the American magician Harry Houdini was also a prominent member of the Spiritualist movement of the 1920s. Houdini believed that Spiritualist mediums were in fact tricks and frauds to make people believe things that really did not exist. However, Conan Doyle was a firm believer that the supernatural forces did exist. He claimed to have conversed with the spirits of dead people. This led to a bitter public dispute between these two legends.*

After this, there were a number of pages from a book about the Russian monk Grigori Rasputin and the spread of occult in Russia. The next three pages were about Hitler's Nazi Party and their belief in the Aryan race stemming from occult pioneers of that time. Yet another article talked about a demi-god in the field of science.

> *Isaac Newton was initially worried to go public with his theories of gravity. His laws on gravity also had a deeper implication. He was suggesting that everybody has an effect on other bodies which acts from a distance. This capability in each body which cannot be seen was pulling others towards it in spite of physical separation. This was a concept similar to magic or when witches cast spells or put curses on people who are not around them. Since the number of people killed in the two centuries before Newton as part of the campaign against witchcraft was more*

*than forty thousand, Newton was genuinely worried for himself. Also, he had once stated that false text was inserted into the Bible in the 4th century to further glorify Christ. This coupled with his reading of Greek and Egyptian texts during his twelve years in Cambridge. In addition, his pursuing of Alchemy and experiments to trap the elixir-of-life put Newton in danger of being persecuted by the establishment.*

As she flipped the pages, Devika's attention was caught by an article about a legendary mathematician.

*The club started by Pythagoras encouraged its students to think out of their belief systems. Pythagoras himself had researched ancient Egyptian and Mesopotamian texts on rituals and magic. The club members were encouraged to harness the knowledge of the more ancient civilisations in their study of mathematics, music, astronomy and medicine. The exclusive club made the people of Croton jealous. The club's building was burned down and many of those assembled there were burned alive. Pythagorean brotherhood was suppressed everywhere. Pythagoras himself fled to Metapontum and died shortly afterwards.*

The purpose of maintaining this collection of articles was unclear. Maybe Mehek used it to impress upon her prospective followers that many famous personalities in fields as diverse as literature, science, mathematics and poetry have had their rendezvous with occult or magic. These articles were interpretations of historical events which may or may not be accurate. However, in the hands of a manipulative person like Mehek, these became case-studies proving the effectiveness and reach of magic. All the literature was driving towards one single purpose. To showcase that these famous people rigorously followed occult to reach the level they had, using it to fuel their creative energy and intellect to a whole different level, an aspiration for her followers.

There were a lot of blank pages in the album after this. Devika was pleasantly surprised to see her own columns published almost a year back in the *Konkan Times* featuring in the last pages of this collection. Her columns which Mehek seemed to have liked were titled 'Today's Woman is a Go-getter', 'Don't Save Earth, Save Yourself' and 'Not a Man's World Anymore'.

"I think she liked you!" Anshuman said.

"I never knew I had such a faithful fan among the readers!" Devika looked evidently flattered.

She had received a lot of fan mails when her column started. The number of letters had diminished pretty much recently. Devika had once and only once received an anonymous letter eight months back which praised her fortnightly column in *Konkan Times* in superlatives. The letter also stated that the sender had great respect for Devika's wisdom, feminist ideology and intellect. Since there was no contact address provided, she did not respond. Devika was now wondering if the writer of the fan mail was indeed Mehek.

Mehek's kitchen was neat and tidy with black granite work panels and wooden fixtures. Devika was surprised to see a lot of fried-food snack packets in one of the boxes. "She ate all this and maintained herself so well. All those men swooning over her from all directions," Devika's eyes opened wide, their baffled expression amused Anshuman.

"If she were alive I would have paid for consultation." Anshuman smiled at Devika's remark.

The pattern in the bedroom was visible here as well. 13 china plates, 13 spoons, 13 forks, 6 types of knives, 6 coffee mugs and 13 glasses. She was obsessed with numbers, symbolism and superstition and it had evidently percolated into her home.

Devika wanted to take some photographs of the crime scene but Anshuman asked her not to. On their way out of the flat, Devika went to the adjacent flat and rang the door bell. The name plate on the door read RAGHAV SHINDE. Devika had heard this name before. He was a pretty famous journalist in the local circles.

"Hello ! My name is Devika. Can I take a minute of your time?" Behind the man who had opened the door she saw two children playing Ludo in the hall and a lady who appeared to be their mother.

"Are you Mr Raghav Shinde?"

"What if I am? What is this regarding?"

"Raghav Ji, it's about your erstwhile neighbour Mehek."

"Sorry, Madam. She stayed here but we don't know anything about her. In fact, we saw very little of her around the complex. We have never even talked to her, ever."

"I just wanted to ask a few questions," Devika was assertive.

"I am sorry, Madam, not the right time. We are getting ready to go to my wife's place in Sangli. You may need to excuse us for now," said the man and shut the door.

"Devika Ji, do you want me to intervene?" Anshuman asked.

"No, it's okay. I would like to leave now."

She reached home with a sense of satisfaction. It had been a fruitful day and she'd come back from Mehek's house with enough material to explore the mind of her book's protagonist. As she entered the house she saw Zeenu walking towards her. The cat as it approached her stopped abruptly.

"Come to me, sweety Zeenu! Come!" said Devika.

The eyes of the cat widened as its eyes started to dart all around Devika. Devika looked around her, there was nobody.

"Come to me darling," said Devika as she stepped forward.

The cat's eyes opened wider. It seemed petrified, its limbs trembling and paced slowly backwards in a defensive manner. Devika wondered what was going on. Both of them were looking at each other eye to eye for a brief moment. Then the cat made a threatening sound and displayed its teeth in aggression. It leaned backwards with its claws out. In this crouching position it looked afraid and threatening at the same time.

"What happened, Zeenu baby?" Devika was bewildered as she stepped forward again.

Then after making a loud sound it leaped at Devika. Its teeth bit into her sleeve. Devika tried to flap her hands. The cat fell to the other side and was gone within moments. Devika wondered if the cat had gone rabid. As she looked ahead, she saw Laali walk from the servant's quarter towards the kitchen glancing at Devika for a moment but walking away as if nothing happened. Of course she had seen what was happening. *Did not even try to help?* Devika wondered. *What was that faint smile on her face?*

In the evening, Devika sat with a glass of ginger ale by the table lamp's dim light, listening to Jagjit Singh's songs of love, loss and nostalgia; she was in a trance until she heard the sound of her husband's car. Shravan came into the bedroom with his usual bright smile. It was his habit to appear in the evening for a couple of hours, have tea with Alpesh or Devika and then disappear again for work. However, today he was not planning to go back. Later in the evening, Devika and Shravan visited the Mahadev temple and had dinner at Ching Ming restaurant on the way back.

At night, while trying to sleep, Devika's thoughts revolved around Mehek and the ingenious workings of her mind. One thought suffocated her. Why did she find herself agreeing to most of the things written in her diary? Considering the demonic mind that had written those words, it was blasphemy to even agree in part to her thoughts. Yet, it baffled Devika that she found herself in cognizance with many of the ideas mentioned in Mehek's diary. It was creepy but true.

This woman was an enigma, a dark mind, like the celestial black hole, not allowing any light to escape and constantly pulling others towards herself. But who is not an enigma? Everyone has a side to their personality which they do not reveal to anybody, even the ones closest to them, spouse, parents, children...nobody. The more unstable the mind, the darker its corners. This was what Devika believed was the most exciting part of her assignments. She liked the process of figuring out unstable minds like these. But is it really possible to decipher unstable minds? Maybe you can zero down to some motivations, but who can guess the pattern of ripples in running water?

Devika felt a strong attraction towards such minds; perhaps because her own mind was volatile. *Maybe she was like me, with an evil shade but a mind like mine, dark and indecipherable where there were multi-coloured marbles going in all directions. Red, yellow, green and blue. Bouncing off the floor, off the wall and off the ceiling. Hitting each other. In random directions all around the place. A chaotic fluid mind. A mind, like Mehek's description in her diary about the situation of the earth today, a place where very different people of contrasting characters are crammed together in a limited space.*

There were so many people inside her. An ambitious woman. A bored housewife. A carefree schoolgirl. A loving wife. A gossip-loving college girl. A depressed, suicidal woman. A concerned daughter. A recluse who wants to renounce the world and join a monastery. A nerd who wants to spend hours and days in a public library. An adventure seeker who wants to rush out into the Himalayas. All these different people crammed inside a single body.

The next afternoon Devika was present for her appointment as suggested by her doctor. Unlike the weekends, there were very few patients in the first floor of Holy Cross Hospital. Devika waited for her turn to undergo the follicular study. All around her, women with baby bumps walked to and from the gynaecology clinic at the other end of the floor. *Why always me?* Jolts of despair spread through her mind.

Shravan and she had been planning for close to a year, with no success till finally they consulted a doctor and were asked to undergo follicular study. The process involves putting in an uncomfortable probe into the woman's body every alternate day for ten days each month, followed by a painful injection in the stomach; a painful procedure that offered no guarantees.

In a country of over one billion, they seemed to be among those rare couples who couldn't get it right. She smiled wanly to herself.

The nurse called out, "Devika Soni!"

Devika got up and followed her. Before lying down on the bed she requested the lab technician, "Please be gentle. It hurts."

When Devika returned home, she was exhausted. She asked Radhemohan to make some lemonade and sat on the sofa in the hall, trying to ease the tension out of her mind and body.

The phone rang. In the silence around her, it sounded shrill.

Devika picked up the receiver; there was silence on the other side. After a few seconds a digital voice on the other end said,

"Shemhamforash."

In the background, Devika could clearly hear rock guitar instrumental from *Police*. She remembered the lyrics from her college days.

"Every breath you take
Every move you make
Every bond you break
Every step you take
I'll be watching..."

The word and the instrumental continued in a loop.

*Some creepy bugger*, she thought. But whosoever was doing this was trying to drive home a point.

She dialled Anshuman's number.

"Hello!"

"Hi Anshuman! Devika. There is a call on our landline. Looks like someone is trying to harass me. Can you please ask someone to trace?"

"Sure! You can hang up and I will look into it."

She rang up Shravan but he did not answer his phone; *must be in a meeting*, she thought. She tried his number every ten minutes for the next half an hour but no avail. She sat on the sofa nervously looping the telephone's chord around her fingers.

*Why are all these strange things happening to me?* She looked at the wall clock in front of her and it seemed like time was moving very slowly. It was twenty-five minutes since the call. Then suddenly a loud banging sound came from the next room. Devika jumped up in fear, then sank into the sofa, crouching in a corner. Her heart beat rapidly. There were sounds of things falling and crashing. She looked around in panic. Sweat beads appeared on her forehead.

"I am sorry, Madam, sorry." Radhemohan rushed out of the kitchen. The pressure cooker burst ..."

She did not hear the rest of the words. Relief flooded over her, for herself and for Radhemohan. He could have got seriously injured.

She had to stop getting scared at every noise that came from the house and outside it.

The instrumental went on for an hour, after which it got disconnected. Devika was sure that by now the police department would have traced the call.

Shravan called on her mobile phone. "Shravan, I have been trying your number for a long time."

"I was in a marathon conference call. What happened?"

"We got a crank call on our landline."

"Devika! Just give me a moment I will talk to Karim or Anshuman. We will be able to trace this one."

"No need, I already talked to Anshuman," she said.

"What did the caller say?"

"Nothing. Someone was saying *Shemhamforash*, which stands for 'Hail Satan', followed by an instrumental track."

"You are sure that this is not a prank being played by someone we know?"

"All the people who know us also know that out residence landline is under surveillance and has tracking enabled. They will definitely not play a prank on that number."

"Are you scared, Devika?"

"No, not much, just curious to know who's behind this."

Even though she tried to underplay it, the bullets and then the strange phone call had made her jittery and she spent the rest of the day pacing around her bedroom, taking deep breaths and drinking water.

Later that evening Anshuman called.

"We traced the call to the nearest mobile tower. The location was Sarvanpur Central Park. We questioned people there and an old couple mentioned that they had heard a faint sound of music coming from a bush behind one of the park's benches."

"Did you find the phone?"

"We found a phone taped to an MP3 player placed in the bushes," he said

"What about the SIM card?"

"Stolen. I think the phone was also purchased from Chor Bazaar. Devika Ji, you need to be careful." Devika was not sure whether Anshuman's tone bordered between professional talk and frustration or if it was the creation of her own mind.

"Any other piece of evidence?"

"There were no fingerprints on the mobile or the MP3 player."

"What's with the people who are behind this? Why are they after me?"

That night after Devika went to sleep, she woke up feeling anxious in the middle of the night; she was sweating, the music played in a loop inside her head.

"Every breath you take
Every move you make
Every bond you break
Every step you take
I'll be watching..."

"What happened?" Shravan asked, worried for her.

"Nothing." She got up and drank water. She opened the drawer of the dressing table to take out her primrose tablets. She would take them for the next couple of days.

# May:
# The Second Letter

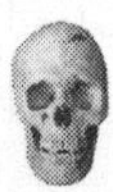

"Shravan's reports are kind of normal, borderline. On the other hand, Devika, it is evident after the follicular study that you have a poly-cystic ovary." The expression on the couple's faces changed. They now knew for sure that it was not a matter of chance, something was out of place. Sitting across the table, the gynaecologist had just confirmed their worst fears.

"What does that imply?" Shravan asked.

"Well, to be frank, conception will be difficult," replied the gynaecologist.

"Are you saying that we cannot have a child?" Devika asked, barely able to keep the tears out of her voice.

"No Devika! With the latest medical technology, HCG injections, IUF and IVF, there is still a decent chance that you can have a baby."

"So we will now have to go through all these complicated medical procedures." Shravan had slumped a little, a defeated man already.

"I guess we have no other option," Devika said. She'd once read about the correlation between these syndromes in a magazine but today her worst fears were confirmed. The mood-swings, the PMDD and this current problem of infertility, all had a single root cause. The magazine had clearly stated that women having an under-performing thyroid gland are more likely to have such issues. In

Devika's case the thyroid problem was hereditary since her mother had also suffered from it.

The gynaecologist scribbled on a piece of paper. "Remember, stress should be kept out of your life if you ever want to have a baby. Take a month off from the follicular study, relax and do some meditation. Yoga and meditation help. I am referring you to the clinic on the 6th floor." She handed over the paper to Devika.

Disappointed, Devika and Shravan walked out of the doctor's cabin. As they walked across the corridor they did not speak a word to each other. The world around them seemed to have come to a screeching halt. Shravan was very sad though his stoic expression revealed little. He had always believed that children brought a sense of purpose and direction to a person's life. Would he have to spend the rest of his life without that sense of purpose? Without a child the road would seem endless, endless and bereft of the satisfaction of crossing small milestones.

As she walked towards the entrance Devika looked at the board showing the hospital's floor plan. She found what she was looking for, the key to her future life and how she would live it. '6th Floor – Infertility and Assisted Reproductive Technology'.

A droplet of tear appeared in her eyes and she tried to wipe it off before Shravan noticed it, but she wasn't quick enough. Shravan had noticed it. He put an arm around her shoulders. "Like all the problems we have tackled before this, we will come through this too." He tried to smile. "Let's go for a weekend trip to Mahabaleshwar. After that you go for some yoga classes and rest."

"Shravan, just because she asked me to relax does not mean I will sit at home and watch TV."

"I think you need to take it easy now onwards."

"No. It does not work that way. I sit at home unoccupied, I get cranky. An empty mind becomes the devil's workshop." Devika tried to keep calm as she fought for control.

Shravan sighed, "Alright, my dear! Do what you want. Whatever makes you comfortable."

Shravan dropped Devika home in his car. After he left, Devika sat on her bed thinking about the gynaecologist's words and started crying. A little later, she willed herself into a more positive frame of mind. *This does not mean the end of the world. I will not take this as a final judgement from above. There are so many destitute children living sad lives in orphanages around the country. What better karma than giving a good life to someone who was deprived of it since birth?*

She decided to divert her mind by concentrating on her work. As she slumped into the chair and thought of her work, slowly, she started to organise her thoughts.

Devika had planned on a fictional narrative with detailed backgrounds for the characters and their motivations. It had to be written like a thriller, not journalistic reportage; her responsibility, as she saw it, as a writer, was to provide facts that the readers did not get to know from the print media, bring alive the reality as she had explored it through various angles, known and unknown.

She spent the next couple of hours typing the first chapter of her book on her laptop. She titled it *Mehek–India's own Aileen Wuornos*. The world famous female serial killer's life story had inspired the 2003 Hollywood film *Monster*. Though she may not have been as manipulative and shrewd as Mehek, there were similarities in their personalities. Like Mehek's words in the diary indicated, Aileen too claimed to be a victim of the system, that she was different from others and society was unable to accept the fact; that the mob always prosecutes people who do not match their definition of right and wrong.

The telephone rang.

Devika picked up the bedroom extension. It was from the *Konkan Times*; she had mail again.

"I'll send my domestic help tomorrow morning," she said.

As soon as she returned to her laptop, the door bell rang. Devika shook her head in frustration; too many distractions. How would she write? Radhemohan would answer the door. She sat at her table again, willing herself to write.

After five minutes Radhemohan stood at the entrance of the bedroom holding a letter. The envelope had a Cherub's logo. She had submitted a proposal for her book with the prestigious Cherub Publishers but she had not expected such a quick response.

*Dear Devika,*

*We are in receipt of your book proposal on the Sarvanpur Serial Murders. The proposal is interesting and we believe that since you reside in Sarvanpur, you will be able to authentically capture the local culture, public opinion and feel of the places and events convincingly.*

*We are glad to inform you that we will be keen to publish your book once it is ready. Royalties, territories, number of copies and distribution network can be discussed once we are in receipt of the final manuscript.*

*Regards,*
*Cherub Editorial Team*

*At last a piece of good news.* Excited, she called up Shravan to inform him about the development.

Hope and despair seemed to have arrived at Devika's doorstep simultaneously.

Radhemohan had prepared vegetable biryani, fried pepper papad and yoghurt-vegetable salad for lunch. After lunch, Devika took a short, contented nap. In the evening, having heard from Shravan about the publishing offer, Alpesh strode into the house, beaming at Devika.

"Devika! You just ask me for whatever help you require from my side for your research. It will be done. I know how important it is for you that this book works."

That night, Shravan and Devika had their celebratory dinner out. Since Devika liked Chinese cuisine they drove to the famous Little China Town near Mohammed Rafi Road in their own car. It was a breezy evening and thankfully the traffic was better than they had anticipated. The restaurant operated on a lavish space. Its walls were bright red, a metallic Buddha occupied pride of place on a centrally located pedestal; the walls had huge images of fire-blowing dragons. Unlike other eateries around town that catered to students, the restaurant was high class and catered to a rich clientele.

"By the way, did Monica mention to you about issues they've been facing at home? According to Alpesh she looks detached and disinterested at home," Shravan said.

"I think her behaviour at home is due to Alpesh being preoccupied with his work and TV all the time. He just seems to be living in his own world, leaving Monica out of it. You know, she was the most sought after girl in her university, guys just craved for her attention and now in her own house she feels unwanted and unappreciated."

"Most marital discords are way too complicated. There are multiple versions and above all one absolute truth. What do *you* think, Devika?"

"Even truth is a very relative term, Shravan. There is nothing called absolute truth."

Shravan now leaned forward and placed his hands on Devika's. "Let's leave the Thapars aside for a moment. You tell me, how does it feel to get the letter from the publisher?"

"When I wrote the first book I didn't know whether it would ever get printed. This time it is motivating to know that this product will see the light of day. There is anxiety, of course, about responses to it, but that is natural, I suppose. Oh crap!" said Devika as she felt inside her purse.

"What happened?"

"I forgot my mobile phone again," said Devika. Shravan looked back at her with a resigned expression.

They had a hearty meal of Wok Tossed Hakka Noodles, Four Treasure Vegetables in Hunan Sauce and a dessert of Honey Noodles with Almond flakes.

The next morning Radhemohan returned with the grocery and a bright red envelope which he had picked up from the despatch section of the *Konkan Times*. As she held the envelope in her hand, Devika felt anxious. What was this imposter trying to achieve with such mail? In her last column in the *Konkan Times* she had changed the heading for fun and titled it - "What's the Objective?" This must be the imposter's response to it.

She opened the envelope and found the familiar white piece of paper. The message was again made of words cut out from newspapers and magazines glued to the sheet.

Dear DeViKa,

I am aghast.
WHY should I be THE Only one to have PAID the price For THINKING Free? WHAT about the OTHERS who betrayed me. What about my present?
MEHEK

*What present was she talking about?* Her hands trembled as she read the message. She opened her cupboard drawer and fumbled through a lot of documents till she got what she was looking for, the photocopy of Mehek's diary. She flipped through the pages and stopped at a particular scribble.

*There has to be a price to be paid for free thinking. The world will oppose us but we all should stand united against it.*

Devika looked at the letter she had received. This was not just any imposter. This imposter surely knew Mehek very well. In fact, he or she was using words so similar to her thoughts that it was creepy. Even the tone of the letter was similar to the tone that was common throughout Mehek's diary. The tone of a victim of the system.

Devika looked closely at the word 'Thinking'; it was a bright blue, almost like a neon sign. She had seen it somewhere. She went to the newspaper pile in the bottom rack of her cupboard and picked out the past week's newspapers.

As she turned the pages she saw an advertisement; the neon word and the words 'others' and 'paid' were taken from the same page. Page number 13 of the *Konkan Times*. The date of the paper was 13th April. Agitated, Devika went to the cupboard next to the hall and took out another stack of old newspapers. She took out the 13th page of the paper for the whole month. All the words were selected from the 13th pages of newspapers between the 1st and 13th of the month. Bright colourful words of advertisements were preferred over normal newspaper text. Newspapers from dates after the 14th were ignored.

Devika wanted concrete answers from the imposter. She looked at the rough draft on the laptop screen. Her next column in the *Konkan Times* was about the multiple meetings between the governments of Karnataka and Goa over water sharing from the Mandovi River. These meetings had been going on for some time without arriving at any consensus over the issue. Devika was now sure that the person trying to reach out to her was reading her fortnightly column and even responding to it.

She would have to create a title that would send the intended message to this imposter and also fall in line with the content of her column.

"Time to come to the Specifics." She found her title; now she would have to wait and watch. Would the impostor respond?

That night as she and Shravan were sleeping in their bedroom, Shravan's mobile phone rang.

"I have an urgent conference call. The Environment Minister will be in Sarvanpur tomorrow morning for an unplanned visit. I am going to the hall," said Shravan as he got up from the bed and went away after picking up a file placed next to the bed. Devika was half in sleep as she murmured, "Okay, just increase the fan's speed on your way out."

It was a silent night. Something troubled Devika and she jumped up from the bed to switch on the bedside table lamp. She looked at the alarm clock. The time was 11.59 pm. One glance around the bedroom, everything was normal. The fan and the breeze from outside were making the curtains fly all around. Suddenly, the door of the attached bathroom slowly creaked open. Wide jawed Devika wondered if the breeze had done this. She could see something behind the door. There was a dark image of a woman standing behind the door. Devika's body turned cold and she could not muster the courage to mouth any words. Motionless, she froze on the bed. The woman in the dark stepped forward towards Devika.

Devika jumped up from her bed, "Damn! It was a nightmare." She said as she took a breath of relief and switched on the bedside table lamp. She looked at the alarm clock. The time was 11.59 pm. Devika had an eerie feeling as she looked around the bedroom. Everything was normal. Suddenly, the door of the attached bathroom slowly creaked open. Devika was mortified. She could not breathe as she could see something behind the door. She felt a shiver run down her spine. Someone stood there behind the door in the dark. "Oh God, Shravan! It was you. I was scared to death."

"Why is the light on in the hall?"

"Let me see!" Devika got up from bed, took a bottle of water in her hand and drank some as she walked towards the hall. As she approached the hall Devika's heart skipped a beat. She saw Shravan in the hall, still on the conference call. He lifted his palms to signal 'five minutes more'. Shravan wondered why his wife had a flabbergasted expression on her face with her drugged looking eyes wide open. Devika looked behind her at her dark bedroom. A feeling of self-doubt crossed her mind. How could she discuss this with Shravan? What if his response was in the same lines as his initial scepticism, *I told you so in the beginning! Look how these things have started to mess up your mind. Why didn't you listen to me?*

Devika decided that it was better for her not to discuss this and get into an un-necessary argument with Shravan. She walked towards the refrigerator in the kitchen to drink some cold water. Near the kitchen sink stood Laali washing a utensil. She turned her face and looked at the visibly baffled Devika. Then she turned her face away and went ahead with her work.

"What are you doing here?"

"Father was not well, so I asked him to take rest while I cleaned the utensils for him," replied Laali with her eyes still focussed on the kitchen sink.

Devika's eyes narrowed on Laali. "What's that smile on your face?"

"Nothing," said Laali looking at Devika.

"Of course, you had a sly smile on your face. Anything funny or amusing?"

"I don't have a smile on my face madam," said Laali as she placed the utensil after cleaning and left.

# May: The Deserted Farm House

The police jeep moved slowly along Vasco Road after crossing Sarvanpur Public Library. Inspector Anshuman, driving the jeep, was cautious on the potholed road. Seated next to him, Devika looked at the passing scenery.

It was the peak of the dry season. The patches of yellow were slowly becoming more prominent compared to the green on either side of the road. The breeze was hot. A stray dog and its lean puppy came towards the middle of the road and jumped backwards as the jeep passed them.

"The road department closed this road for four months; they worked on the steep curves and broadened the road, yet the number of accidents on this road has not decreased," Anshuman said.

"It has been like this from the 1980s. Vasco road is like the Bermuda Triangle for vehicles plying on the road to Goa. Tell me Anshuman, do you believe the legend that this place is cursed in some way?"

"Devika Ji, I don't know about it being cursed, but one of my constables driving on this road at night claimed that he saw a disturbing sight of a strange old lady dressed in a gown walking backwards on the side of this road in the dark. This constable from my team is a very stable person and not the sort who would cook up a story for amusement. I really wonder what the issue is."

"Reality is a complex term, Anshuman, and it often makes a fool of us. Once verified, the big, concrete, real world may take just a moment to crumble, like a house of cards. In a way, you should treat it like government files."

Anshuman was puzzled. "Government files?"

"The government files which state that there is a dam on this river, there is a public park over here, this road was repaired two times in three years, there is a bridge across that stream, the drinking water pipeline was totally replaced, the sewage lines were completely revamped etc. None of these exist or happened on the ground. It's an illusion which some people claim, others propagate, and most believe without verifying."

Anshuman smiled, "An illusion which is making some people rich. The general public who don't verify it become fools. You're right, Devika Ji."

"My point is that one should verify everything before believing."

The jeep crossed Saint Francis Church on the way to Goa. Devika looked around at the wilderness. "I wonder; what could be the root cause of all the weird accidents and deaths that take place on this road."

"According to an old local saying, this place has an undesirable effect on people because of which they start behaving strangely when in this area."

"Undesirable effect? Like what, Anshuman?"

"It magnifies a person's negative traits, triggers the dark areas of the human mind. So you could have adventurous drivers become foolishly reckless, depressives turn suicidal, the absent minded go into deep sleep, and the ill-tempered enter a state of mindless, self-destructive rage."

"So what you essentially mean is that there is something here in the air or water that triggers the darker elements of a person's mind."

"No Devika Ji. Not air or water. There is negative energy around this place," Anshuman glanced momentarily at Devika, his eyes intense. "I have been to numerous macabre crime scenes where murders or suicides have taken place, like the place we are visiting today. Believe me, these places still have a creepy air even years after everything has been cleaned up and sanitised."

"Sounds more psychological than actual fear. The fear that repulses people from leasing flats where a previous tenant had hanged to death," said Devika.

"Madam, my take on this is simple. There are millions of believers for positive energy. They all believe that there is high positive energy around places like temple complexes, around mosques and church premises; then going by the same logic there must also be places where there is high negative energy as well."

"Interesting, but not quite believable. I am not buying that. When will we reach the farmhouse?" she asked.

"Just round the corner," he said.

Anshuman looked a little upset at Devika's lack of enthusiasm in his concepts; now he wanted to quickly get done with the job. Jyoti was right; she often told him that Devika was unpredictable. He was getting a firsthand experience of it. When they reached, he got down from the jeep and opened the gate. Then he drove the jeep through the mud road surrounded by trees and grass on both sides. The jeep came to a halt and Anshuman escorted Devika between the tamarind and kokum trees to a structure in the middle of the farm.

"Devika Ji, welcome to the devil's playground."

As Anshuman pushed open the door of the shed, they were greeted by a strong, stuffy smell and a cloud of dust. The dark and suffocating place was like a hidden world concealed by the greenery around it.

"This is the altar where they used to conduct their rituals."

Devika stepped forward and took a photograph of the giant pentagram with a goat's face. The expression on the goat's face was rather unpleasant and cruel. A small rat dashed across the pentagram and Devika instinctively jerked backwards.

There were empty bottles of vodka, brandy, injection syringes, broken vials and plastic covers littered all around the place. A room freshener was lying on top of the toolbox on the other side of the shed. The forensics team had taken away the spade, shovel and the other items that were in the toolbox. Below it was a litter of half melted black candles and used matchsticks.

"Where was the Western Ghats Centre?" asked Devika.

"Adjacent to this compound but visible from the road. There was a brick wall separating the compounds but it caved in, making it easy to cross over," replied Anshuman, pointing to his left.

They walked to a corner of the shed where the burial pits were located. Devika counted 11 such pits. The number of missing people from Sarvanpur in a year was estimated at between 120 and 180. These included young people eloping with their lovers, aspiring young people fleeing to Mumbai, casualties of college politics or gang rivalries, victims of crimes etc. The local police was having a tough time trying to identify at least three of the badly decomposed bodies. Devika looked at Anshuman and said, "This must be the place where the ritual ended."

"Devika Ji, you should have seen this place when we were digging out the skeletons. The media was covering it like they had covered the Nithari serial killings of Noida. Every skeleton found was flashed on televisions as national news."

"The media coverage was baffling. Our local home-grown psychopaths along with the tales of their antics got enough air-time and advertisements to help companies sell colas, chips, holiday packages and mobile connections worth crores of rupees to unsuspecting audiences across the country."

A praying mantis had sneaked into the shed and stood poised near one of the graves, looking as though it was praying.

"Must be really weird people. Using such a place for implementing such atrocious rituals," Devika said, an eye on the insect-at-prayer.

"Happens all around. Yesterday a family in Arvinwadi made their son walk on a path of burning coal embers outside a local temple to bring good luck. Today's newspaper says that the boy was admitted to hospital with very severe burns to his feet. I am convinced that the number of insane people is growing all around us," added Anshuman.

"Anshuman Ji, have you ever wondered about this? Sanity and Insanity can easily switch places depending on who has more numbers. If the number of insane people increases, these people will run governments and large corporations. We on the other hand will be sent to mental asylums for not being like them."

"I believe there are already enough insane people running governments and large corporations around the globe," Anshuman laughed.

Curious, Devika looked around the whole place. After she'd taken some photographs, they left the place while it was still day time. The cool evening breeze made the drive back a pleasurable experience. Looking at the tree branches swaying in the breeze, she thought about the people she was writing about. Was it a coincidence that all these eccentric people got together at one place? Or is there a weird eccentric element inside every person waiting for some external stimulus to break free? What uncanny ability in some shrewd people arms them with the capability to elicit such filth out of others?

When they reached home, Alpesh and Shravan were enjoying their evening walk in the lawn. Anshuman wished his seniors and sat with them while Radhemohan served tea. Once she was inside her bedroom, Devika called up her father in Delhi.

"Did you get the result of your blood test?" There was a brief pause. "The haemoglobin count is decreasing. How much is it?"

Devika tried to conceal the anxiety in her voice. "Eat broccoli, soya milk and leafy vegetables. You should not eat dates, so forget it...You are losing weight, Papa! Is your sugar reading under control? Take care, Papa. Otherwise I will catch the next flight and come to Delhi."

She was happy to hear that her father's diabetic condition had stabilised after the daily insulin injections. However, she was worried about his blood report. The doctor had assured her father that having iron rich food would help.

A week later Devika enrolled for the 'Art of Living' course. She had done their week-long beginners course when she was in college and wanted to repeat it. She had little faith that yoga and meditation could lead to the miracle she was hoping for. One thing she liked was that unlike other spiritual groups they never talked about earthly relationships being the root cause of all sorrow with the accompanying advice to renounce material relationships or things. Relationships can give heartbreaks and grief but they are also the spice of life. Devika believed that the logic of renunciation was best suited for people who can live on a lifetime diet of boiled oats and sprouts because everything else that is a delight to eat has fat, sugar, cholesterol and spices. After completing the course she tried to sit at home and relax. Instead, she became very restless.

Two days later she attended the meeting of the local chapter of 'India Against Corruption' and the subsequent demonstration on MG Road. The meeting and the subsequent demonstration were responses to the *Konkan Times*' exposé of a land grabbing mafia who operated along with state officials. The mafia forced poor farmers whose plots were around Mar Ivanios Road to sell their land below market rates to the mafia members. However, with bigger scams getting unearthed at the national level, media coverage of the local issue lost steam midway.

A week later, Devika was engrossed in reading a current issue of the *National Geographic* magazine in the afternoon, when the landline phone rang shrilly. Irritated, she picked it up. "Hello!"

"Devika Ji, Anshuman. I have something very interesting to show you."

"What is it?" Devika was puzzled.

"I suggest you come to the fallow ground behind the Sambhaji Memorial. There is something of interest to you there," Anshuman sounded confident.

"Okay! I'll take an hour to reach there, Anshuman."

"No problem."

An hour later Devika walked along the dirt road behind Sambhaji Memorial. At a distance she saw a police constable on an endless stretch of open fallow land. A shaky sign post read 'Mandigaon Public Burial Ground'. The constable led Devika through a dirt road along the side of a hedge to a small two room structure near the entrance. On the steps leading to the rooms a mentally ill woman was squatting on the floor; her hair cropped short and brown with dust, red bloodshot eyes darted from side to side. She had a running nose and long grey fingernails, the ugly scar of a deep cut ran across her left cheek. She was a wearing a dirty dark green gown torn at many places.

Devika was shocked when the woman greeted her with a smile displaying her partially broken teeth coated with shades of brown and red.

"She is harmless. Roams around here all the time. God knows where she came from," the constable said. He searched his pocket and came up with a small packet of peanuts that he gave to the woman. She snatched the packet out of the constable's hands and said in a low husky tone, "*Hya jagacha anth jawal yet ahe....Hya jagacha anth...*"

"What did she say?" Devika asked.

"Oh! She keeps saying that the world is coming to an end," said the constable.

Inside the room seated on either side of the table were Anshuman and a dark bald man wearing a black shirt and brown trousers.

"Devika Ji, this is Emmanuel, the caretaker of this burial ground."

"Namaste, Devika Ji." The dark, bald man gave her a broken-toothed grin.

Anshuman got up from his place. "A rather bizzare issue was reported from here this morning. You may need to come along with me to have a look."

They all stepped outside the office and walked along rows of graves. The mad woman in her ragged clothes followed them at a distance, her eyes full of fear and suspicion. Each grave had a small white tile with the name of the buried person or a reference number mentioned in the file maintained by the burial ground.

'Here Lies Kevin Fernandez'

'Here Lies Samuel Gomez'

'Here Lies Mini Periera'

All the tomb stones with numbers were unidentified dead bodies. The ones with names were unclaimed bodies of people who died in encounters and other criminal actions.

Burial grounds have an eerie feel about them; layers of soil over hopes, aspirations and dreams. Man reduced to his true worth, without self-awareness, self-preservation, or ego, humble food for rodents, worms, germs and insects. Why did they ask her to come to this place? Emmanuel seemed to be showing them a botanical garden, not a burial ground.

They all walked past a number of 'Here Lies' tiles until they reached an empty grave, a solitary empty pit in the ground. It looked as if someone had dug it out hastily.

"It's strange, but she is missing," said Anshuman as he pointed at the pit.

"Who is missing?" Devika asked.

"Mehek was buried here after she was used as a cadaver in the dissection room of the Sushrut Medical College. This grave was her final resting place. This morning when the caretaker came in here, her dead body was gone," said Anshuman.

"I found this first thing in the morning," said Emmanuel with the triumphant smile of a young boy happy at the first faint trace of a moustache on his adolescent face.

Devika allowed the information to sink in. It was strange to even think about something like this, let alone carrying it out. *Who would do such a nasty thing?* It is known that some psychopaths have a fascination for dead bodies. They have even made a provision in law for the same. IPC Section 297 – 'Trespassing on burial places'. Devika wondered what kind of necrophilia ridden mind would dig out a coffin with a badly decomposed body inside; the rotting skin and muscles over the bones, the disgusting liquids and filthy slime smeared around it. Yet, someone had shown the will power to do this dirty job.

*Why just this body out of all those in the burial ground?* She could think of only one possible reason for that. Maybe some dark mind thought that Mehek's mortal remains or bones may have some magical powers. Whatever it was, this was a chilling reminder to everyone of the cult and Mehek's legend in this region.

"Why was she buried and not cremated?" asked Devika.

"They went by her school records where the religion mentioned was Christian," replied the broken toothed caretaker.

"Strange. Her surname is a Hindu surname. Also, she had renounced religion altogether, so how does it matter whether she was cremated or buried. Doesn't anybody guard this place at night?"

"There is one guard in the night shift. He was unwell last night and left by midnight," the caretaker said.

"What do you suspect?" asked Devika.

"Not sure! What will someone do with a dead body?" Anshuman asked.

"Black magicians consider dead bodies and bones to be of immense power especially if it belongs to someone special," said Devika.

"Considering the state in which the dead body was, I don't think anybody would do this even if it guaranteed heaven," commented Anshuman with a puzzled look.

"Ever heard of the *Aghoris*? This stealing of corpses from graveyards is not a new happening in these parts," she remarked.

"Devika Ji, there is something inside the pit we wanted to show you. I saw it before anybody else came in," Emmanuel announced, again with a sense of accomplishment. The caretaker jumped inside the pit and pointed at a picture cut out of a magazine which was placed inside the pit. He was careful not to pick it or touch it.

Devika walked to the other end of the pit and her eyes narrowed. This was not some bit of paper that had blown in the wind into the pit. It had a meaning. Devika looked carefully at the picture and said, "It is a picture of a broken chain. It is a symbolic statement."

"It means?"

"Broken chains mean freedom."

"Freedom from what?" Anshuman seemed clueless.

Devika was equally clueless. At this moment the mad woman who was leaning against a tree and standing at a distance started to laugh hysterically. Devika turned and looked at her. Her blood shot eyes were now looking at her.

"*Ti kal ratri nighun geli. Kal ratri,*" she said in her low husky voice starting to laugh again. Devika looked at her face puzzled. Then the mad woman stepped backwards repeating the words and laughing. Devika looked at the constable standing behind her.

"What is she saying?" asked Devika.

"Nothing, Madam! She just blabbers things," said the constable.

"*Ti kal ratri nighun geli!*" The woman repeated.

"She is saying something. Can you please tell me what?" Devika was impatient.

"She is just saying that some woman walked out of here at night," said the constable.

# June:
# Light Fades Out

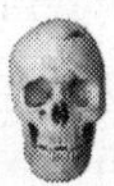

Nelson Pereira became an introvert in his adolescent years. Engrossed in his books and plaster-of-Paris modelling, he lived in his own world.

After his schooling at The Bishop's School, Pune, he completed his BA and MA in English from Sorabji Pestonji College at Sarvanpur. Nelson liked the climate of the small, educational town. Its peace, natural beauty and people. A place with which he shared old ties that attracted and repulsed him at the same time.

Nelson decided to settle down in Sarvanpur to work on his first book. His father, an author of many failed books, had used a small portion of the family fortune to buy a small house for his son near Old Church Road, Sarvanpur. After a year of working on various ideas and breaking his head on multiple drafts, Nelson finally abandoned the venture. He had many relatives in the USA and the UK, and a cousin in France. He wanted to go there and see the world, he told himself, and so, when his cousin informed him of a vacancy for an English teacher at Villejean University, he jumped at the chance. After multiple telephonic interviews, his cousin's recommendation, and a video conference, Nelson got the job. He used his France sojourn to travel to Paris, Florence, Rome and Brussels but he preferred the European countryside, especially

Normandy and Brittany. On weekdays he spent his evenings in open air coffee shops in the town centre of Rennes called Republique. On weekends he would take the TGV bullet train to visit the Louvre and other museums.

He fell in love with a French girl named Anne Cecile who worked at the university and they got married six months after their courtship started. Excited and animated, he applied for French citizenship. Six months after their marriage, life became mundane. Nelson was introduced to weed at a friend's party; it took him only a year to turn it into a habit. As weed took the better of him, Anne Cecile decided to call it quits.

Nelson spent the next two years travelling between Rennes and his now favourite destination Amsterdam. Despite the excess of drugs and women, Nelson was a very lonely and unhappy man.

After a failed suicide attempt, his cousin sent him back to India.

Once he completed a painful drug rehabilitation programme, Nelson decided to travel around the country. It was a different country from the one he had left many years ago. Globalisation had brought about changes that left him cold and feeling unwelcome. Old college buddies were too busy with their careers to spare an evening for some beer. Nelson felt unwanted, but not for long. When he reached Sarvanpur, it seemed to be largely the same except for a few more colleges that had sprung up. Old acquaintances greeted him with open arms. It was like an outcast high-school 'uncool' friend whom you befriended out of sympathy, but a friend who even after years gave you the same welcome smile, easy approachability and affection.

Nelson decided to attempt writing a book one more time.

Two years later he was ready to publish his debut novel.

His book, *Loss of our Innocence*, explored the themes of faith, atheism, coming-of-age and the ups-n-downs of two brothers with divergent views on faith. It failed to pick up in India, but critics rated it highly and Nelson was surprised when the book was shortlisted for the Booker Prize. It did not get the coveted prize as the book was the least likely to win, but it ensured good publicity for Nelson across the country.

With this unexpected recognition, Nelson began to believe that he was unusually gifted and could make an impact as a social reformer and activist.

When Nelson founded his Atheists & Intellectuals Club at Sarvanpur Public Library, he had an unexpectedly high number of guests turn in to register themselves; these men and women, influenced by the themes in Nelson's book, had put their faith in his ability to shape their lives.

The guiding principles of the group were to tap the hidden power within each individual, uproot social evils, and the philosophy that there is no god who will come to help, so each man should take the responsibility for himself. Though the initial enthusiasm wore off in two months' time, the 30 core club members organised picnics, discussions, book-readings and other events; at every platform, the dominant theme of their discussion was atheism.

Mehek and her group were very active in organising various events for the group. However, Nelson could not stay rooted at one place for long. For the launch of his book's international edition he went on a tour of Europe and North America. Once there, he was invited as a guest lecturer at various universities. In Nelson's absence for such a long duration, the club he'd started degenerated.

Devika knew she had to contact the erstwhile members of this club and get more information on Mehek and the other cult members.

All she could get were random inputs but nothing concrete.

*They were a closed group, content among themselves.*

*Mehek was very shrewd, she used to control each move, each word and each activity of her group.*

*Once they had made up their minds, they picked up petty fights with other members to walk out of the club.*

Devika tried to contact Nelson Pereira also. However, she realized that this man was a nomadic vagabond who had just temporarily paused in her town. Now he was like a high flying kite whose string had snapped. Even he did not know which direction he was going and where he would land. Devika decided to concentrate on the people close to Mehek.

On a hot June morning she ventured out to the town centre of Sarvanpur. Her destination was the culturally vibrant Mohammed Rafi Road.

She entered the narrow lanes of the road leading to the Babla Masjid. Despite its commercial buildings and a few shopping complexes, the lanes seemed to be living two decades in the past; the only connection to the present being a few shops selling cheap mobile phones. While everything else around it moved ahead, this place seemed to have been left behind. The road was lined with various kinds of shops. There was the lemon soda stall, the watermelon slice stall and the sugar cane juice shops doing brisk business. Eateries frying chicken and roasting tandoori rotis stood in close proximity by the roadside. There were shops selling carpets, prayer mats, and in one of the lanes, there were more than 20 shops selling only leather footwear. Two shops stood out: one displaying numerous coloured bottles of local perfumes, 'itra'; the other exclusively selling flavoured betel nuts and pan masala of various kinds. With the municipal elections due in October, the marketplace had also turned into an arena for some kind of a hoarding war with the Islamic Liberals Party competing for space with the Mathrubhumi Morcha.

As she walked along the street, Devika felt uneasy. She switched off her MP3 player, took off the headphone and turned around. Was someone following her, or was it just her imagination? It was a normal day with passersby, street vendors and shoppers.

She shrugged away the feeling and continued walking. Next to Babla Masjid was Patil Lane leading to the railway overbridge. On the overbridge there were hawkers selling belts, bangles, mobile covers, and handkerchiefs among other things.

Devika looked behind from time to time, the feeling of being followed too strong to ignore. Once Devika crossed the overbridge to the other side she reached a lane of shops selling dresses and dress material owned by Sindhi businessmen. They dealt in textiles; she could see three textile units in the vicinity. The lanes were getting narrow. Devika stopped in front of a DVD-VCD and gift shop named 'Khemani Gift Mart'.

"Bhaiyaji! Where can I meet Aftab?" Devika asked a fair, tall man standing outside the shop.

"I am Aftab. Namaste Devika Ji! I was waiting for you. Shall we sit in the eatery on the other side of the road?"

Devika followed the man to Jaltarang Hotel across the road. Once there, they ordered for tea and butter bun. Devika looked at his big ears. She smiled at a sudden image that presented itself to her; the man before her sitting on a plank of wood on a river while his ears were the wind sail guiding the wooden plank across the river.

Aftab refused to make eye contact with her, his eyes transfixed on the table between them. Devika wondered whether he was scared of something.

"As I mentioned on the phone, my name is Devika, I am a writer...."

Aftab interrupted rather nervously, "Madam, I have seen your photograph in the *Konkan Times*. You are the ACP's wife. You had written a book sometime back." He hesitated for a while. "Can I ask you something? I have already faced police grilling four times since Mehek died. What more do you people want?"

"Well! Being the ACP's wife is not my identity. I came here, like any other commoner doing my job. I need your help."

Aftab did not hold her gaze, nor did he look at her. "You make it sound good, but I don't think I have a choice. Alright. Go ahead and ask." His ears had suddenly turned red and Devika felt that she would get nothing out of this jittery young man.

"If this makes you uncomfortable, I will leave immediately, Aftab Bhai. My objective is not to get information out of you by putting you in discomfort. However, your answers will lead us to some really useful truths."

For a moment Aftab glanced at her face and Devika held him with her friendly gaze.

Aftab took out a handkerchief, wiped his sweating forehead, then slumped back into the chair, more relaxed. "Fine. Now that you took the pains to come all the way here, I won't disappoint you."

Aftab kept his eyes on the table as he spoke.

Devika picked up the glass of water in front of her and took a sip, "I am aware of how you met Mehek and your harrowing marital experiences. It is there in your statement which is a part of the police file. Your marriage of horrors has got extensive coverage. I am curious about only one part."

"Go on!"

"Aftab, in your statement to the police you mentioned that Mehek claimed to be sexually abused as a child. According to her version, where did that take place, in the Government Shelter for Girls or her school?"

"I don't remember correctly but I think she said it was the school."

"Tell me Aftab, was your mother against your marriage?"

"I suppose she respected my choice. I am from a pretty well known Sindhi family and Mehek was from an orphanage. Considering these facts, I think she resisted only mildly." Aftab looked defensive when questioned about his mother.

"She was suffering from lung infection. For how long?"

"Devika Ji, she suffered from lung infection for four years. When we got married, Mehek was surprised that we kept oxygen cylinders and a mask in her bedroom."

"There are textile mills here which makes it worse. So your mother died a couple of months after you got married. What were her symptoms?"

The tea arrived with the butter buns. Devika and Aftab sipped their tea quietly. Aftab started eating the bun quickly in between short, quick sips of tea. Devika thought he was still very nervous; the experiences of his past had made him a man perpetually in fear.

"In the later stages, my mother started vomiting, having diarrhoea and convulsions. Mehek requested a young lady doctor known to her to visit our home everyday to keep a check on mother's health. In spite of our efforts she sunk into a coma and died."

"Any other symptoms that your mother had?"

Aftab's eyes narrowed as he tried to recollect, "Towards the end, there was a bit of blood in her urine. There were white patches on her fingernails too."

"Aftab, one last question. The lady doctor who came for your mother's treatment. Did she have any peculiar features or characteristics?"

Aftab was relieved that this was the last question. "Yes, she had brown eyes. You know her?"

Devika nodded. "She is known to me. Thanks for your time, Aftab."

Devika walked out of the eatery into the street. The crowd on the street had increased. As she approached the railway overbridge she felt somebody's presence behind her again. Someone was stalking her. She was sure of it. When she turned back she saw a lot of faces. She started to walk fast, almost barging into passersby. She quickly climbed the steps to the overbridge and looked behind nervously.

*I am sure someone is following me!*

Several burqa clad women and men with prayer caps surrounded her. Devika walked very fast. She stopped an auto rickshaw. Once inside the vehicle, she felt relieved and called Anshuman from her mobile phone, informing him about her morning meeting with Aftab. Her doubt about his mother's death was correct after all. The woman had not died a natural death. In all probability his wife Mehek had killed her by regularly administering what seems to be mild arsenic. Mehek even managed to rope in an imposter for her treatment on the basis of false diagnosis.

She described the doctor to Anshuman.

"Brown eyes! Ma'am, that is the doctor's daughter."

"Precisely! Poor Aftab is not even aware of the real truth behind his mother's death. I did not have the courage to tell him that his marriage cost him his mother's life."

"If he ever reads your book, which he surely will, he will get to know the truth," said Anshuman.

Devika sighed. "I hope he does not read my book."

"Devika Ji, *maybe* you were right that the full body count of Mehek's victims is not a complete list yet." Unlike his regular self, Anshuman seemed to be compliant today.

"I think this is just the start. There are more skeletons about to tumble out of the closet."

Devika was in high spirits.

On the way back home she stopped the rickshaw at the pharmacy on MG Road to buy a kit. As she put her hands inside her leather bag to take out her purse, she saw a blue folded paper inside her bag. Her bag had two buttons but no zip; it would be easy for anybody to slide objects into the folds created on the sides when the bag was buttoned.

Devika opened the paper and read. "Just do what you are supposed to do. It's not a choice."

What was required of her? She was baffled by the message and the constant harassment. Devika decided to ignore it.

On returning home Devika went directly to the washroom, her hands shaking as she tried the pregnancy kit.

The two lines on the pregnancy kit strip made her jump in happiness.

She called up Shravan. Her voice shook as she gave him the news of her pregnancy. "Today you have made me the happiest man on earth. I am winding up everything at work and coming home right away."

Devika felt good. Yoga and meditation had come to her rescue. Finally, she was going to experience the pleasures and pains of motherhood; life would not be an endless road without milestones. All she had to do was to be happy, control her mind for the next 9 months and stay away from the anti-depressant Serta tablets which could seriously harm the unborn baby. Devika decided to hand over the Serta strips to Shravan in the evening. From the window of her bedroom, Devika saw her cat Zeenu walk across the garden. She tried calling it. The cat looked at her. Its eyes widened in fear and she ran away as fast as she could.

Excitedly, Devika punched her father's mobile number. It rang for a long time. For the next one hour she called every ten minutes but there was no reply. It was strange because her father Rameshwar never switched off his mobile phone.

Something was really wrong.

Devika was impatient; he was about to become a grandfather and she wanted to hear his reaction to the news. After all, he too had waited a long time to hold her baby in his arms. Two hours later, her father's phone was still not reachable. Devika was restless with anxiety when her uncle, her father's brother, called.

"I was trying to reach Papa. Where is he?"

"I don't know how to tell you this beta..."

"Tell me what?"

"The biopsy results of the samples taken during the endoscopy procedure have come." Her uncle's voice cracked.

Devika stopped breathing, her palms began to sweat.

"Your father has stomach cancer."

In a moment, Devika's world changed; life came to a standstill.

In a low tone, she said. "Ask him to get ready. Shravan and I will catch the next flight to Delhi to bring him here."

Slowly, she replaced the receiver in its cradle. People go through bitter phases and sweet phases in life; this was the first time that the two came together in hers, hand in hand. 'You have no right to be happy.' She murmured to herself.

Yin and Yang, the opposing forces which run the universe; today they were together at her doorstep making a cruel joke out of her life. It was as if the powers above were playing a game in bad taste. This should have been the happiest day of her life. God's sense of humour was at a new low. In one place life was slowly getting created and nurtured, in another, it was slowly self-destructing. Tonight, even her primrose tablets will be of little help.

# July: Making Father Proud

The doctor scanned the reports. "This is the problem with this form of cancer. While other forms of cancer have some symptoms or the other, stomach cancer remains untraced till it reaches a fairly advanced stage." He looked at Shravan, his expression grim. "People mistake it to be just normal stomach ache and indigestion. That is what gives the cancer more time to grow." Devika was hanging on to every word spoken by Dr Makhija, the senior oncologist at the Sushrut Oncology Centre in Sushrut Hospital, the biggest medical facility in Sarvanpur.

On the table were the slides with the samples that had been sent for biopsy. Devika looked at them with unexplainable disgust. She was face to face with her enemy for the first time. Those small stains on the glass, those were after her father's life, an enemy so small that there can be no argument or negotiation with it; so miniscule, yet so feared.

"What stage is the cancer?" Shravan asked.

"It's spread to other organs around the stomach. I am sorry, the truth is that we have crossed Stage 3," the doctor said with a sigh. It was always difficult to break such news to the family.

Devika closed her eyes for a brief moment; the truth needed time to sink in. She was still not crying. It felt like a bad nightmare which had paralysed her mind. Only her hands trembled.

"Is it curable?" Shravan asked.

Dr Makhija said, "We will start the treatment immediately..."

"He asked you if it is curable." Devika interrupted.

Dr Makhija took a deep breath; this was an occupational hazard, something one signs up for when one chooses the stream of oncology. Most oncologists end up becoming poker faced after some time. It's difficult to go ahead without being stoic. More often than not, they are the ones who end up speaking the dreaded words to people, words that shut out hope from the patient's life, like light from an underground dungeon. The gynaecologist, more often than not, gets the sweets and the memorabilia, the oncologist nothing but cold stares, anger and gloom. In a compassionate tone the doctor replied, "We will try our best, but it looks highly unlikely that we will be able to cure him fully. It's at a stage where it is like diabetes or high BP. You can only hope to keep it under control but will not be able to get rid of it."

The comparison to diabetes and BP was supposed to be a feel-good statement. In reality it sounded like a blatant lie making fun of its own stupidity.

"How much time do we have?" Shravan's voice trembled.

"Let's face the truth! I know it is difficult for you," the doctor groped for the right words,

"At this stage we have observed life expectancy to be six months to a year, on an average."

"Six months!" said Shravan.

"I am sorry. I understand your trauma but I need to give you a realistic picture. What we need to do now is a surgical procedure to insert a chemo port," the doctor scribbled something on his pad. "He may need to get admitted in two days time." He handed Shravan a slip of paper. "Please show this slip at the reception."

"Thank you doctor." Shravan mumbled. On his way out he whispered to his wife,

"Relax! Remember, if you look petrified it will knock Papa out of his calm."

As they were about to step out of the doctor's cabin, Devika took a deep breath and smiled. She was preparing herself for the endless lies she would have to mouth after this. Outside the cabin Rameshwar was seated in a wheelchair; his haemoglobin reading was very low, he could not walk and had a terrible backache. The cancer was causing havoc inside his body tissues causing blood loss, turning his robust structure to bones, a distorted shadow of his former self.

Rameshwar asked, "Which stage?"

"Stage 1." First lie.

"Is it curable?"

"Yes. You will be as fit as an athlete, Papa." Second lie.

"When is the surgery to remove it?"

"You don't even require a surgery. It will be gone with some chemotherapy." Third lie.

Rameshwar asked in a low tone, "Devika, beta, I will survive this, right?"

"Yes! Don't worry, Papa, just a couple of months of discomfort." Fourth lie, the most difficult.

In the early years of his career, Professor Rameshwar Soni was known to be a strict disciplinarian who would make the most difficult students to comply with his rules. Today his body was rebelling. Throughout their lives her parents had saved for their retirement. While her father worked at the Deshbandhu College in Delhi, Devika's mother had a small beauty parlour in their locality They saved a little money every month and put it away into post office deposits to be used after their retirement.

'To be used on a rainy day,' they would say.

Devika's mother had once told her when she was a teenager, "I would not like to live beyond the 50s. I feel sad when I see very old people losing their loved ones around them one by one. They keep staring at the empty chairs and vacant rooms of the departed. In our lifetimes we are used to people, places, relationships and material objects in a certain way; all of which change with time. It's better to exit when everything is familiar than feel lost in an unfamiliar world."

The divine powers had granted her wish. She died of meningitis while still in her early fifties.

Her father still sprayed her mother's favourite perfume on his hands and remarked, "People may think I am weird, wearing ladies perfume. How can I tell them that this makes me feel her presence around me?"

Now barely four months after his retirement, her father was detected with cancer. The futility of their whole exercise of saving money in deposits was evident. The couple had saved all their life for nothing. There would be no 'retirement life' for either of them.

Shravan and Devika had flown to Delhi to pick him up from their small flat in Malviya Nagar. They packed up everything, even shutting off the main gas pipeline and electricity mains. As they prepared to leave, Devika took one last look around the house. Everywhere she looked, she could see her younger self with her parents: lighting the lamps on Diwali night, renting a VCR and video tape to watch movies with the neighbours, replacing the old black-n-white TV with a new colour TV, devouring watermelon after dinner at the dining table, making thermocol models for school assignments, playing carom on Sunday afternoons, her parents' surprise gift for her – a brand new Ladybird bicycle for topping her class. Small things provided immense excitement back then. Cheap country-made dolls, Bambi pencil-boxes, Camlin ink bottles and her first fountain pen, a new set of butterfly hair clips, a new stamp for her stamp collection album, a new pair of shoes and along with these, the excitement to flaunt it in front of friends. She knew that the next time she returned it would not be the same place; it would not evoke happiness.

As they spread white sheets over the furniture and locked the flat, Devika's heart sank.

When she locked the main door from outside, it was like putting a lock on a chapter of her life. The next time she would enter the house, the people inside would not be there. Not even their images, only memories to welcome and haunt her. Her childhood and youth spent in a house which was now under a white sheet, like a dead body.

One thing Devika understood was that pregnancy would render her incapable of work after a couple of months, especially for research related outings. She also knew that she had to complete the book, get it edited and published in the five months she had before she was compelled to rest. This was her chance to make her father proud.

Rameshwar had always wanted to write a book and had kept it aside for his retirement. He would now live his dreams through her. Devika's first book was a disappointment, this time she would give it all she had. She was working against a tight deadline. The creation of life was going to take nine-and-a-half months. The creation of death had an uncertain tenure. Nature was setting its own deadlines.

Lost in these thoughts, Devika stood near the gate in the evening. Two fakirs clad in shining green robes with long grey beards approached the gate. One of them was holding a small earthen pot which was giving out fumes of burning incense and the other a bunch of long peacock feathers tied together. Between them they held a green sheet – a chadar for alms. Devika went inside and returned with a 50 rupee note. As she opened the gate the fakir in the front looked at her carefully and withdrew backwards. When she tried to put the money into the chadar he showed his hand gesturing her to stop. "There are some really dark energies around you, beta! Be very careful," he said. Devika stood motionless looking at them. "We don't need your money. Allah willing, you will be freed from all this, my child." They left after saying, "Take care of yourself and pray." Devika's gaze followed them to the end of the road where they disappeared. She couldn't help but wonder why these strange things were happening around her every now and then.

A week later Rameshwar underwent the surgical procedure to insert a chemo port inside his chest. He would have to undergo at least six rounds of chemotherapy and the port inside the body was necessary to administer the chemo-medicine without any difficulty.

Devika was having a difficult time with her morning sickness in the first trimester of the pregnancy besides having to juggle time between her own health and her father's ailment. Rameshwar was bedridden with terrible pain throughout his body. Shravan had to take 12 days off work to stay home and manage the situation. These were trying times.

# July: Hidden Objects

The reply took longer than usual. Maybe the person on the other side was taking some time to make the decision. Probably there was some thinking or planning going on at the other end.

Dear DeViKa,

How ARE you?

Like you wanted. COMING to the Point. Some objects are below the Victim of the Mob.

MEHEK

The strange pattern of the previous letters continued in this one too. All the words were made up of letters cut out from the 13th page of the *Konkan Times* between the 1st and 13th. The imposter's belief in numerology was evident. The communication was force fit into the words available on that page, even at the expense of confusing the reader.

At the local chapter meeting of 'India Against Corruption' later that morning, Devika found herself distracted by the letter she'd received. The words echoed in her mind: *'The Objects', 'Victim' and 'Mob'*. Those words were clues but she was unable to decipher them. When the group members asked her to speak, she was at a loss for words.

On her way back home, her mind drifted back to the letter again.

In the afternoon, she was due for her regular tests at the hospital but before leaving she went to the guest room which was now occupied by her father. Placing a hand on his forehead, she leaned over her father and whispered, "Papa, I'll be back in a couple of hours."

On her way out her eyes strayed to the painting of a flower pot on the wall opposite the window. It had a layer of dust over it.

"Radhemohan! Tell the maid who comes for dusting that she should not just clean the floor but also the tables, showpieces and wall hangings," she instructed. Picking up her bag from the table she went out but stopped short. The picture had reminded her of something.

*'Victim of the Mob'*

Who was this victim of the mob? A person who perished in a riot, revolt or revolution. A victim would be a person who had suffered injustice. A mismatch in the crime committed by the person and the punishment inflicted upon them by the mob. This rang a bell inside Devika's head. She had recently seen a victim of the mob. Framed, quite literally.

She put her bag down and dialled Inspector Anshuman's number.

"Hello Anshuman, Devika here. I think we need to search Mehek's flat again."

The voice on the other side did not answer. There was an uncomfortable silence. "Devika Ji, this would be the third time. I will not be able to get the permission unless there is something substantial."

"Anshuman, I got a letter from my imposter pen-pal today. There is a very strong reference there to something inside her flat."

"How can you be so sure, Madam?"

"The letter mentions the victim of a mob. It clearly hints that there is something placed in Mehek's bedroom below the sketch of Marie Antoinette," Devika was excited. "What surprises me is that whosoever wrote this letter knows Mehek so well that he knows what hangs on her bedroom wall."

"Devika Ji, it's highly unlikely that we will get the permission but I will try my best. Many people in the department strongly believe that following the leads in this case is a futile exercise." She heard the disinterest in his tone.

"Thanks Anshuman. This time we could use sniffer dogs. Whatever we are looking for is somewhere close to that painting."

Instead of leaving for the hospital for her tests, Devika sat down near the door, her mind a whirlwind of thoughts.

*Anshuman must be thinking that I am an albatross around his neck. Something he has to carry along because his boss may get offended.* She fervently hoped they would find something important in Mehek's flat or else she would lose her credibility with Anshuman.

Devika and Shravan were present the next day for their appointment at the Holy Cross Hospital. This was their first ultrasound of the baby. As they saw the tiny pea-sized image of the seed of life, they forgot all their worries and problems. They hurried home and showed the report along with the images to Rameshwar. The expression of a worried man facing a terminal disease changed to that of an expression of a child on a merry-go-round.

On Sunday, Devika and Shravan took Rameshwar to the Sarvanpur Public Park and for dinner at the famous Patiala Grill restaurant. Though the C-word dominated their thoughts, everyone tried to behave as if it was a normal weekend. Chemo-therapy was an integral part of their life with its brief interludes of normalcy.

A week later Devika got a call from Anshuman. He was calling from Mehek's house.

"Good news. We found a loose tile in the floor below the painting. Guess what we found?"

"Not sure... drugs?"

"Yes! Two sachets of cocaine, a country made pistol similar to a Beretta, a log book full of betting details on various cricket teams maintained to track profit-and-loss; a list of bookies along with transaction done with them, worth crores of rupees."

Devika was elated; she was on the right track after all. "It looks like we need to track down the person who is sending me the letters. This person seems to know a lot about the internal details including the cult's finances."

"Devika Ji, I think if we shake up the postal department we can track this person."

"This Mehek is an enigma. She was laundering all the money received from the doctor. Placing it on illegal betting..."

".....And losing a lot of money. I am not sure if even her fellow cult members knew of her dealings. The good thing with the log book is that it provides names, address and the numbers of bookies from as far as small towns in Rajasthan like Jodhpur and Ajmer. Goddamn useful!" Anshuman sounded excited. Devika wondered whether the letter sent to her was a vengeful act by the sender. Perhaps to punish the illegal betting network for causing financial loss to the cult?

"Anshuman, my biggest fear is that these people may have been planning something big with all this money. I had told you earlier that I'm sure there are more untraced cult members out there. Are we sitting on a landmine without realising the seriousness of the problem at hand?"

"Madam, I think even if there was a sleeper-cell it would have disintegrated by now without a leadership. I believe there is nothing more to investigate," Anshuman said rather assertively.

Devika felt frustrated. Why couldn't the man take her views seriously? Wasn't she too researching, exploring the cult and its activities? Hadn't she already given them vital clues in the case?

# August:
# Police Check Post

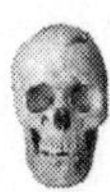

The red post box stood on the roadside in front of the huge white wall around the Holy Cross Hospital. Some 300 feet ahead was the famous hotspot 'The Club,' complete with a swimming pool, a tennis court, cafeteria, gym and an indoor games section for members and their families only.

Devika and Anshuman looked around the narrow road, empty even during the rush hour. This was the Annie Besant Road, an alternate road connecting Sarvanpur to Goa. Occasionally there were some trucks, vans and pickup vehicles carrying goods plying on this road. There was a police check post across the road set up to keep a check on vehicles carrying goods without permits, papers or documentation.

"We tracked the letter to the post office based on the seal. One of the postmen confirmed that he collected the bright red envelope from this post box along with 20 wedding cards in the afternoon collection," said Anshuman.

"Let's go across to the check post and ask the constables there if they have seen the person who posted it or observed anything suspicious." Devika was halfway across the road even as she spoke to Anshuman.

The check-post smelt of beedis. There were stray glasses of tea from the nearby tea stall. A Marathi local newspaper, some files, a desk and a few plastic chairs were scattered inside. An old radio played an old song from a 1963 Hindi film, *Jo waada kiya woh nibhana padega...*

At the approach of a senior officer the check post drifted into momentary fluster, like a businessman's office during an income tax raid. One of the constables quickly switched off the radio while the other stood up out of respect. Both constables were middle aged; one of them was very thin with betel-stained teeth, the other was what Devika called 25-75. He was bald, so he used the 25 percent of the hair on both sides above his ears to cover the 75 percent bald patch between them.

"Salaam Saheb!"

"Do you keep an eye on who drops letters into the box across the road by any chance?" Anshuman asked.

The constables looked at each other.

"Not many people post letters in these parts. They are using computers to send letters now, Saheb."

"I know that. Just answer my question. Have you seen anybody?"

"Sir, when?"

"21st July."

The thin constable reached below his table and took out an old ragged notebook. He flipped the pages.

"What is this?" Devika asked.

The bald constable smiled and said, "We have no entertainment here other than the radio. Few vehicles pass along this road. So we play a silly game of keeping bets on the number of letters that will go into the box on any given day between the morning and afternoon."

"You place money on your bets!"

"No, only beedis, and sometimes cigarettes, Madam. Then we write it in the notebook and do a consolidated clearance every ten days."

"It's because of people like you that the general public think policemen in these parts just come to while away their time." Anshuman was angry. In the momentary silence that followed, the constables busied themselves with the pages of the betting book.

"Look Saheb! 21st July was a special day and I won the bet. The number of letters posted was abnormally high; 22! Most of them were big wedding cards which were pushed in one-by-one. There were 20 of them." The thin constable smiled triumphantly.

Anshuman intervened. "Yes! We know that a family posted 20 wedding invitation cards on that day. What about the others?"

"Saheb, from what I remember, one letter was posted by an old man who lives in the nearby lane next to the drainage stream. His wife is ill and bedridden. Once every two weeks, he sends one mail to his son who is in the army."

"The other letter was from the tea stall owner a little ahead on this road. He belongs to Valsad. Sends occasional letters to his family there," added the thin constable.

Devika asked, "There were no more mails posted that day?"

The constables looked at each other and the notebook. They shook their head.

"So when the postman came here to collect the letter he found the bright red envelope along with the other 22. How could that letter come out of nowhere?" Anshuman was incredulous.

"Any chance that you were out for lunch or doing something else?" Devika asked.

"Madam, at least one of us is here at all times. There is nothing on the road on the opposite side except the post box in front of the big white wall. We can clearly see anybody coming or going."

"We will do a background check on the two suspects. The old man living near the drainage stream and the tea stall owner belonging to Valsad," said Anshuman.

"False leads," Devika said, crestfallen.

She sat down on one of the plastic chairs in the check post. "This is where you people sit the whole day?" She looked around, puzzled.

The constables nodded.

From where she sat, Devika could see the top of the post box. She narrowed her eyes. After some time, she left with Anshuman.

"Is it a possibility that the person we are looking for is short? The narrow road, the high parapet wall around the cabin and the raised position of the check post blocks visibility across the road to only above four and a half feet," said Devika.

"Yes! If these constables were seated on that chair then the person posting the letter had to be of average height to be visible," said Anshuman as he kept his eyes on the road.

Devika looked askance at her companion. Was he always like this at work or was he getting tired of helping with her research? This was the wrong time of the month and Devika was a little over-aggressive. "Such a shitty situation! I can't believe we missed this person after coming so close. Whoever he or she is, the person knows too much. He or she even sounds like Mehek. That's creepy."

"We will get the imposter next time," said Anshuman.

"There may not be a next time. Dammit! Who knows if the letters will stop after this?" Devika knew that she was getting more anxious than usual; she should take the primrose oil tablets.

"Let's see." Anshuman tried to calm her down. "By the way, this evening Jyoti and I are going shopping to buy new dresses for our little one."

"Little Arjun going to school. It will be very difficult for Jyoti to stay away from him even for a couple of hours."

"Devika Ji, all parents have to go through that pain. Some in the beginning, some later."

When Devika entered her room she saw a courier packet with a familiar logo on her table.

It was from Cherub Publishers.

Dear Devika,

We are writing this letter to look at the possibility of advancing the submission deadline for your manuscript. It would be great if we could have the manuscript by 30th November instead of 30th January as decided previously. With time, the public fascination for the Sarvanpur Serial Murders is waning. Getting the book out into the market when the subject matter is in vogue will ensure instant success.

Also, we are told that a popular publishing house is pitching with their authors to come up with a book on the same subject matter. I hope you understand how important it is for us to be the first in the market. Considering these points, it would be great if you could finish the work on the manuscript promptly.

Regards,

Cherub Editorial Team

*As if I did not have enough on my plate already.* Devika sighed and kept the letter down. Her first reaction was to write to the publisher that she would take her own time to finish her work and that they could withdraw their offer to publish if they wanted. Then she looked at the light coming from the guest room where her father slept and decided against it. If she went out hunting for an alternative publishing house, it would take time and she had to get this book out soon, no matter what. Time was running out. She would negotiate with them and see if they would agree to a December deadline. She sat down at her laptop and typed the finishing lines to the third chapter of her manuscript.

Before going to sleep Devika spent time with her father. He took out his most prized possession, the old Sony Camcorder which worked on small video tape. In the display he showed Devika the videos of her parents' trip to Nainital, Mussourie, Shimla and Mount Abu.

"Your mother enjoyed boating a lot," Rameshwar said as he showed a clip of their boating trip in the middle of Saptatal Lake.

In his eyes Devika could see the longing to go back to those times. There was a sudden outburst of enthusiasm and energy in his tired body when he revisited the past through old photographs and videos. They talked for some time before she retired to bed.

Shravan did not return from work till midnight.

"Devika! Devika!"

Devika rushed to her father's room but found Rameshwar seated on a sofa in the hall.

He was furious as he stared at the ground.

"Ask these people to go!"

"Which people, Papa?"

Rameshwar pointed behind Devika, "That nurse behind you. Ask her to go!"

Devika turned around. "There is nobody behind me Papa!"

Rameshwar looked around the room bewildered, "They were here. They saw you and must have left."

"There was nobody in this room," she said.

At her words he lifted his legs on the sofa, bent them towards his chest and started to rub his head hard with both hands.

"I know what to do!"

"What are you saying, Papa?"

"I know the remedy for this!" Rameshwar yelled.

"Papa, calm down." Devika sat next to him.

Rameshwar started to cry. "Beta, everyone is making me go mad."

"No no. Come with me. Let's try to sleep."

Hearing the commotion Radhemohan entered the room asking Devika as to what happened. His daughter Laali was standing behind him at a distance.

Devika and Radhemohan took Rameshwar to his bed, made him drink a glass of milk and sat there till he went to sleep. She was aghast to note than even in this moment of panic he was tightly clutching the Hanuman Chalisa to his chest.

> *Faith is not a choice you make depending on your convenience. On the contrary, Faith chooses you, depending on whether you have the courage to take the first few steps without having any idea of the path that lies ahead.*

Devika shut her eyes as she recalled her father's words. After the events of the past few months Devika found herself at the crossroads between faith and its absence, and here was a man who could, if he wanted, cry hoarse at the injustice meted out to him by fate, proclaim against the uselessness of his god, rant at the death warrant issued against him, yet he held on tightly to his faith.

Rameshwar's faith was not fragile enough to crumple under the weight of his misfortune; his faith was not dependent on his fate. He would often say that faith was the most ultimate form of outsourcing. A person outsources his problems to the divine power and he should go ahead with his normal life without any worries, believing that his troubles will be taken care of. "That is the most precious gift which faith provides to you, peace of mind," he would often say.

"The hallucinations are due to deficiency of sodium. Give him ORS solution five times a day," advised Dr Makhija the next day.

At the end, it seemed like a minor issue. However, the previous night's incident had terrified Devika. It was her introduction to her new role. This disease, 'the king of malaise' brought suffering for both the patient and the people around him. One day there would be swelling, next day indigestion, third day body pain, fourth day headache... both the patient and the caregiver lived a day-to-day existence; daily there are new issues and new hurdles to be crossed. The acceptance of the truth is half the battle won. It mellows the treacherously painful journey towards the inevitable. The only thing that can save when grief hits the roof is not mental strength but detachment – the ability to unplug the mind is sometimes the only way to preserve one's sanity and do one's duty.

Relieved from an immediate crisis, Devika started to draft her column for the *Konkan Times*. This time her column was about corruption allegations and a court case against a local politician, Satyaraj Kale. The prosecution was unable to prove most of the charges against him. The courts imposed a fine of 50,000 rupees for negligence and awarded no jail term. Devika read her column closely trying to understand what she wanted to communicate to the imposter. She was sure the person sending her the letters was in all probability angry with the betting network for having caused monetary losses. The person on the other side was vengeful, in a perfect state to solicit more information. After thinking for some time she came up with a title, 'Is that all?'

# September: Number Games

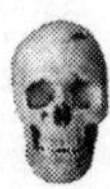

The next time Devika received the bright red envelope, the intention and the subject matter of the sender were even more unclear to Devika.

Dear DeViKa,

How is LIFE?

Sharing my Happiness. 102 will make THE country and its people Stand up and TAKE notice unlike 815 and 825

MEHEK

The numbers in the letter were cut out of advertisements appearing on the 13th page of *Konkan Times*. All the other text was also from the 13th pages of issues between the 1st and the 13th.

The numbers signified something. What did the sender mean by 'Sharing my Happiness?' What was 102? Some event, some place? This weird open challenge baffled her. She quickly switched on her laptop and then the modem to connect to the internet.

What were 815 and 825? Maybe they were postal pin codes.

She typed 'Pin code 815' into the India Post website. Satara.

She then typed 'Pin code 825' into India Post website. Jalgaon.

She decided to research terror attacks that had taken place in Satara or Jalgaon. If the number signified a postal code, that meant the upcoming attack would take place in pin code number 102 – this was a non-existent postal pin code. Nonetheless, Devika decided to revisit it later. She looked at the numbers 815 and 825 again. Maybe it was a date. Looking at the digits she knew that the first digit could be the month and the second two the date. No other combinations looked likely.

She typed 'August 15th attack' into the search engine. The search results mostly pertained to Iraq bombings on 15th August, 2011. A string of roadside car suicide bombings in Baghdad, Kut, Najaf, Tikrit and other places that had left 64 people dead and 287 injured.

Devika typed 'August 25th attack' into the search engine. There was a list pertaining to the 25th August, 2010 Iraq bombings. The attacks happened across Iraq killing 53 and injuring 270 people.

The world was in such a sad state that if you picked up any random date and searched, it was very likely that a terror attack would have taken place somewhere in the world on that date. However, these attacks had nothing to do with India. Since the letter clearly implied attacks pertaining to India, it meant that 815 and 825 did not mean calendar dates. If not dates, these numbers could mean anything, even street numbers, house numbers or building numbers. Devika wondered if the digits meant latitude and longitude coordinates. She searched in the search engine 'India Latitude Longitude Extent'.

India's extent is 68 degree East to 97 degree East.

India's Latitudinal extent is 8 degree North to 37 degree North.

Devika tried to play with the numbers 815 and 825 to see if they could be adjusted to fit inside the range but to no avail. The search for numbers signifying telephone codes also proved unfruitful. '82' was the international code for South Korea and '81' for Japan.

Deep in thought, she looked up to see her father dressed in his favourite white checked shirt, khakhi trousers and a white cap to conceal hair loss. He stood at the entrance of her bedroom.

"Ready to go?" he asked.

They had to be on time for their appointment at the Sushrut Cancer Daycare ward for chemotherapy. Devika switched off the laptop, kept the letter aside and got ready to go.

The Cancer Daycare Ward is one of those rare places in the world where extreme hope and extreme despair coexist in equal measure. As Devika and her father went past the other patients towards the nurse's desk, they exchanged compassionate smiles with the others in the ward; the smiles belied their individual thoughts and fears. She knew their stories as they knew hers. In the eight-hour long procedure, lying next to one another, the patients get to know one another's life stories.

There was a seven year old boy suffering from leukaemia; as Devika accompanied her father she heard the boy laugh as his father tickled him, unaware of the pain awaiting him at every turn.

In the next bed was a young man with a towel wrapped around his face that was disfigured by frequent tobacco chewing. A middle aged housewife sat with her husband who had a scarf wound tightly around his head to conceal the bald patch due to the treatment.

Cancer, the lord of malaise, was slowly sucking the happiness away from all these people and taking away their health, looks, dignity, modesty and hope. For them it was the fourth round of chemotherapy, the procedure that injected toxins into the blood stream of cancer patients to damage the cancerous growth. These toxins damage the health of the individual and attack the healthy cells too but there was no alternative. The disease did not leave one with too many options. Today her father would be given Epirubicin and Oxaliplatin again; previous sessions had caused mild vomiting, loss of hair and darkening of nails.

All senior police officers of the state had been summoned to Mumbai by the state home minister for an important briefing. In Shravan's absence, Devika had to manage everything on her own. After admitting Rameshwar in the ward, Devika stood in the queue at the main reception of the Sushrut Hospital for billing. The total cost of the six-hour procedure was 30,000 rupees. Devika looked at the bundle of notes she was about to deposit. When she was in college Devika had wanted to earn huge sums of money to make her parents happy; money to pay for lunches and dinners at five star hotels, for expensive clothes, exotic vacations and so on. She had drawn up a long list. Today she was paying money to buy expensive poison to be injected into her father.

At least she was able to provide the best medical facilities to her father. A clean hospital and good medical care was a luxury in any third world country where government hospitals were so crowded that patients had to stay for months in the corridors, on stairs, roads and footpaths outside the hospitals. Doctors in such places often prescribed expensive medicines and medical procedures which either had cheaper alternatives or were not required at all. Greedy physicians making their cut at the cost of a poor man's malaise because the government had largely washed off its hands from the responsibility of social security and health care. In these third world countries life was messy and death more so. Whenever she read about all this in newspapers and magazines Devika often wondered how low is low?

After the billing, Devika had to call up the health insurance company for reimbursements. As expected, the company initially tried to evade processing the claim on grounds that chemotherapy was not a 24 hour procedure. She would have to call up multiple times, fax the documents and proof to remind them that policy covered the illness.

She returned to the Cancer Daycare ward. Her father was in bed reading the day's edition of *Konkan Times* while the nurse prepared the bright pink bottle of the dreaded liquid to be given intravenously to him.

Rameshwar was smiling as he read the *Konkan Times*. He pointed to an article and said, "Interview of your mother's favourite author."

Devika peered over his head at a faded photograph of the author Ved Prakash Sharma.

Devika's parents hailed from Sagar in Madhya Pradesh. Before migrating to Delhi for higher education, Devika's father did his schooling in the steel township of Jamshedpur where her grandfather worked with Tata Steel. Devika's mother came from a family of silver jewellery makers and did her primary education in her hometown. When the couple lived in Delhi, they used to regularly travel to their hometown by train and at every railway station her mother would look frantically through the window for book-wheelers. AH-Wheelers have a 100 year old legacy in the country. From their stalls Devika's mother would buy Hindi crime fiction; these thrillers would usually have the standard cover of a man, a woman, a gun or knife and some blood. Devika's mother was a big fan of Surender Mohan Pathak and Ved Prakash Sharma. Even Devika's name was a slight modification of the famous Hindi author Devaki Nandan Khatri.

"You seem to have inherited your love for English from me," Rameshwar said, the smile still around his mouth, "but your love for bizarre crime stories from your mother."

As the nurse proceeded to inject the medicine Rameshwar turned his face towards the wall and said, "Once I recover from all this I want to visit Kedarnath. It has been a long standing unfulfilled wish of mine."

Every time her father expressed a desire to be fulfilled, Devika felt upset and would be shaken to the core of her being.

Rameshwar believed his disease was in its preliminary stage and therefore curable. Devika never let him read the CT scan reports and handed him only the images or initial summary page with its confusing medical terms. She also removed the 'High Risk' and 'Extreme Caution' stickers or covers on medicines purchased from the pharmacy before handing it to Rameshwar – anything that would give him the slightest hint about the severity and extent of his disease.

So Rameshwar was full of hope. Every time he said 'Once I recover', he would look into Devika's eyes for confirmation and Devika had a hard time keeping up appearances.

After the 6th chemotherapy session it was time for the next phase of the CT scan.

The results were encouraging. The cancerous growth had shrunk by 50 percent and it was not spreading. Instead, it showed very little metabolic activity.

# September: The Post Box

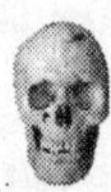

"We're in luck!" Devika pointed towards the bank's security camera.

The Indudurg Cooperative Bank branch stood right opposite the post box from which the previous letter had been sent.

Anshuman looked at the camera fixed above the entrance of the bank facing the road, in the direction of the letter box on the other side. The road between them was a narrow single lane. This post box stood in front of thick vegetation growing on disputed property which was the subject of a long running legal battle between its erstwhile residents and a redevelopment builder.

"The postman had been sure that he had picked up the envelope from the same letter box on the 13th of this month. I hope the camera was working properly and the recording took place," said Anshuman.

Devika was excited. "I am so glad that we will finally get to see the face of the enigmatic person who is sending these letters. Does the postman recollect how many letters he collected? This was just a couple of days back, wasn't it?"

"Devika Ji, according to the postman, there were three other letters besides ours."

Wearing his Inspector's uniform, it was easy for Anshuman to gain entry into the bank along with Devika. There was a huge rush of customers inside the bank branch which had been recently computerised. Not yet familiar with the technology, the staff was slow at processing transactions. Most of the staff looked baffled as they peered at the computer screens before them.

After a ten-minute wait, Devika and Anshuman were with the bank manager in his cabin.

"This is for the investigation of a criminal case. We would require the security tapes of the camera fixed at the entrance for the 13th of September."

The branch manager, a pleasant, bald, middle-aged man, replied, "I will call the security officer to help you with that." He gave instructions on the telephone.

"Would you like some tea and snacks?"

"No. Thank you."

"Hey Anshuman! I forgot to tell you about the content of the letter I received. It has three numbers 102, 825 and 815. Does that ring a bell in your mind?" said Devika turning to Anshuman while the bank manager was busy looking at his computer.

"102, 825 and 815. No!"

"Any address, pin code or number that appeared on any of the crime scenes."

"No!" Anshuman said narrowing his eyes.

Fifteen minutes later a Safari suit-clad, dark, well built man with a prominent moustache came into the cabin. He led Devika and Anshuman to the rear of the premises where the security control room was located. Seeing a police inspector in uniform, the staff started to fumble with the tapes of the previous day. The control room had two flat screen wall mounted LCD displays. They were displaying live feeds from the cameras. There was another display screen placed on the desk attached to the archive storage device.

Devika and Anshuman sat on plastic chairs, their eyes glued to this screen while another employee fast forwarded the tape to the time when the postman arrived for his morning pickup on the 13th.

Thankfully, it was a bright day and the recording was clear. Devika and Anshuman stared at the black-n-white tape carefully as if their life depended on it, their eyes scanning the screen for every detail.

At 10.15 am, a street vegetable vendor took his cart near the post box and put a white envelope inside the box. Then he went behind the post box closer to the vegetation beyond and returned after some time. Obviously, he had relieved his bladder.

"Poor man had no idea that he was on camera!" Devika laughed. Then she looked around at all the men standing around her and felt slightly embarrassed.

At 11.12 am, a local madman in ragged clothes came and sat on top of the post box. He hugged it, played around it. He tried to put his hands inside the opening of the letter box and later pulled out his hand with some difficulty. After some time he left when a street dog started to chase him.

At 12.25 pm, a crippled young man on crutches came slowly near the post box and took out a big dark envelope. He looked at it for a while, folded the big envelope and put it into the box. He then slowly crossed the road to enter the bank.

"Looks like one of your customers," said Devika. She knew that this was not the man they were looking for; the envelope was too big.

At 1.15 pm, a school bus stopped on the other side of the road and twelve children came out of it. A street dog barked at them. One of the boys threw a stone at the canine which ran away.

At 2.45 pm, a group of housewives carrying metal plates for puja at the local temple went past the post box. One of them took out a white envelope from her blouse and put it inside the letter box.

At 3.20 pm, a young man with long, curly hair and wearing a jacket came on a motorbike and parked his bike in front of the letter box. He took out a dark medium-sized envelope.

"Now that is our man!" Anshuman exclaimed. Devika narrowed her eyes and looked closely at the young man. Long hair, bandana, French beard, thick bracelet...

The man looked at the envelope, kissed it and went near the letter box. He then paused for a moment and thought of something. Devika and Anshuman looked on with baited breath. The man looked at the letter and the letter box for a fairly long time. He just stood there. Finally he decided not to post the letter for he placed the envelope back into his jacket pocket and left.

'Ah!' Devika heaved a sigh.

Later when the postman came to collect the evening pickup, it was clearly visible that there were two white envelopes, one big dark envelope and one dark envelope of regular size. The last one was in all probability the red envelope addressed to Devika. Anshuman and Devika looked at each other, totally bewildered.

They thanked the security officer and bank manager before leaving. On the way back Devika and Anshuman did not speak much but their minds ran riot. The source of the letters was a mystery. It was as if a ghost had posted them. As he dropped Devika off at her house, Anshuman asked, "When are you going to meet the doctor?"

"I may have to wait till the end of September. The procedure is cumbersome."

"Oh okay! I am off to the hospital because the little one is feverish since morning."

"Jyoti told me it is a mild fever. He will be fine. Do let me know if you recollect anything pertaining to the three numbers 102, 825 and 815."

# PART - II

# The Cult's Final Days

# PART – II

# The Cult's Final Days

# What Happened in January

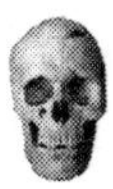

Raghav Shinde placed his laptop bag on the centre table in the middle of the hall and drew all the curtains. He then looked out through the eye hole. As he looked through the eye-hole at the lobby on the other side of the door, Raghav forgot to blink.

After a long, agonising wait, the door of the flat on the opposite side opened. Clad in an elegant red sari with black patterns, she appeared from inside the flat. Her eyes were bright and lined by dark kaajal. Large sparkling earrings dangled from her ears while a red-black bindi was prominent on her smooth forehead. Her curly hair was untied and flowed down to her elegant midriff.

Raghav inhaled the mesmerising scent of her perfume behind the closed door. It had the effect of an aphrodisiac. Her name was perfect for the effect she created.

Mehek – an effervescent fragrance.

He pushed back the stool and picked up his laptop bag. Pretending as if he was in a hurry to leave for office he opened the door and immediately looked surprised.

"Oh! Good morning, Mehek!"

"Good morning, Raghav Ji." The sound of her voice was enough to give him goosebumps.

He tried to appear calm, "Got a bit late for work." They waited at the lift door. "Can I can drop you to work?" He asked.

Mehek smiled and replied, "Sure!"

Raghav could hardly conceal the rush of excitement on his face. He felt like a high school boy in love for the very first time. In the parking lot, Raghav fumbled with the car keys. Inside his car, her heady fragrance was overwhelming, intoxicating. He started the car and drove out of the Sahyadri Hills residential complex.

When his wife was around, Raghav would give a mere hint of a smile of acknowledgment to Mehek, while at his children's birthday party, he would behave as the smiling, silent host. But the moment his wife left for her home-town, Raghav would be a transformed man.

Sitting next to the object of his fantasy he was feeling helpless, almost drugged. Unlike the clichéd Hindi film depiction of the seductress, this woman sounded strangely erotic but in a pleasant and mild way. Her piercing but dreamy eyes and her husky voice were the root of all unholy thoughts clouding his mind. Her language was sophisticated, her voice, that of a young seductress, had the power to arouse the average male's carnal desires. Raghav believed that even if she were to read out the daily stock market update from *Konkan Times*, it would arouse some men. He felt powerless before the sexual pull she exerted.

He was trying hard to figure out an interesting topic for conversation. In their last three trips together he had managed to strike descent conversations with Mehek. Today he had the usual starting trouble in her presence.

"So, what is your contribution to this month's *Ratnagiri Tarang?*" Mehek asked.

As a journalist, Raghav was well respected in the local journalistic circles. "I am writing about the water shortage problem in nearby regions this month. It's sad that we don't care about the most precious resource man requires. Once this resource is destroyed, we will have only useless salty sea water for our use," Raghav said, trying to appear intellectually sound.

"True! I think earth is now truly incapable of handling the burden of so many people. You will need to read out and translate the article to me when it is published," she added with a smile.

"Sure!"

"What next?"

"Next month I will be interviewing Satyaraj Kale."

Mehek turned towards him. "Is interviewing powerful and influential politicians a bit intimidating? Are you worried at any time that what you ask them or what you print about them might offend them and there can be repercussions?"

"It's our job, Mehek. We always walk on thin ice, probing sensitive subjects without offending powerful individuals. Satyaraj is an exception as he's a powerful politician and a gentleman."

"Can I ask you for a favour, Raghav Ji?"

"Sure!"

"Can I come along with you when you meet Satyaraj Kale?"

Raghav was surprised, "It will be difficult. Why do you want to meet him?"

"I am affiliated to an NGO GreenWorld which works for environmental causes. I was looking forward to a donation and also wanted to request him to be the chief guest at the World Environment Day ceremony organised by the NGO."

"World Environment Day is almost six months....." Raghav couldn't complete his sentence. Mehek had placed her hands on his thighs and pleaded with a bewitching smile, "Please help me, Raghav Ji. It's for a good cause." Raghav glanced at her brightly painted fingernails.

Beads of sweat broke out on his forehead and his heart stopped beating for a moment. "Er....sure...of course...yes...I will try."

Her hand had a scar from a corrective cosmetic surgery and did not look beautiful. However, the touch brought the blood rushing through Raghav's body as if he was about to explode.

Sweating profusely, he took a while to recover from the effect. He was wondering what to say next to break the awkward silence.

"So Mehek, how is life otherwise?"

Mehek looked outside and replied in a stoic tone, "Lonely. Trying to save my marriage."

"I don't see Aftab around these days." Even though he sounded very concerned, Raghav hoped that Aftab, Mehek's husband, would never come back.

She started to twirl her hair rather nervously. "Raghav Ji, it's getting more and more complicated. It has always been like that. For people who want to leap high to achieve something in life, there are always some compromises and sacrifices on the way."

Raghav could not understand the context of Mehek's rambling but he nodded nonetheless, trying to look concerned and compassionate.

Mehek sighed. "I am not an ordinary person and there are flip sides to being unusually gifted. If my marriage has to be sacrificed for those bigger causes, then so be it."

Raghav found himself nodding to this rather incoherent blabbering.

At that moment the car turned right from MG Road and stopped in front of Mehek's workplace. She got out of the car and said, "Thank you, Raghav Ji. It's always a pleasure to interact with you."

"See you. Bye." Raghav could barely speak through the lump in his throat.

After she left, Raghav let out a breath of relief. No woman he had met before had the kind of effect Mehek had on men around her. In their residential complex Raghav had noted other married men behave like nervous lunatics in front of her; wherever she went, male attention shifted to her. As Raghav drove his car to his workplace, he thought of the long, boring day ahead. The relief was that next morning he would be meeting Mehek in the common area again, a 'co-incidence' that would take place daily till his wife and children came back from Sangli.

That afternoon Mehek walked across the road to Sagar-Ratna, the air-conditioned Malwani restaurant opposite her workplace. She wore her uniform minus the cap. At the table next to the door sat a tall, fair, unshaven man with prominent ears that turned outwards, as if leaning towards the listener. He had a handsome face except for the dark circles around his eyes. The man looked tired.

"Aftab! I am so happy to see you here." Mehek tried to keep her hands on his hands but he withdrew them.

His gaze was fixed on the table between them. "I came here to tell you something, firmly and face to face. Can you please stop harassing me by calling at the shop and on my mobile phone?"

"That is not harassment my dear, it's love. You came here and that means that somewhere deep inside you still love me."

"Don't be under any such illusion. I have not even told my sister about my coming here. She will kill me if she comes to know about this."

Mehek's expression changed to one of disgust. "Are you a primary school boy that you need to inform your elder sister every time you want to take a leak?"

"I am leaving." He got up from his seat but she caught his hands and made him sit down. He still did not look into her eyes.

"Alright. Let's talk about something else."

"Go on." Aftab took a deep breath, his expression cold. His shifting eye balls made him seem like a prisoner, constantly terrified of being punished.

"I am shifting jobs next month. Guess where I am going?"

Aftab looked back but did not react well to her enthusiasm.

"I am going to Holy Cross. They are giving me a 50 percent raise."

"Good for you." Aftab was disinterested.

"What happened? Why are you always so cold?"

"Nothing."

"Remember the good old times we spent together. Those golden days. I miss those days when I used to come dressed up early morning to college to impress the young handsome manager in the administrative section," Mehek looked at Aftab with affection. "Love is all about remembering and cherishing some episodes. It is also about forgetting the bad ones."

"I don't have any sweet memories, Mehek. Those were harrowing times because of which I still don't get enough sleep. I still do not sleep well with all those goddamn nightmares and I know that you are responsible for it." His eyes darted from side to side.

"How can I be responsible? We have not met for such a long time."

"You know what I am talking about. Don't deny it. You don't need to be physically around people to mess with their minds. You're doing a good job with psyching me out with all your tricks. Your way of getting even with the people you don't like."

"People you don't like! I love you, Aftab. Let's give it one last try. Breaking a relationship is easy; mending it takes a lot of patience and effort." She kept her hands on his. His hands were shivering; he withdrew them.

He picked up the glass on the table and gulped down the water. In a low and nervous tone he said, "After what you did to me, I see no chance of any reconciliation."

Aftab got up and walked out of the restaurant quickly. The physical distance from her temporarily reduced his fear of Mehek. He shouted back at her,

"Stop calling me! Leave me alone. I will pray to God that he blesses you with some sanity."

Mehek swore under her breath and looked at the waiter who was overhearing them. "What are you looking at? Get me some rice and a plate of pomfret curry," she yelled.

After she finished her lunch, paid the bill and left the restaurant, the waiter came to clear the table. He saw spots of blood on the white table cloth. *What the hell is this?* he thought. There was something else too and he picked it up. He dropped it as soon as he realised what it was. It was a bright pink nail-polished human nail. There were droplets of blood on one side. It was crumpled on one side as if bitten and seemingly pulled out in rage. The waiter slumped on the chair to catch his breath.

That evening Mehek returned from work to the silent walls of her house. She hated the silence. Sipping her glass of vodka, she tried to read a book called *Unleashing One's Inner Power* but put it aside after reading only a page. Given to restlessness, she hated sitting at home on lonely evenings. She was not meant for such a dormant and unexciting life; she was special. In these inactive hours, her mind became a cacophony – the noises within insistent, demanding, till she did their bidding. Then there were faint knocks on the windows. *Thud! Thud!*

"Not today! I am tired today."

Now there were faint knocks on the door as well. *Thud! Thud!* Mehek looked around as a faint but desperate banging started from all four sides. She popped in her sleeping pills and gulped them down with the vodka. She switched off the light in the room and slumped on sofa trying to ignore the noises. The knocking intensified.

"Go away, you wretched bastards! I am not letting you in today."

Her head started to ache as the banging became more agitated. The door, windows, the walls, the glass on the painting on the wall – everything seemed to rattle in unison.

"You can all go to hell where you came from."

The phone rang. Mehek fumbled in the dark, following the sound of the ringing, and picked it up. The noises around her ceased.

"We have got one. Let's fix up for tomorrow," said the voice on the other side.

Mehek smiled. Tomorrow would be exciting.

# September: Researching the Shaman

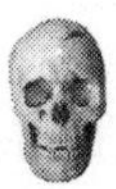

*Shrewd*
*Excellent at networking with influential and powerful people*
*Objective driven*
*Magnetic*

These were the words used by friends, acquaintances and neighbours to describe the Shaman-the leader, Mehek. In the second trimester of her pregnancy, Devika decided to travel and meet those who had been in touch with the slain cult leader.

One thing that fascinated Devika was the way occult rituals were conducted. Her initial insights came from attending the court proceedings of the cult members. The rituals were an absurd mix of Satanism, Thelema and Aghori practices. Mehek gave her own original touch to the rituals. Devika singled out that one cult member who was the most passive. Her name was Vandana and she was in the Sarvanpur Women's Jail. Devika was slated to meet her next week. If she turned out to be a tough nut to crack Devika would require more meetings.

Devika was one her way to Pune to meet a certain man named Jagannnath who was in Pune on a four-day business trip. She had tracked down his name and number from the police records and wanted to ask Jagannath about his nephew and niece who had been cult members.

Like other cult members, they were social misfits. They were confused, driven by instinct, pretending to be normal members of a society to which they could not relate. Their childhood and past had left them with the scars of a lifetime, making them impressionable, gullible – ideal material to mould as the cult pleased.

What she found out from Jagannath and later from Vandana revealed to Devika the full extent of the horrific rituals that the cult had practiced.

# What Happened in the Last Week of January

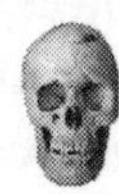

It was a rather cold evening. Mehek got out from her workplace wearing a black top over a long, black skirt. The sari and uniform were inside her leather bag. She walked to the bus-stop in front of her workplace. A van stopped in front of her and she got in.

In the rear of the van, she saw the brother and sister seated comfortably on a stretcher.

"*Shemhamforash!* How are you Vishakh, Vaishali?"

"*Shemhamforash!* We are fine. How are you Shaman Mehek?"

"Good."

The siblings were in black as well. Mehek gave them a quick lookover; Vaishali, slightly plump, wore three sets of earrings and a thick layer of eyeliner and had prominent tattoos of fairies, large flowers and mermaids covering her arms. Vishakh, fair, with a goatee and a hooked nose had a single tattoo of a vampire bat with its wings spread open between his neck and chest.

From her bag Mehek took out two sets of photocopies and handed them over to the siblings. "As promised last time, *Introduction to Practical Hypnotism*. This will help you in your journey towards the discovery of your hidden powers. After you finish reading this, we will start with your practical sessions."

"That is if we feel interested," Vaishali remarked.

Mehek did not respond.

Outside, it was getting dark and the wind was strong. After the initial hesitation, Vishakh finally gathered the courage to ask, "What are we going to do today?"

"You will see," replied Mehek with a slight smile. "It will be fun, that's all I can say for now. We will feel powerful and you will get your stuff in plenty."

"Vishakh and I were talking at home," Vaishali interrupted, "and we thought it was the right time to share our thoughts with you. Mehek, when we were all part of *Nelson's Club*, things were different. We were in a liberated and joyful state of mind. Now we are not sure where we are heading."

"What's the worry? This is the problem with you people, constantly evaluating things as right or wrong from a conventional viewpoint. Vaishali, free your mind," said Mehek, her tone imperative as she observed the two faces. They were not convinced.

"Tell me something. Are good things happening to you at work or otherwise? Are your enemies suffering at this point of time? Are you looking at a bright and exciting future ahead? The answer to all these questions is *yes!*"

She continued after a pause, "All this is because of what we do, and are not coincidences. The energies of the universe are now working towards your advantage, manipulated to serve your interests."

"But there is right and there is wrong! Are we not indulging in too much hedonism?" Vaishali retorted.

"Hedonism? Some famous guy once said that God is supposed to be the manifestation of one's inner self. Let's be very frank and admit that lust, greed and wants are also parts of the inner self. So why is that unholy and wrong?"

"To tell you the truth, we are increasingly disillusioned with whatever you have been telling us. It appears to us now, after traversing the full circle, that faith is not all that futile," Vaishali raised a hand to stop Mehek from interrupting. "I was having this conversation at my workplace with a colleague. His brother met with a road accident, there was a fracture in his skull with internal injuries and the doctors had given up on him..."

"Then what happened? Some crazy miracle! They prayed and his brother came back to normalcy. Is that the bullshit story you are telling me? His brother would have survived even if there were no prayers." Mehek tried hard to put a lid on her rage.

Vishakh looked back stupefied as Mehek continued, "You people are used to following this 'herd' mentality. Think about it. Any lie accepted by intelligent people and inculcated in every little child by its mother is more dangerous than mass poisoning. There is no God, my dear! Since these are man-made concepts, we should be able to shatter them and liberate ourselves! Faith is just a superstition created by naïve people. Religion is a refugee camp without a caretaker."

"In my past life, I was more at peace with myself," commented Vishakh.

"I accompanied my friend Janet to the Holy Cross Church last Sunday. Let me tell you that after a long time, I felt for some strange reason, extremely at peace with myself. All our rituals have not even come close to that," Vaishali asserted.

"Instead of rationally evaluating whether occult is giving us the promised benefits, we are busy rubbishing everything all the time, hell bent on proving there is no god," Vishakh remarked.

Mehek interrupted again, "Listen! We also believe in a supreme power but not in the conventional sense of the word god. This force we believe in maintains the balance in the universe. The proof of its existence is not because we have seen good things happen to good people but because we have seen bad things happen to everyone in some form or the other. However, this balancing force is far too impersonal to care about the happiness and misery of every person. You really think that there is someone up there who cares about you? I am sure that the powers running the universe have long given up on mankind, perhaps hiding after they figured out that they cannot manage their own chaotic creation."

Mehek's eyes were two slits in her face, her voice loud. "Where were the saviours of the universe when your parents died of chemical gas poisoning? What was their or your fault? You were just two children enjoying a vacation with your grandparents in Cuttack while a multinational company's negligence took away your parents' life."

The siblings were listening to her silently, carefully.

The van took the Vasco Road towards the wilderness outside the city. There was silence at the back of the van. The Sarvanpur Public Library passed by in a flash. The terrain was partly hilly and the road took hairpin bends along the slopes. The Sahyadri hills engulfed the town of Sarvanpur on two sides. They crossed the old Saint Francis church which looked overpowering at night. Mehek peeped outside the window for a moment; at the horizon there was the outline of a mansion lit by the moonlight. Her eyes were transfixed on that mansion till it disappeared out of sight. For a moment Mehek was bothered by this faint dissent that had not started to surface in some cult members. She had painstakingly built this group and its structure; she would not allow the cracks of dissent to topple it.

"I guess we are just trained to go back to the lessons of faith instilled inside us from childhood. We know it is trash but that is our tendency." Vishakh tried to lighten the mood.

Mehek said, "Understand this, my friends, religion asks you to plead for solutions to your problem. Atheists ask you to go out and solve your problems. On the other hand, the dark forces give you the solution to your problems."

"But what we do cannot be even classified as Satanism," said Vaishali without sounding assertive.

"No one will tell us what to do and what not to do!" Mehek laughed mockingly. "Only we will decide where to stop! Even Thelema is an optional reference point."

The siblings knew that Mehek had a long-standing argument with the Church of Satan. She had managed to find communication addresses in forums over the internet and written to their black pope. However, she got no response for the five times she wrote to the black pope or to the secret council of nine. It frustrated her and she was disheartened. However, she still believed that such affiliation to established organisations was important. Mehek's roadmap for the future of their group was way too ambitious; to the siblings it appeared impractical.

The van turned left and stopped in front of a gate. The driver of the van got down and opened the gate with the keys he had. The van moved inside a farm house. After going down a mud road for a little distance, it stopped. At a distance they saw a large wooden storage shed in the middle of the farmhouse partially concealed by tall shrubs and trees on all sides. The young man Kunal who was driving the van escorted Mehek, Vishakh and Vaishali along the path between the tamarind and *kokum* trees towards the storage shed which was a fairly big structure made of strong wooden planks fixed on a metallic framework with a hollow foundation. The door opened and the young man said, "Father, they are here."

It was a family of five; father, mother, son and two daughters, all of them clad in black. They all wished each other. "The boys will be here on their bikes shortly," said Mehek.

She had suddenly transformed into a smiling, pleasing and caring figure in the presence of this larger group.

Vishakh and Vaishali entered the shed behind her. The shed seemed ready for the ceremony. There was a small wooden altar in the middle on which a pentagram symbol with a goat's face was painted. Around it where five black candles. A small gong was hanging on a stand next to the altar. Next to the altar sat another woman dressed in black, drinking from a bottle of vodka. They knew her name. Vandana.

"*Shemhamforash!* How are you doing, Vandana?" The woman did not respond to Mehek's greeting.

On one side of the altar was a table on which there was a body underneath a black cloth. A caged pigeon, a copper chalice, a dagger and a wine bottle were placed at the corners of the table. One side the wooden flooring had been removed to expose the ground. There was a black casket and a newly dug pit five-feet deep in the corner of the shed.

"So this is our man today. Who is he?" Mehek asked.

The head of the family of five said, "A bum who lived inside the premises of the nearby Shiva temple. His audacity is commendable as he entered our premises riding his bicycle fully under the influence of *cannabis*."

"Oh! So he is a believer. I like that. Is he cleaned and dry?"

"Yes. I personally cleaned him and later we drained him out as much as possible."

"When are the recipients coming?"

"Tomorrow early morning onwards. I will be doing my job back to back," said the head of the family.

Mehek now looked at the body and said, "I think we can clean up these people even better. They have more to offer to us than what we utilise."

"I know what you mean, but we don't have the capability to do that."

"I have told you many times before, my dear. Hire that capability!" Mehek sounded stern.

"This is the best we could do. It's difficult to satisfy your demands like infant babies – where do we get them from?"

"That I understand since I am in a better position to arrange for those, but this I don't understand. I hope you people appreciate that I am being flexible by performing ceremonies over the dead foetus provided by Vandana."

There was a roar of motorbikes outside. The door of the shed opened and five young men entered. They were already masked and did not reveal their names to anybody. Only Mehek knew them. She had befriended these men on the internet. The group identified themselves as 'Anarchy' and were clad in black t-shirts. Two of them were wearing messages on their t-shirts: 'Dead Artists Society' and 'I love my girlfriend, I love her brother more'. One of them was wearing the t-shirt of the rock group *Lucifer's Noise*. Another young man was clad in the t-shirt of the video game *Urban Mass Genocide*. The fifth man was wearing a t-shirt of a joker holding a knife with the quote 'My Personality is Split'.

The rest of them wore black cloth masks over their faces. Mehek went near the body placed on the table and said,

"Hail Satan! *In Nomine Dei Nostri Satanas Luciferi Excelsi! Shemhamforash!* May the energy of the departed sacrifice be distributed equally among all of us faithful followers attending this ceremony."

She raised her hand and out of thin air appeared a black book. She flipped to the portion called *The Book of the Dark*. The light of the candles started to flicker. She raised her other hand and a metallic pentagram with a goat's face appeared.

Mehek spoke out aloud, "The powers of the Cosmos! I stand forth in front of you to question the wisdom of the world, to investigate the laws of man and his so called supreme power."

A gong sounded and everyone chanted,

*"Shemhamforash!"*

"I question everything that goes around me. As I stand in front of you, the innocent bodies who have faced unnecessary misery throughout their lives. Awaken! All that they tell you is a facade!"

*"Shemhamforash!"*

"Lo and behold! For too long good and evil has been inverted by fake messengers of the so-called God. Deceptive godmen who have vested interests and dubious intentions. I stand here to set you all free."

*"Shemhamforash!"*

Now Mehek started to read the 'invocation of the dark lord' written in the book. The language was Enochian. Then she read out the 'Conjuration of Desire'. The assembled people were in a frenzy. Mehek was sweating profusely while her hair flew wildly around her face and shoulders. Her hand, which was holding the pentagram, moved upwards. The sound of the gong was now more frequent.

"Hail Lucifer! Hail Azazel! Hail Pan! The dark energies of the world, come here! Come here and enter our bodies. This world is a sad place and only you can lead us to the bliss we deserve."

For a brief moment her body levitated, her skirt fluttered. Then she appeared to come back on the ground. From her handbag she took out a small metallic box. Inside there was a syringe with a yellow liquid.

She showed it to all the assembled people and said,

*"Shemhamforash!"*

The father of the family of five stepped forward and requested, "Allow me to enjoy the privilege." He then proceeded to the table on the altar on which the body was placed and injected the liquid into the body.

Mehek, who was behaving like a maniacal religious preacher, instructed, "We have set this man free and sucked his energy into all of us. He has died for a purpose, he was useless otherwise. Now it's time to bury this body which is devoid of any energy."

The five Anarchy boys picked up the body and placed it in a casket. It was dropped into the pit dug up in the corner of the shed by the son from the family of five. They then covered it with soil. Vishakh and Vaishali were bewildered but, as always, they played along with the group in anticipation of their reward at the end of the session. Mehek pulled out the pigeon from the cage and walked towards the burial pit. She raised her hand and a knife appeared. They could see that her left ring finger was bandaged around the nail. She held the pigeon by its neck as she repeated,

*"In Nomine Dei Nostri Satanas Luciferi Excelsi!"*

Blood dripped into the burial pit. As she beheaded the bird, she accidentally cut her own left index finger, dropping the pigeon and the knife into the pit. It looked intentional to everybody in the audience and was her regular habit. Vishakh took a bottle of water from the side of the podium, walked to Mehek and poured it on Mehek's injured finger. He then took out his handkerchief and tied it.

"See. This is true unconditional love. I like that. This is how we should behave towards one another," Mehek said as she leaned forward and kissed Vishakh's lips. Vishakh blushed behind his mask. She glanced at the head of the family of five, who in turn looked at his son who brought forward a rolling tray of liquor bottle and glasses. Mehek raised a piece of paper and pen.

"Now everyone, write the names of your enemies on this paper. Satan will take care of them for you."

She took out the chalice and poured the wine into it. Then the head of the family of five took out a dagger and profaned it. She then raised it into the air and said,

"Lucifer! Protect us all!"

Everyone formed a queue in front of the table to write down the names of their enemies on the piece of paper. Mehek handed them the chalice of wine and they all took a sip from it after writing the name of their foes. Mehek picked up the piece of paper after everyone had finished. She moved her hands in a circle three times and a packet of white powder appeared.

Mehek looked at the masked faces in front of her. "This is for you all. Enjoy! Remember, life is the ultimate indulgence. Death is the ultimate abstinence. Here and now is all you have. You have always rewarded yourself after rewarding others around you. Now reward yourself first. Redeem yourself!" she yelled.

The group plunged into a collective maniacal frenzy.

After this, everyone drank from the liquor bottles and snorted cocaine. Only Vandana sat motionless drinking her vodka.

Mehek raised her arms and said, "Any substance that takes you on a journey of self-exploration and a higher degree of awareness is not bad for you. Snort in the white powder and see where it takes you."

One of the girls from the family of five suddenly gripped an Anarchy boy and pulled him along to a corner of the room. Ripping open his t-shirt, she began to bite him all over his chest while her sister locked lips with another.

"Yes! Shed your clothes. Clothes are the innermost wall of your self-image. Drop your clothes and become what you truly are. Make love so that the power of life engulfs this place of worship."

As soon as she stopped speaking, one of the Anarchy boys started running around the shed, his hands outstretched like the wings of a bird.

"I am fucking free!" he screamed through his LSD haze.

Another slumped to the ground like a house of cards.

"Good shit!" Vishakh muttered as he snorted cocaine, his eyes bloodshot "This is good shit".

Vaishali was high on vodka. As she stumbled into the arms of one of the Anarchy boys and as she tried to rip off his mask, he caught hold of her arms and pulled her towards him. She slapped him and laughed hysterically before trying to bite his lips. The father of the family of five was already high on cocaine. As Mehek stood reading aloud from the *The Conjuration of Vengeance*, he stepped up behind her and grabbed her breasts.

The dance of hedonism continued for hours. At dawn, when everyone else was asleep Vishakh woke up his sister. Slowly, they walked to the main gate of the farm house, took a rickshaw from the Vasco Road and made their long journey home. Once inside their flat, they slumped on the couch. Vishakh saw tears in Vaishali's eyes.

"What happened, Vaishali?"

"No, nothing!"

Vishakh Held her hand. "Tell me."

"Vishakh, every time I do this, it seems like a lot of fun, but later, I feel terrible. Today it is worse than ever."

"Why are you feeling terrible?"

"They killed an innocent man. It is wrong!" She sobbed loudly.

There was a knock on the door. Vaishali dried her tears while Vishakh opened the door.

Mehek stood at the door with the five Anarchy boys. For a change they were unmasked and looked younger than Vaishakh had anticipated.

"Can we come in?" Mehek asked with a smile.

"Sure. We were not expecting you. Boys, you have finally revealed your faces to us."

Inside the room, Mehek looked sharply at Vaishali who was still wiping her tears.

"What happened, my girl?"

"Why are you all wearing rubber gloves?" Vishakh asked.

"Look what we got for you? Your favourite stuff!" Mehek held up the white powder.

"That is not the answer to my question."

"You will get your answers," Mehek replied with a smile.

"We are getting late for office," Vaishali said.

"What's the hurry? Let's take a quick sniff and let me tell you something," Mehek said.

That evening, when the cook arrived as usual to make dinner for the siblings, she found the door wide open but the house empty.

In the bedroom, the big metallic trunk in which Vishakh kept his belongings was missing. Everything else was in place. Presuming the brother and sister had forgotten to lock the house, she cooked dinner and bolted the door from the outside when she left.

When she came the next day, the house was still bolted from outside and the dinner untouched.

The siblings were untraceable.

After twelve days of no communication from the siblings, their uncle, Jagannath, arrived from Cuttack and filed a missing person's complaint at the local police station. Even after a week there was no sign of Vishakh or Vaishali.

A month later, the bodies of the siblings were eventually found in adjacent graves at a mass burial place outside the town.

# September: Rachel's Nursing Home

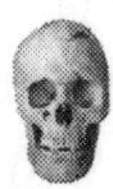

It was right in the middle of the town's commercial district. The police barricades and tapes for cordoning off stray visitors and media had been removed a month back after the court judgement on the cult members.

As she entered the premises, workers pulled down the tattered signboard which said *Rachel's Maternity Home* and placed it near the entrance. Paint tins, ropes, bamboo sticks and cement sacks littered the place; after the renovation it would be put up for sale.

As Devika walked to the reception area she looked up the flight of stairs that started from the corner and ran up to the first floor. She remembered verbatim each sentence of the first newspaper reports which narrated the events of the fateful night catapulting the nursing home to overnight infamy across the country.

The contractor who was undertaking the renovation work saw the pregnant woman walk inside the premises and walked towards her, "Madamji! Can I help you?"

"Just having a look around," replied Devika with a smile.

"There is renovation work going on here and in your situation it is not advisable for you to be here for a long time."

"Just give me ten minutes. I want to go to the first floor and have a look," said Devika and climbed the stairs slowly without waiting for the contractor's response. When she looked at the reception area from the top floor she felt dizzy. Anshuman was right, places like this retain the eerie feel of their past. She could almost hear the wailing and screams all around this ghoulish place. Devika took some photographs and left with enough images in her mind and camera to write about that dark fateful night in February.

# What Happened in February

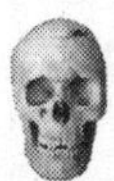

As he cut the umbilical cord the baby's cry filled the delivery room.

After cleaning the baby, the nurse standing behind Dr Carlton placed the infant on a weighing machine.

"2 kilos, 900 grams."

Dr Carlton smiled as he looked back at the healthy baby boy for a moment; he still had to stitch up the mother, his wife.

The paediatrician checked the baby's heart beat and other parameters. "Like his father, he is in good health. Okay from my side!" he remarked.

It was the delivery of Dr Carlton's own child and the team was a closely knit one. The atmosphere was cheerfully informal.

The nurse said, "Congratulations, Doctor, on being blessed with a healthy baby boy!"

"Praise the Lord!" said Dr Carlton.

"Doctor, I'm sure whatever good has happened to you is due to the blessings of all the expectant mothers and newborns you have saved with your expertise," the paediatrician said.

"Just doing my job, my friend."

"A really good job, to say the least," remarked the paediatrician.

The nurse added, "For women with complicated gynaecological

conditions in Sarvanpur, Dr Carlton is like a lighthouse in a turbulent sea."

"So let's continue the good work. Why are you leaving us?" Carlton asked as he turned towards the nurse.

The nurse smiled and wordlessly handed the baby to his mother.

Mrs Carlton's face lit up as she looked at her baby and the pain and discomfort of natural birth was forgotten.

"Cynthia, are you okay?" Dr Carlton asked his wife.

"I'm fine, great in fact."

"He is cute, isn't he?" Carlton whispered.

"The epidural made it less painful this time. When you gave birth to Katie, I remember how you raised hell in the labour room," said Carlton as he washed his hands in the nearby basin.

"You rest, sweetheart, I'll leave now and will be back at night. These people will take good care of you." He took off his gloves and touched her cheek.

"Call me in case of an emergency!" Carlton instructed the nurse before leaving.

In the span of 24 hours he had assisted in the successful deliveries of three women in labour, including his wife. Now he was fatigued. He badly needed to get home, break the good news to the rest of his family and get some sleep.

Dr Carlton changed out of his work clothes and looked at himself in the mirror. He was not handsome but looked young for his age. A red birth mark ran down from his left ear to the jawbone. Usually after assisting so many deliveries his face would have displayed fatigue, but today his face looked brighter than ever.

The doctor walked to his scooter parked outside the maternity home. He wished he had the car but the mechanic was still trying to repair it. He looked back at the board. *Rachel's Maternity Home* was named after his mother, built on land bought by his father 25 years back at dirt cheap rates; it was worth a fortune today, yet it was not doing well. *What grand plans I had for my venture. What has happened of it!*

The last six months had been turbulent. On his way back to his house outside Sarvanpur town, his mind was full of positive thoughts for a change. He was going to break the good news personally to his mother and his little daughter Katie.

He rode the scooter across the small bridge over the irrigation canal leading to the Old Church Road. After that there was a stretch of fallow land followed by the St Anthony's Church. It was a 45 minute drive.

As he parked the scooter outside his house, he saw the mechanic on his way out.

"Repaired?"

"No, *Saab*. It will take some time. I am going to shut down my workshop and have some evening snacks. I will come later in the night to fix it."

"Even if it is late night by the time you fix it, ask your brother to drive down my mother and Katie to the maternity home."

"I will tell Jerry to drive them to the maternity home. Any problem?"

"No. Cynthia delivered a baby boy an hour back."

"Many congratulations, Saab!"

Carlton kept his hand on the mechanic's shoulder and said, "Thank you. We will have cakes sent over to your home shortly."

Rachel was watching the daily soap. He looked at the scenes flashing across the screen and shook his head. She had been watching the serial for almost a decade now, but the story had not moved forward for the past few months. The characters neither aged nor did they stop discussing the same old issues. Carlton's nine year old daughter Katie was on the carpet concentrating on a sheet of white paper before her. He peeped over her shoulder. Katie was busy colouring a picture of a coconut tree with crayons.

"Guess what! Katie has a baby brother!"

Rachel and Katie sprung up in surprise. "Hurray!" Katie was overjoyed and threw herself into her father's arms. "We want to go to the maternity home now." Rachel said.

"Mamma, let's get the car fixed first. Even if it is late, Jerry will drive you to the maternity home."

Rachel didn't wait to hear him. She was already at the phone calling up relatives with the news.

Katie was happily skipping around the place. Her forehead had a red welt.

"Katie! What did you do? How did you get this mark?"

"Andrew said if I rub my finger continuously on my forehead 101 times, I would see Jesus Christ."

"Ah! So your classmate took you for a ride."

Katie smiled, "Wait, Papa! Listen to what I did. I went to the school canteen and emptied the salt container into a paper; later, when Andrew went out for football, I put all the salt into his water bottle. You should have seen his face after he drank from the bottle."

"Katie! That was mean."

"No, Papa! It was well deserved. This does not end the matter. I will make sure that every week I trouble Andrew."

Carlton picked her up off the floor and sat her down next to him. "Katie, this kind of behaviour is bad, it is revengeful and does not suit you, sweetheart."

"I know what to do, Papa. I'll trouble those who trouble me, I will." She stamped her foot.

Carlton did not pursue the argument. No point. They had spoilt her. He would look into the matter after bringing his wife and son home.

"Anyway, your coconut tree here is shaping up pretty well." His daughter was indeed good at drawing. "Now I am going in to sleep so don't make any noise."

Carlton went into his bedroom, changed into his t-shirt and pyjamas and collapsed on the bed.

Two hours later, he was woken up by a punch on his leg. Katie stood by the bed, feet apart, wearing the leather gloves Carlton had bought her during the family's visit to Shimla the previous year. She looked like a tiny boxer.

"Get up, Tyson! Mary Kom is ready to fight you."

Carlton got up and mock punched her and the fight continued for some time. It was their favourite game. When he finally collapsed on the bed, Katie gave a triumphant cry, "Yeah! Mary Kom won by a knockout!"

She ran out to give the news to her grandmother.

On his way out to the hospital again, Carlton called out to Rachel. "Mother, I am getting late. See you at the maternity home tonight."

"I am coming along with you to meet the baby!"

"No Katie! It's windy outside. You come in the car along with grandma. Bye."

"No! Please!" Carlton had to spend the next fifteen minutes trying to pacify his daughter and convince her that she should come later. He had to finally bribe her with the promise of chocolates.

MG Road was bright with the lights from various shops and restaurants. One particular sign blinked temptingly at Carlton as he entered the commercial heart of the town. Haveli Bar & Restaurant. He had sobered down after he got married, but the day called for a celebration. Just a pint.

He parked his scooter outside the restaurant. Everybody told him that he was unpredictable person and sometimes he surprised even himself. Inside the hotel, he knew he would have to deal with the suffocating, acrid smell of smoke and food. But tonight was different.

The restaurant had Mughal-themed decor with tacky chandeliers and curtains. He was dressed a little too formally for the place and time; Carlton noticed people staring at him. A famous qawwali played in the background, the singer's soulful voice expressing anguish at having lost his deceptive nomadic lover. The music was supposed to evoke pain and encourage liquor consumption; for Carlton the only pain this song evoked was in his ears.

He found an empty table at the other end of the restaurant.

With beer and salted peanuts before him Carlton was lost in thoughts. A Vaastu-Shastra and Feng-Shui expert was scheduled to visit his maternity home the next day. Carlton hoped to find some answers from him. What ailed his maternity home rendering it unprofitable? The previous week a team of pathologists had conducted a full-fledged hygiene survey, hunting for germs in the air, water supply, furniture, equipment, and fixtures. Everything was in order. Yet, most people around town knew Rachel's Maternity Home to be jinxed; four out of ten infants placed in the infant ICU in the last three months had not survived. Another five infants died within two days of birth due to heart failure and two infants were partially paralysed post pregnancy. When Carlton started the nursing home, he had put in place a highly trained team and the best equipment and facilities in the town. Yet, the mortality rate was higher than normal. Carlton had initially approached an NGO working for poor people and offered drastically subsidised service to expectant mothers below the poverty line. Yet the number of people admitted to his maternity home had fallen sharply in the past couple of months. Since most of his patients were poor, nobody took legal action for negligence. Until now Carlton had been able to avert investigation but if things continued, it would not be long before law enforcement came knocking at his door. Carlton admitted his wife to his own maternity home, just so it would encourage people to come.

Suddenly he felt as though somebody was watching him. He turned to look. The man at the next table was staring at his face and his eyes were transfixed on the birth mark on Carlton's jaw. He looked familiar except for the dark circles around the eyes, the unshaven stubble, and shabby hair.

"It has been years, but I cannot forget your face, my friend."

"Aftab! What a pleasant surprise. How can I forget those big ears?" Carlton got up and walked towards him, enveloping him in a hug.

"It's been such a long time! Come sit here," Aftab said.

"Want to try out Richards facing Kapil after the drinks?" Carlton asked, referring to their childhood when they lived at Sunshine Cooperative Housing Society and played cricket all day long.

Aftab smiled. "The old stamina is gone. I am likely to collapse due to heat stroke if I play in the sun for even half an hour. What happened? I never expected to meet you here."

"A personal celebration. I was blessed with a baby boy today."

"Congratulations, my friend! May God bless you and your family." He slumped back into his seat.

"What happened to you? You look like...."

"I am in a mess. I know, I know. Fate! This past year has been very difficult for me and things have gone haywire," he slurred.

Carlton tried to calm his friend, "Don't worry. Whatever it is, it will get resolved!"

"I am going through a divorce to resolve it," Aftab replied with a wink.

"You got married?"

"I had got a job as the Admin and Facilities manager at Sharada College and fell in love with one of the students. I sent you my wedding invitation but I came to know that you had shifted out of Pearl Avenue."

"Yes, I bought my own place on Old Church Road and shifted there. What was her name?"

"Let's leave the name out of this. It's a small town and we all keep bumping into one another. Besides, what's the point? The marriage is over." Aftab sighed.

He gulped down the beer. On a small podium on their side of the restaurant, the helpers started to set up microphones and speakers for the live performance. A local ghazal singer was to entertain them. The alcohol sloshing in their stomachs, the two friends walked cautiously to the wash room.

"You should never get married to the most beautiful girl who comes your way." Aftab was having difficulty speaking clearly. "It is a mirage."

"Aftab, I married the most grounded and mature woman I met. No regret on that front. The first six months were like a fairy tale."

Aftab started to ramble. "My fights with my wife started in the first month itself. Bitch! Every day she would nag me and I would give her a piece of my mind. I never thought I would lift my hands on a woman but she deserved the occasional thrashing. Daayan!"

They returned to their table.

"I cannot imagine a person like you involved in domestic violence, Aftab. It's something to be ashamed of but if the two of you are so frustrated, it's better to get out of the relationship in the beginning itself."

Aftab laughed. "Two months after the wedding, my mother died of a lung infection."

"I am sorry, Aftab. My mother came to know about it from the obituary section of the *Konkan Times*. I was in Delhi for a doctor's conference at that time. Mummy was present for aunty's last rites."

"That's the last time I met your mother. Rachel Aunty looks pretty fit for her age. God bless her! Anyway, I went into a bout of depression since my mother was a pillar of strength for me and my sister ever since my father's early death."

Carlton took a big sip from the beer mug. As Aftab spoke, he forgot his own worries.

"My wife offered to make me feel better with some trashy hypnotic therapy she had supposedly learned from a friend in her younger days."

"That's interesting."

"Initially I felt better. I was able to sleep well and divert my mind; later, I tried to slit my wrist once...," he showed the blade mark on his wrist. "I drank pesticide at home on another occasion..."

Carlton listened in disbelief.

"My sister came here from Dehradun and took me away with her for a month."

"Afreen works in Dehradun?"

"No, she's a housewife. Her husband is a mathematics teacher in a school there. Anyway, she took me to a psychiatrist; the treatment and the fresh air helped me recover quickly."

Aftab leaned closer to Carlton and spoke in a low voice, "They told me there that my wife was the reason behind my suicidal tendencies."

"How can that be?"

"It seems she planted some distressful ideas into my head during her therapy sessions. Since I was already on the edge, it was enough for me to fall off. The cunning bitch!"

"Your wife seems like one hell of a player."

"I can take legal action against her but all I want now is redemption and my peace of mind. I have started a small DVD-VCD store cum gift shop near the railway station and stay alone in my mother's ancestral house nearby."

When the waiter approached them, they repeated their order. It was getting late. Carlton knew he ought to be by his wife's side rather than in this bar, but Aftab's story had engrossed him.

"My wife is a weird woman. Often staying back overnight at her workplace, and then leaving home to meet friends for some private meetings during weekends. There were other eccentricities as well."

"Like?" Carlton was feeling drunk.

"Every other day she would get some injury or bruises on her body. A burn from the stove, a cut from kitchen knife, a sprain in the leg, etc. I think she intentionally did it to draw attention. She would frequently claim that she was pregnant when she actually wasn't..."

"That is strange," Carlton was suddenly interested.

"Once I was walking behind her down the stairs. She intentionally tripped, fell down the stairs and hit her head on the railing. I bandaged her head and took her to the local dispensary. All through the day, even when she was getting the stitches, she was beaming with happiness and smiling, as if she was enjoying it. Weird!"

"Your wife needs a psychiatrist. I had a roommate in my MBBS hostel who later went on to specialise in psychiatry. We still have long talks over the phone and discuss among other things, rare ailments. I don't know much about it but there is a disorder called Münchausen Syndrome where people behave like that," said Carlton.

"What is this Manchurian thing?"

"Munchausen." Carlton laughed. "Patients harm themselves to get other people's care and attention. They will go to any extent to get sympathy and care. There are famous cases of a British woman called Beverly Allitt and another woman Wendi Scott from America because of whom this disorder got a lot of media attention. It is seen in many people who had a disturbed or lonely childhood."

"My wife had a bad childhood for sure. She grew up in the Government Shelter for Girls. She once claimed that for many years, she was sexually molested as a child in her school."

"Lies – only to grab attention. There is another more dangerous variant of this disorder called Münchausen by Proxy where the patient harms other vulnerable people around him or her to drive attention towards them," said Carlton.

"Like?"

"Well, there are cases of mothers physically harming or maiming their own children to attract attention from everyone around. I have read about a british woman called Petrina Stocker who was jailed for contributing to her own son's death by excessive salt poisoning."

"Unbelievable!" Aftab gulped his beer and said, "Now I am very worried. I think I need to do something quickly. Since my wife works at such a place where she can get dangerous....."

Carlton interrupted, "Wait a minute! You told me that you met her at Sharada College where she was a student. Sharada is a college of nursing. She is a nurse?"

"At Rachel's Maternity Home, two blocks away from here".

The blood drained out of Carlton's face.

"What is her name, Aftab?"

"Why are you so obsessed with her name?"

Carlton leaned forward on the table with both hands and yelled, "What is her name?"

"*Mehek! Mehek*, if that makes you happy."

Like a man possessed, Carlton gave 500 rupees to the waiter and ran out of the restaurant. Aftab slumped further into his seat.

As he drove his scooter like a madman to his workplace, Carlton's mind was racing with thoughts. Mehek had joined the maternity home shortly after it had started six months back. If she was indeed having mental issues then she could have harmed the infants in numerous ways like injecting air bubbles into the infant's blood or cutting off the oxygen supply while the infant was on life support. All these could never be traced during an autopsy.

*Damn it! Why couldn't I have guessed this before? An insider was causing all the harm!*

Carlton swore at himself. She had resigned from her job and it was her last three days at the maternity home. Carlton knew that patients of Münchausen get more aggressive when they know that they have an escape route. Mehek would be deadlier than ever before.

He parked his scooter, ran across the reception and up the staircase. He saw Mehek, still in her uniform. She was in a panic. "Doctor, your wife was sleeping and I took the child aside for the Vitamin K injection."

"What happened?" Carlton was furious.

"I don't know, Doctor, your son has stopped breathing and the other nurses have taken him to the infant ICU section."

Carlton could not control himself anymore. He gave Mehek a tight slap. She looked baffled.

*"If anything were to happen to my child, I will strangle you!"* he screamed.

Mehek stood motionless, her hand on her burning cheek.

He ran across to the other end of the corridor where two nurses came out of the infant ICU red faced. They looked at each other before one of them started crying. "We are sorry! We were not able to save the little one. The sugar level went abnormally low..."

Carlton opened the mini refrigerator placed near the infant ICU section and ransacked its contents. He took out a small glass vial, read it, and smashed it on the ground. "Damn it!"

He looked at the nurses and pointed towards Mehek who stood at the end of the corridor. "The sugar level went low because of that bitch there." He held his head in his palms and tried to control himself.

"She injected my baby with insulin. I am going to kill her for that!" Tears in his eyes, Carlton picked up a pair of scissors from the cupboard above the refrigerator.

Mehek had locked herself in the nurses' room.

Carlton banged on the door like a madman, "Open the door, you bitch! I will bleed you to death today". He could hear faint conversation inside. The doctor now started to kick violently to break open the door. Hearing the noise from one of the rooms, Carlton's wife came out. She could barely walk properly. "What happened to you, Carlton?"

He dropped the scissors and walked towards her, "Cynthia, please go inside."

"Carlton! What happened?" He wanted to touch her cheek and comfort her but his hands were shivering.

"Nothing! Just go!" Carlton punched the wall and walked back towards the door, kicking it violently.

"No! I want to know why you are behaving like this. Where is our baby?"

Carlton looked at his wife and walked towards her like a man who had lost everything; he knelt before her, his hands folded, his voice choked. "Please baby, go inside. I'll handle this."

"Carlton, where is my child?"

She repeated her question to the two nurses; they stood silent.

Before she could ask anyone else, the door to the nurses' room opened and Mehek made a dash for the exit.

Carlton ran behind her. "Wait, you whore!" he yelled.

By the time she reached the stairs, Carlton had caught up with her, clutching at her shoulders from behind.

Desperate to flee, Mehek bit Carlton's hands. Carlton's reaction was immediate and violent. As he pushed her away, Mehek fell over the railing, hit her head on its metal bars and landed head down near the reception on the ground floor. The railing had caught her above her left ear, cracking her skull. Mehek lay in a pool of her own blood, her body still shuddering.

Carlton rushed down the stairs unable to believe what he had done. "Get the OT ready!" he yelled.

He checked Mehek's pulse. Nothing. She was dead.

"Jesus! What is this happening?" Rachel exclaimed.

Kneeling next to the dead Mehek, Carlton whirled around at his mother's voice. Rachel and Katie stood at the other end of the reception, horror and shock distorting their faces.

Little Katie screamed in horror and hid her face in her grandmother's back.

Rachel looked at the pool of blood and the dead body and collapsed.

The next day the police search party sealed the hospital premises and later in the day, broke into Mehek's house.

Sarvanpur's reputation as a peaceful town plunged overnight.

# September: Mumbai Visit

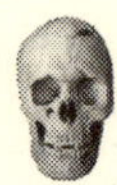

At 9.30 am, Devika and Shravan crossed Dadar station. Throughout the journey the three numbers from the previous letter 102, 825 and 815 floated around her eyes. Devika looked outside the window of their AC taxi at the thousands of faces starting their hectic day in the megacity. Shravan was on official duty to attend a felicitation ceremony for constables who had completed a long tenure of service with the department; Devika accompanied him for her own research. She wanted to meet the Carvalho family, without whose inputs her story would be incomplete. At Prabhadevi, Devika got off in a lane running parallel to the Ravindra Natya Mandir.

"I'll take a taxi to the guest house," she told Shravan as she got off.

"Bye and take care. Call if there is any problem." Shravan shouted out as the taxi sped away towards Appasaheb Marathe Marg.

Devika looked at the apartments around her. Right before her stood Gulmohar Co-operative Society.

On the first floor she knocked on a door with the nameplate *Carvalhos*.

Inside the apartment, Devika heard a story that made her Mumbai trip seem worth the trouble.

# What Happened in Mid-February

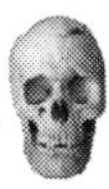

Sophie's car was a new one and a joy to drive but it was getting dark and visibility was poor, the darkness accentuated by trees on either side of the road. Gradually, sharp twists and turns loomed without giving away much of what lay ahead.

She had planned this trip since her student days in the Mudra Institute of Communications. The trip occupied the pride of place on her wish list; she'd always wanted to take her parents by road, in her own car, from Mumbai to Goa. Indus Public Relations paid her well, and she'd made the down payment for the Chevrolet car with savings from her initial three months' salary.

"Mumma and Pa, next year, I will send you on a week's vacation to Singapore," she said.

Her mother Anna, known in her locality for her penny-pinching lifestyle, was not amused. "Don't throw away money like this on lavish activities," she retorted.

Her father Roy agreed with Anna. "We don't want to go to exotic places, Sophie. You just save enough to buy yourself a flat."

Anna looked nervously outside the car's window. It was unnaturally dark. She felt as though she was going down a coal mine in a rail cart. "I think it was a bad idea to drive through this place so late in the night," she complained.

"Mumma, we will be in Goa in 90 minutes. Don't worry."

"We would have reached Goa by evening had it not been for your mother who took so much time to pack for the trip. There are restaurants on the way. Why get everything from home?"

"Why blame only me? Your dear friend Vinayak came in the morning; instead of telling him to spare us today at least, you indulged him with your expert comments on the newspaper headlines and then that lengthy discussion on what is going wrong in the country."

"Mumma, Pa, please stop! We are here to enjoy, not argue over trivial issues. Also, it was the broken-down truck on Old Church Road and the resulting traffic jam which delayed us by an hour at least."

Roy took off his seat belt and relaxed. Sophie was driving well around the sharp turns but they would take more than the 90 minutes she'd promised.

"People say that this road is not safe to drive through at night," remarked Anna again.

"Now that the atmosphere is so spooky, let me scare you a bit, Mum. One of my office colleagues Ravi was driving a bike through this road at midnight on his way back from Goa. He claimed that in the dark he saw an old woman wearing a pink gown walking backwards on the side of this very road. Wooooooo!" Her eyes on the road, Sophie imitated the eerie sound and thrust her left hand backwards like a claw at her mother's face.

"Don't be silly! It's not a joke. My sister used to tell me about strange incidents that happened on this road as far back as the 80's and 90's." Anna was jittery.

"Mumma! I don't believe Ravi's story. He is a lunatic who says atrocious things. What happened that night was probably one of those midnight-post-booze bike rides followed by drunken imagination."

"I really hope so!" her mother mumbled.

Silence enveloped the three inside the car. And then Roy started to hum along with the Boney M's '*Sunny*' playing in the stereo. His wife had no musical inclination but he had always enjoyed music, especially the old classics. He looked at his cell phone every now and then. No signal. "I don't understand why telecom providers don't install towers here so that people don't feel cut off on this stretch."

Anna looked outside, took out a miniature copy of the *Bible* from her handbag and started to pray.

Sophie felt excited thinking about the exotic resort she had booked for her parents in Goa. She had already enrolled them for water sports and a motor boat ride to see the dolphins. Another half day was reserved at the ayurvedic spa inside the resort. Sophie had it all planned out, one surprise for each of the four days they would spend in Goa.

They were coming down the slope at a decent speed when there was a loud sound. Sophie looked behind to see what had happened. There was a jerk and before she could react, the vehicle swerved and went off the road on to the grass.

"Sophie! What is happening?" her mother shrieked.

"The brakes, Sophie! The brakes!" Roy screamed.

Panicking, she tried to step on the brakes but the car skidded and smashed into a tree. A loud crashing sound broke the silence of the night, sending birds flying out from the trees in panic. From the rear passenger seat her mother screamed in panic,

*"My God! Oh my God!"*

Sophie turned to look at her. Anna had bruised her head and was holding an injured wrist. Next to her, her father was unconscious and bleeding profusely from his nose and mouth. She kicked open the door, her nose bleeding and her head spinning. The front left tyre had burst.

"Roy! Roy! Your father is not speaking! *Sophie!*"

Sophie pulled her father out from the other side of the car and laid him on the grass. She grabbed a bottle of mineral water from the back seat and sprinkled some water on his face. He murmured but was not fully conscious.

"Mumma, just wait here. Take care of Pa while I go to the road to get help."

Sophie walked on the slippery grass surrounded by the trees to the road. There were no vehicles as far as she could see on either side. Not even the distant light of one. She took out her mobile phone. No Signal. Wiping the blood dripping out of her nose with her handkerchief she started walking on the road towards Sarvanpur. A truck full of goods appeared on the other end of the road. Sophie waved out to it to stop. The vehicle accelerated and zoomed past. She looked at herself. Clad in a black shirt and black jeans with blood stains around her mouth, she must be looking hideous. Given the legends surrounding this road, she must have scared the hell out of the poor truck driver.

A little later, a van appeared at the turn towards Sarvanpur. Sophie stood in the middle of the road and frantically waved her hands for it to stop. The van skidded to a halt; she could see a young man wearing a yellow t-shirt at the wheel.

"Bhaiyaji, my car hit a tree and my father is seriously injured. Can you please take us to some hospital nearby?"

The young man gave a welcome smile and replied, his tone sophisticated. "You are in luck. This van belongs to the Western Ghats Hospital and is used to carry supplies, equipment and medicines. Give me a minute; let me park this on the side."

He parked the van on the side of the road and walked with Sophie to her car. He lifted Roy onto his shoulders and started to walk towards the van.

"He is lighter than I expected!" said the young man.

"Go to the front and turn the keys to start the vehicle."

Sophie followed as instructed and returned to open the van's backdoor. A small yellow lamp illuminated the cramped space and a weird mix of acrid smells, a mixed odour of copper, bleaching powder and spirit hit her nose like an invisible assault. The floor was covered with a blue plastic sheet; there were five big brown cardboard boxes, two big oxygen cylinders and three metallic IV stands stacked in a corner. Sophie entered to pick up a brown mattress rolled in another corner. She unrolled the mattress; it emitted a pungent smell.

"I sleep on that sometimes," said the young man as he placed Roy on the mattress and asked Sophie and her mother to sit next to him. There was a small opening on one side of the van facing the driver's seat; the back door was left open. Anna held the Bible in one hand and her nose with the other. As the van started to move Sophie asked from behind, "What is your name, Bhaiyaji?"

"Is that important for you to know? As of now we need to save your father," he replied from the driver's seat.

"Don't get angry brother! I need to call you by some name."

"Okay! My name is Tommy, if that makes you happy."

"Bhaiyaji, the place you are taking us to. Is it a good hospital?" Anna asked.

"No need to look any further. This is one of the best hospitals in town!" The man stepped on the accelerator.

The van roared along Vasco Road. Fifteen minutes later, the vehicle entered through a large gate into a compound with a modest single-storied building. A neon light display read 'Western Ghats Diagnostic Centre'. The van crossed the building, took a sharp turn and moved towards the back of the structure with a display on the roof, 'Western Ghats Hospital'. It appeared strange to Sophie that the diagnostic centre faced the main road while the hospital had a quiet existence at the rear. The young man placed Roy on a stretcher and rolled it to the Casualty Ward of the building, adjacent to the small reception area. Sophie and Anna followed them from behind.

The Casualty Ward had five empty beds and two nurses who woke up from what seemed like deep slumber on hearing the commotion. One of them had a pimple-pitted face and the other had brown eyes. The beds were like those in government hospitals with metal frames, white linen and green curtains. The plaster on the walls was peeling at many places. Roy was placed on the bed in the corner. The nurses immediately started to clean the wounds and attached a clip to his fingers which routed the pulse rate to a display monitor on the side of the bed. One of the nurses called up the duty doctor who appeared after five minutes.

The doctor was a middle aged woman dressed in a blue sari and white coat. She looked at Sophie and her mother seated on two plastic chairs at the entrance of the Casualty Ward.

"Doctor! My father....."

"I'm Dr Leela. Don't worry, we'll take care of your father."

She went to the patient's bed, examined Roy, dilated his eyes, checked his chest with a stethoscope and gave him an injection.

Dr Leela walked over to Sophie and said, "Your father has suffered serious injuries to his head. I have asked our senior doctor, Dr Mrinal, to come here. He lives on the other side of the premises. We will take a decision on what to do once he is here." For some strange reason she kept looking towards the casualty door.

"Doctor is there a bigger hospital nearby where....." Sophie was interrupted before she could complete the sentence.

"There are no big hospitals nearby. Also, the nearest hospital is an hour's drive from here. Why are you trying to go to some other place? This is one of the best hospitals in town."

Sophie did not reply.

"By the way, what is your father's blood group?"

"O+ve."

"Good! Let's wait for Dr Mrinal." Once again, she glanced at the door of the casualty ward and left.

Sophie was puzzled. What should she do next? She was stuck in the middle of some godforsaken place at this time of the night. For once she agreed with her mother, it was not a good idea to have undertaken this trip. They could have stayed at a motel in Sarvanpur and started early the next morning. There was no point thinking about what had happened. Instead she needed to focus on the situation at hand. With a muddled mind, she stepped outside for some fresh air. The young man stood next to his van, smoking a cigarette. She walked towards him trying to see if she had any alternatives.

"Bhaiyaji, do you have your cell phone with you? I need to make just one call."

"My mobile phone is sans signal when I am here," he said.

"Can you please drive me down to Sarvanpur? I will pay you as much money as you want," Sophie requested.

The young man did not make eye contact when he replied, "I don't need your money. I just checked the fuel meter; there's not enough fuel for us to reach Sarvanpur. One of the ward boys in the morning shift has a moped. I guess, I will go with him at dawn and fetch a can of fuel for my van."

"Just a second, Bhaiyaji. I saw the dashboard of the van while turning the keys, there is enough fuel."

The young man reacted as if he was not expecting that remark but almost instantly, the casual look was back on his face. "Ah! There is a problem with that needle on the dashboard. It is always at half way mark. Besides, why are you trying to go to some other place? This is one of the best hospitals in town." He looked away from her.

"That's up to me to decide, don't you think so?"

"You are free to do whatever you want. All I know is that the van is low on fuel and I cannot help. Sorry."

There was no use talking to him. When she returned to the entrance of the Casualty Ward, she saw that the brown-eyed nurse was offering coffee to her mother. Anna placed the Bible on her lap and gratefully sipped from the Styrofoam cup.

"I think my mother has also injured her wrist. Can you please have a look?"

"You should have shown it to the lady doctor. Wait, I will call her on her extension," the nurse replied.

"I think it just requires some preliminary first aid. Just to pull through the night. In the morning we will go to some hospital in Sarvanpur and get a proper scan done," said Sophie.

The nurse was visibly affected by the suggestion. "Why are you trying to go to some other place? Please don't go anywhere else. This is one of the best hospitals in town."

As she spoke, the nurse with the pitted face came up from behind asking about the commotion. "She wants to take her parents to some other hospital in Sarvanpur."

"You know that it is not polite of you to say that. Don't you?" the second nurse shouted.

"Excuse me!" Sophie was livid.

"What is all this planning to go somewhere else?"

There was a momentary silence in the casualty ward. Sophie was bewildered. "What is the problem? I will do whatever I feel like, none of your business."

"Then you can go ahead with whatever you want to do," the brown-eyed nurse replied.

"You people know how helpless we are right now and you can treat us with arrogance," Sophie retorted.

"We are arrogant? We? Can you believe this woman? You must hear how you speak, young lady." The pimple-pitted nurse spoke.

"Alright! Let's not create a scene here," said Sophie.

The brown-eyed nurse whispered to her colleague. "This woman has a Bible."

Sophie was getting increasingly upset at their eccentric behaviour. There was something creepy about the hospital, the whole place in fact.

The beep on the monitor connected to Roy slowed down at that moment and the nurses rushed back to his bed. A middle aged man with grey hair and brown eyes entered through the casualty ward door, followed by the lady doctor on duty.

"I am Dr Mrinal. I'm sorry I took time to come." They both went to Roy's bed while Sophie and Anna looked on from a distance. The doctor had piercing brown eyes and was smartly dressed. Dr Leela trailed behind him like a tail.

Dr Mrinal looked concerned. "I think he is sinking. We need to take him to the ICU." The nurses swung into action and called in the young man who had driven down the victims from the accident site. They placed Roy on a rolling stretcher and took him to another section of the hospital behind the curtain.

"Doctor! What is the problem?"

"His condition is critical due to the blood loss. You people sit here while I attend to him in the ICU," Dr Mrinal told Sophie.

From the other end of the room, Anna called out frantically. "Sophie! Sophie! I'm feeling weird. Hold me, please!"

"Mumma! Are you giddy?"

Sophie held her mother's hand as she was about to collapse. With the help of Dr Leela, Sophie placed her mother on the other bed. Anna was weak, sweating and pale. Dr Leela took out a diabetes test kit, pricked Anna's finger and put the drop on the test strip.

"Sugar reading is extremely low. I will put her on drip." The doctor prepared for the intravenous drip for Anna, but she kept looking towards the door from time to time.

"What is your mother's blood group?"

"B+ve. Dr Leela, she has had no blood loss, so why is her blood group detail required?"

"Who is the doctor here? You or I?"

Sophie was now fully convinced that she did not want to continue treatment for her parents in this godforsaken hospital. *Did they inject something into her father?* It was dark outside. Quietly, she sneaked out of the casualty ward and dashed to the reception area.

*Did they drug her mother?*

She walked fast towards the reception. There were a lot of empty chairs; at the main desk there was no receptionist, just as she had anticipated. Behind the reception there was a flight of stairs to the first floor. She could hear the faint echo of two women talking on the phone.

"Yes! Three people. Today."

Sophie tried to overhear the conversation but she could only barely make out the words.

"Two fine, one hurt."

*What kind of a place was it?* She tried hard to eavesdrop.

"What do you mean later? We don't have time. Get your act together."

Sophie knew that it was time for some quick decisions and actions. She looked around nervously as her heart beat had increased and droplets of sweat appeared on her upper lip. All the hospitals in the state had a prominent display of the Nursing Homes Registration Act 1949 framed in their reception area. It was strange that this hospital did not have one. There were two landline phones on the desk – a white one and a black one. As she looked around, her terror mounted, almost choking her. She picked up the white phone with trembling hands. Dead. Nervously, she picked up the black phone, a board line.

She pressed 0. It did not connect to the direct line.

She pressed 9. It did not connect to the direct line.

A voice came from behind her, "I am sorry. It's not good manners to snoop around someone else's property at this time of the night.

Are you looking for something here?" Sophie's heartbeat stopped and her knees trembled as she turned to face Dr Leela.

"No! Nothing...."

Dr. Leela smiled. "By the way, you did not tell me the blood group."

"I told you that my mother's blood group is B+ve."

The doctor narrowed her eyes. "I was not talking about your mother's blood group. I was asking about yours, young lady."

Sophie stepped backwards. "Stay away! Stay away from me!" she screamed.

She looked outside and dashed out of the reception into the darkness, running on the green grass past the tamarind and kokum trees. She looked behind and she could not see anyone following her. She looked in front of her but she could still not see clearly. She was sprinting into the unknown hoping to plead for help. Momentarily, she stopped to catch her breath. It was a wrong decision to have run into the wilderness; she should have run to the other side of the building towards the gate. Her mind was numb with fear. Running among the trees through thick grass, her blood froze when an owl hooted from a nearby tree.

*What sin had she committed to be put through such an ordeal? She had just wanted to ensure a good time for her parents.*

She could smell something. It was similar to the smell of burning wood. Maybe there was a house nearby. At last she saw something ahead of her – the dark outline of a house in the moonlight. It was more like a big shed she realised as she drew nearer. As she approached it she saw someone standing in front of its door. The wind was blowing gently but Sophie was sweating. She was panting heavily. Finally, she gathered the courage to approach the stranger standing in the dark. As she cautiously approached him, the stranger switched on his torch and pointed at her. Sophie stopped. Her heart stopped beating and she could not breathe. The man then pointed the torch at himself. Two piercing brown eyes looked at her illuminated in the torchlight. *Dr Mrinal*!

He smiled and said, “Why are you trying to go to some other place? Please don’t go anywhere else. This is one of the best hospitals in town!”

Sophie turned cold. A loud scream of helplessness echoed around the farm house. It echoed in the uneven terrain around the premises.

Dr Mrinal, Dr Leela, the two nurses, and the young man who drove the van assembled in the reception area of the Western Ghats Diagnostic Centre.

“Kunal, you take the towing van to the crash site and push the car over the cliff near Silent Villa. Don’t be an idiot to drive it over the nail traps you have yourself placed on the road, else you will have to fix the flat tyre yourself,” Mrinal instructed.

The young man replied, “Okay father, as you say.”

Mrinal drank a glass of water. “I am going to the terrace to pull up the signboard at the back,” he said.

“Any work for the two of us, father?” the brown eyed nurse asked.

“You remove the ‘Casualty’ board from the back. And you...”, he said pointing at the pimple-pitted nurse “....call up Shaman Mehek and the others to tell them that we will have another ceremony shortly. This time it will be a triple!”

“As you say, father!”

“Have you informed the recipients?” asked Dr Leela.

“Of course, my dear wife. They will start coming in from tomorrow morning. We need to put up a board outside the diagnostic centre stating that we are closed till Monday for renovations,” said Mrinal.

“What about the abortions and ultrasounds scheduled by Vandana for the next few days?” Leela asked.

Vandana, the gynaecologist, was Leela's cousin and worked at the diagnostic centre.

"What if we don't comply with the appointments? Will they go to the police and complain that we did not comply with their appointment to terminate their future girl child?" Mrinal was furious.

He was the boss of this family of five; any difference of opinion with him was not permissible. "Don't tell me what to do or I will bend over and slap your wrinkled, ugly face, sweetheart!"

The others in the room hoped the thunderstorm of rage would pass soon. Their father was someone with whom they could not disagree. Their lives had been altered living under his terror for so many years. Twice, the girls had failed to clear the medical entrance exam. One of them was interested in Accounting while the other loved History. Because they had let him down, their father forcefully enrolled them in Sharada College where the sisters befriended another student of the college named Mehek. She soon became their closest family friend. When Kunal failed to clear IIT and engineering entrance tests, even he had to face the wrath of his father. In an act of rage his father forcefully enrolled him in the Bachelor of Home Sciences course, a course generally undertaken only by women. Mrinal ensured that his son completed the course with distinction as well.

He was almost yelling now. "Did you people hear me properly? Did you? Now get to work. Leela! You tell Vandana to be here in the morning tomorrow; considering the amount of work we may need her help."

After everyone left, Mrinal went to the terrace to pull down the sign board.

Later, he slept for a couple of hours. There were long hours to be spent at the operation theatre in the next two days.

The next day as he proceeded with his work inside the concealed operation theatre in the diagnostic centre, he heard the ward boy who had gone to Sarvanpur town mention a bizarre midnight murder that had caught the town's attention.

Out of curiosity, he read the morning *Konkan Times* but there was no mention of any such incident. The national TV news channel did not cover anything either. In the *Dusk Star* evening issue, the news was the front page headline:

## Sarvanpur's Medical Horror Story

The victim's name made Mrinal slump in grief; the grief was overtaken by worry after reading the article further.

The police had raided the deceased woman's house and confiscated her diaries, phonebook and some literature written by her. All throughout that sleepless night, Mrinal planned his next course of action. Occasionally he would look at the tall framed portrait of his illustrious father which he had next to his bed. The only person he had ever loved and respected in the whole wide world. He had never been close to his mother, a detached and mute individual always busy with her work. However, he had always idolised his father and wanted to be a known personality like him. All throughout his life he had feared to be labelled as a robust shrub growing below the shadows of a tall tree. Just when Mrinal thought he was going to make his mark, achieve his well deserved fame and associated pleasure, this misfortune had to strike.

Dr Mrinal started to cry silently, something he rarely did. At one point of time Mrinal had fancied being much more influential in life than his father had ever been. Tonight he was struggling to save himself from a world that did not understand him.

Dr Mrinal's worst fears came true the next morning when a police party stood at his doorstep with a search warrant in hand. The search party found three heavily drugged bodies in the basement of the diagnostic centre – a middle aged man, a young woman and a middle aged woman. The middle aged man covered in a blood stained white sheet, had a prominent scar on his body from which one of his kidneys had been removed. An IV unit on his hands indicated that a certain amount of blood had been drained out of his body as well. The young woman had injury marks on her head and she was barely alive when they found her. The middle aged woman had a bruise mark on her face and an injured wrist. She had a copy of the *Bible* next to her bed.

Sophie Carvalho, Anna Carvalho and Roy Carvalho were the last victims of a horrendous medical practice that would shake up the sleepy town. They were lucky to have got out of it alive.

# September: Meeting the Beast

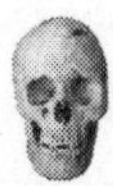

Devika sat in front of her laptop trying to write an initial introduction to the subject matter she now had to research, the hideous mind she would have to face at Sarvanpur Central Jail, Doctor Mrinal Tenmala. The man who she believed knew too much but had revealed too little. Under third degree torture, he had revealed all the crimes he had committed as well as those of the other cult members but he had not mentioned in detail the functioning of the cult, its psyche and long term plans. This was what interested Devika. She tried to organise her thoughts in the form of a paragraph around her perception of the image of this man. The next day when she would meet him personally, she could use the paragraph as a good yardstick of her assessment and compare the man and the myth.

## Chapter – VII
## Doctor Death of Sarvanpur

There have been people in the medical profession who have had a larger list of victims than Sarvanpur's Mrinal Tenmala. Dr Harold Shipman, a British doctor, was rumoured to have caused 215 deaths. More recently, a Brazilian lady doctor, Dr Virginia Soares, was accused of being allegedly

> responsible for around 300 deaths. Her reason for killing the patients was equally bizarre. Apparently, she wanted to free her hospital's beds. Mrinal had fewer victims but there is something special, something different about him, something not visible at first glance. The difference is in the business acumen of this savage mind.

There are times when no matter how hard a writer tries, she does not get the words to flow out of her mind. Devika was having such a day. She felt she was not getting it right, but she tried. She was thinking what to write next when loud music started playing from the guest room. Nazia Hassan singing the evergreen *Aap Jaisa Koi*. She went to her father's room and watched him enjoy the song. For the moment she forgot everything; the murders, the cult and the psychopath. The mesmerising voice of the beautiful singer overshadowed everything. She sat next to her father and for the next hour, father and daughter together listened to other songs by her – *Disco Deewane, Boom Boom, Ankhein Milane Wale*. The same songs which during Devika's childhood played out loud on weekends from the old tape-recorder from the hall of their house at Delhi.

The next morning, Shravan left early for work. Since Devika was in the second trimester of pregnancy, her morning sickness had reduced substantially. Before leaving for Sarvanpur Central Jail, she went through her notes on Doctor Mrinal one final time.

Mrinal Tenmala was born in Arvinwadi town 25 kilometres west of Sarvanpur. His father, Ashok Tenmala, was an IAS officer and a well-known member of the community at Arvinwadi. A known philanthropist, Mrinal's father had political ambitions for his post-retirement life. His mother used to run a small scale industry employing only women to make jams and pickles. Mrinal was a class topper throughout high-school. He did his MBBS and MD from Imperial Medical College at Belgaum specialising in Nephrology and was especially skilled in Nephrectomy. After rejecting multiple lucrative job offers from big cities he decided to take up a job in Sushrut Hospital, Sarvanpur. At that time he believed that the villages and small-towns of India required doctors more urgently than the big cities and participated in village polio camps and rural health check-up drives around Sarvanpur. His life went for a tailspin when he sent his retired parents on a trip to Nainital with the first salary he received from Sushrut Hospital. Mrinal's parents got off the train at Kathgodam railway station and hired a jeep to take them to their hotel at Ramgarh. On the way the driver drove recklessly and the jeep skidded off the high mountain road, plunging the couple to their death.

Mrinal drowned in his own depression and could not come to terms with the thought of having funded the death of his own parents. Their community at Arvinwadi named a small road and a mini memorial after Mrinal's father. Mrinal found solace in alcohol. He was asked to leave Sushrut Hospital when he turned up for work on multiple occasions sloshed on whiskey. This was followed by a six-year stint with Holy Cross Hospital where he was famous for yelling at all the junior staff in the hospital and creating a ruckus on small issues. At home he was known to be brutal to his wife, two daughters and son. They were all slaves to his decisions. Mrinal had a major tiff with his hospital's management over procurement of dialysis machines and other equipment for his wing. He was adamant that the management should give their go-ahead for the brands he wanted while the hospital was adamant on procuring the equipment from lower cost vendors. Mrinal quit his job, used the couple's life savings and took a loan to open the Diagnostic Centre on Vasco Road. Since the Diagnostic Centre was way outside the town, patients were few and it started making major losses. At one point of time the bank funding the project issued warnings of a takeover if their dues were not cleared. The family was under great duress.

That's when Mehek, who had studied nursing along with his daughters entered their life. She suggested other lines of business to Mrinal. After venturing into the field of illegal organ transplants, the Diagnostic Centre started making money. They also roped in Leela's cousin Dr Vandana, a gynaecologist who ran their sex-determination ultrasound and illegal abortion business. Mehek was their friend, guide and consultant in all their initiatives. Mrinal had little faith in black-magic but enjoyed the thrill of money, sex, drugs and alcohol that came his way after joining the cult.

A couple of days after Mehek's death, Dr Mrinal Tenmala was arrested along with his family members.

Devika waited at the bus stop across her house for 45 minutes for the rickety bus going to Puranwad near Sarvanpur Central Jail. Once she got down from the creaking bus she walked for another ten minutes to the main gate of Sarvanpur Jail.

At the guard room she introduced herself. "Please tell Jail Superintendent Jaykumar that Devika Soni is here."

Jaykumar had already received instructions from his senior, Alpesh Thapar, about this visitor. Devika was asked to go inside towards the drinking water unit in the courtyard. At the gate a lady constable checked her clothes and bag after which she walked towards the main courtyard where families of convicts and their advocates stood around, discussing individual cases. The main jail building was old and had cracks at multiple places. Inside, it was dingy and acrid.

She waited in front of the drinking water unit for twenty minutes.

"Devika Ji, Namaste."

The man who stood before her was dark and well-built with curly hair. He was dressed in a white shirt and white trousers, the uniform of the jail authorities.

"I am Jaykumar. Please come with me."

She followed him across the registration desk into a corridor where on one side the guards were checking the relatives of the convicts. They were putting in the same big spoon inside all the tiffins which the relatives had brought for the convicts. This was their way of checking if some object was concealed inside the curry. Once when Devika was working with NDTV, a colleague who had interviewed a convict had mentioned this practice of using the same spoon dipped in all the tiffins, that too without being washed between the dips. This interviewee convict once supposedly had peas in spinach gravy made by his mother which also tasted of fish made in coconut gravy topped with flavours of mutton roganjosh.

Once again a lady constable checked Devika's dress and bag after which they went through a dimly lit corridor leading to the Mulakat room. Devika could see a mid-sized hall where relatives met the inmates across two layers of wire mesh in a dim room. Jaykumar led her to an adjacent room which was more brightly lit with a large glass window on one side of the wall. On the other side of the glass window, there were metal railings placed at a distance of one foot; the room had a chair in front of a metal door. The glass window had five equidistant holes in the middle. A modest wooden table and chair were placed in front of the hole in the middle. The walls were cracking, the plaster peeling off. Cobwebs clung to the ceiling.

"I thought that this will be a better place for you to have a proper talk with the madman."

"Mr Jaykumar, what is this room?"

"This is our new Mulakat room. We are yet to start using this and some wooden partitions are being made. I will leave now," said Jaykumar.

"Thank you, Mr Jaykumar."

"One word of caution. Please be careful not to put your hands across the hole on the window or hand him anything. This man is a beast. He had tried to molest a hapless woman on the way to the court. So please be wary," Jaykumar sounded concerned.

"I understand. Thanks."

Devika kept her bag on the table and sat down on the chair. She looked at the clock on the wall. It was a longer wait than she had expected. Probably the prison staff were doing their work at leisure. Devika wiped the perspiration on her forehead with her handkerchief, her eyes transfixed on the door. The door on the opposite side opened and a middle aged man with curly greying hair entered. Two police constables entered behind him. Mrinal was in handcuffs and padlocks. He had a flat, short nose like that of a wild boar and a ridiculously round double chin which looked like a miniature buttock on his face. However, it was his eyes that caught her attention. The two brown eyes were piercing.

She stood up from her chair and said, "Good afternoon, Doctor Mrinal."

The doctor looked carefully at her slight baby bump.

"Good afternoon. What is your name? I am unable to recollect." His welcome smile revealed a clean white set of teeth with prominent canines.

"I'm Devika. I am a housewife and an aspiring writer. I am writing a book on the events that took place in Sarvanpur in the beginning of the year, so the request for an interview. Thanks for accepting my request for a meeting. I need a minute before we can start." Devika fumbled with her leather bag and opened it to take out her notepad.

A white pack inside the bag caught Mrinal's attention for a moment. Devika took out her mobile phone, switched on the voice recording and placed it on the desk.

"Devika, have you ever been to a psychiatrist?"

"Excuse me!"

"Have you ever been to a shrink?"

"Hmm. Well, to be honest with you. I was once asked to go and meet a psychiatrist." Devika managed a smile in a bid to appear pleasant and friendly.

"Can I ask you why?"

"My doctor suspected that my mood swings were because of Bi-polar depression. They sent me to the shrink for a diagnosis."

Mrinal now looked her in the eye. "So you were diagnosed to have Bi-polar?" His stare made her feel uncomfortable and jittery. Like a wave of electric current it passed through her body. This man had something very repulsive about him.

"No! Not at all. It was finally diagnosed as a hormonal imbalance due to thyroid." Devika could feel a certain bit of nervousness in her voice. A lizard was crawling on the other side of the wall. Mrinal looked at it and his glance shifted back to Devika.

"Tell me Devika. How was your experience with the psychiatrist?"

"I thought this was your interview, Doctor, not mine," she stated but her voice broke midway through the sentence.

Mrinal looked stern. "It's not fair that I tell you all about myself and you don't tell me anything about yourself. Is it fair, Devika? We will start with you first."

After what looked like a long uncomfortable silence, Devika felt that this interview was not going as per plan. She decided to comply with the doctor for the time being to make him comfortable. There was no point being stubborn with this psychopath. If he went into his shell it would be difficult to get the information she wanted.

"Alright. I felt like trash. The psychiatrist had an intern also with him when I went for consultation. So the psychiatrist asked me questions, heard the response, turned to the intern, gave insights and reinforced his observations with him. I was very uncomfortable. As if....."

"As if you were some strange creature or exotic animal who was being observed. As if you do not exist as a person but are a case-study, a specimen. Correct?"

"Very true!"

"Devika, I came here to have a good conversation. And I liked you at the first glance. But then you did something insulting. Don't you think your voice recording and scribbling makes me feel the same way? An animal in a circus or a zoo?"

She was taken aback by his remark. "I am sorry if that upset you."

Devika switched off the voice recording and placed the notepad back into her bag. Her stomach muscles seemed to shrink, squeezing her breath. She told herself to relax and breathe slowly.

*Why am I choking like this?*

Trying to regain her composure, she said, "So as I told you, writing books is my hobby. You must be aware of what authors in this country earn. However, my purpose is not money. It is to bring out the truth for the general public."

"Very noble indeed!"

"Doctor Mrinal, your father was a great man, a public figure respected by his colleagues and the community. I am sure that a son born to an exemplary person like your father cannot be as evil as the media has portrayed him to be."

"Sadly, nobody realises that there is my side of the story also." said Mrinal. He constantly touched his face and moved the strands of hair falling on his forehead. Devika could see his grey long finger nails with dirt between them.

"Precisely! That side of the story should be out there. I am sure that you will be appealing to the higher courts against the death penalty awarded to you."

"Sure I will!" Mrinal said with a smile.

"I hope you also realise that it is important that the public opinion is in your favour. That the media should not write atrocious and malicious things about you like it is doing now," she asserted, slowly getting into her rhythm. "Nobody wants a media driven trial-n-judgement which is prevalent nowadays. Even before courts could listen to testimonies, the media paints a demon or a victim out of the accused. The judiciary, even if they do not acknowledge it, comes under a lot of public pressure. To prevent that, the accused's version of the truth should be out there as well."

"That's the bitter portion. Nobody is willing to hear my story."

"Doctor Mrinal, I am here to document your story. I have read your files and the first thing that caught my attention was the starting point of all this, the accident involving your parents. It transformed you forever."

"I don't think many people realise that, Devika. They are so busy throwing stones at me."

Now Devika felt was the right time to start probing, "Tell me, Doctor Mrinal. Was Mehek the bad influence which brought about this change in you?"

"Ha! Not so soon, sweetheart! What's the hurry?" Mrinal gave a hearty laughter.

"Is there anything funny we are discussing here?" Devika was annoyed with his hysterical laughter.

He continued, "Ha! My dear, you started off pretty well, I must say. Your 'housewife and aspiring author ' story was a very good effort at removing the threat perception and breaking the ice".

"What do you mean?"

"Devika, I have seen your photograph in the *Konkan Times*. I know you are the ACP's wife and hence we have this meeting in this special room. You might have a perception in your mind that you are a feminist but the truth is that all the privileges come to you because of your husband's position."

"I can do without these privileges." Devika felt offended.

"I have read your first book. Incidentally, Mehek gave her copy to me. She was glad that you, her favourite columnist, were making an attempt to explore the dark side of human nature. I love reading gross and macabre stuff, but your book let me down. There were so many errors. Your research was shallow, and you did not get inside the head of that female murderer or her motivations. A pathetic waste of time, paper, trees and effort."

Devika was silent.

Mrinal continued, "I can see through you like glass. Cheap quality glass. That talk about my father's greatness was a lousy trick at getting an emotional connect with me. The whining on authors not getting enough money was a dumb attempt to tell me that you have no vested interest in this book. That it was my golden opportunity and not yours! Bullcrap!"

"I was honest. It's up to you whether you buy my argument or not." Devika asserted herself.

"Nice attempt at showing me the carrot as well. Appeal in higher courts, positive public opinion and a stop to the media bashing. Of course, the masterstroke was the empathy card you played – my parents' accident making me a different person. Ouch! I am touched."

Mrinal leaned his face against the glass and pulled a sorry face.

His voice rose as he spoke, his piercing brown eyes looked into Devika's eyes. "Guess what? Poor homework, poor skills and a wrong person to direct your charms at. Now you can stop wasting my time and push off."

"Let me tell you, Doctor. I can write my story with or without your inputs." Devika tried hard to appear calm.

Mrinal leaned forward and said, "I saw a white packet of CAPAD in your bag. Are you suffering from cancer?"

"No. It's for my father."

"Devika, isn't it heartless of you to be here wasting your time with me while he is at home suffering, about to die a painful death? Shouldn't you be with him, my dear? He will be gone soon, dammit!"

His resistance toughened Devika's resolve. "That is none of your business," she mumbled as she tried to fight back her tears.

"Devika, let's stop talking about me and let's look at you. Your plain look, shabby clothes and the couple of grey strands in your hair that you do not bother to attend to. Tell me, Devika, are you disinterested in life as a whole?"

"No. On the contrary, I enjoy my work and I am here because of that."

For a split second Devika could not help but wonder how he could read her so easily. The doctor was slowly but steadily figuring her out and Devika found herself to be increasingly defensive.

"You lie convincingly, Devika. Tell me the truth, have you thought about ending your life ever?"

"Of course not! And even if I did, that is none of your business," replied Devika, feeling vulnerable.

"Oh, acid tongue! Annoying baby-bump woman! Are you in a bad mood? It's quite sad. You are in a pretty helpless state. Putting so much effort when you should be home. If I were you I would stay out of all this for the sake of the unborn child."

Devika was tongue tied as Mrinal closed his eyes and took in a whiff of fresh air.

"Ah! Let me tell you some good news but it is a secret."

"What?"

Looking eye-to-eye in a low tone and leaning towards the screen he murmured, "She is all around you. I can smell her presence."

"Who?"

"The dead woman!" he replied with a sly smile.

"What nonsense?"

"Let me tell you, she will not leave until she totally messes you up. You will figure that out," said the doctor with a confident smile.

"How is that related to this interview? Doctor Mrinal, I am here to understand Mehek's plan for the future of your organisation. You are the only person with whom she would have discussed this. I am not leaving here without that." Devika folded her arms and crossed her legs.

"Can I tell you an uncomfortable truth? You know why you are so interested in people like Mehek?" Mrinal leaned forward. "Maybe it will be difficult for you to accept but believe me, it is true. It's because people like Mehek are like you. You see a bit of your unstable self in them and it is comforting. Isn't it?" The doctor laughed hysterically. "It is comforting. Very comforting. Thank goodness it is not only me. There are others worse than me. Victims of unstable minds. What a relief to know that!"

Devika felt suffocated and tongue tied. She was wondering what to say next when Mrinal exclaimed, "I am ready to speak my mind and tell my story to someone. However, Madam Devika Soni, a struggling, helpless, unstable, suicidal, heartless, pseudo-feminist who is plain disinterested with life and an obvious loser, is not the right candidate. You are hollow and dead inside. What you write will be inanimate as well. An internally dead woman writing about another dead woman. I need somebody more worthy. A more deserving and capable person to speak about me. Not an ugly distorted mess like you are."

With an ailing father who was terminally ill and a fragile self, Devika had shown enough courage in the past few months. Today this man figured out and ruptured the weakest portions of her inner self. She could not take it anymore. Shattered like glass on which a madman had flung a stone Mrinal's words suddenly sounded thought-provoking to her. Her innermost fears and complexes came out in the open with the commotion of a bee hive set on fire.

*Am I a failure? Am I struggling too hard not to face the truth? Am I not good enough?*

"I have a suggestion for you, Devika. Listen to me carefully." He beckoned to her to come near the glass partition. Devika found she was too scared to refuse. She leaned forward.

"I think you really, and I mean seriously, require help. Professional help. You are in a pretty bad state, my child. Get someone to look inside your head and put you on some medication. You are struggling too hard with life. Let it go. Spend time with your father, he will be gone soon. You will repent wasting your time with me here." His tone was matter-of-fact, his fingernails dirty as he scratched his cheek.

A tear dropped off Devika's cheek. She wiped it and left the room without saying a word. Mrinal stood up with a triumphant look, a wide smile lit his face as he walked towards the metal door. She stood at the main gate fighting the tears that flowed uncontrollably down her cheeks.

I should not have got involved in this, she thought, as she walked towards the Puranwad bus stop, her emotions like a flash flood after a cloud burst.

As she waited at the bus-stop, she took off her hair band, feeling its tightness against her scalp. Unhinged, her hair flew around her face, wild, free; the tear-smudged kaajal around her eyes gave her a ghostly appearance and attracted strange looks from curious passersby.

*His words were so true. I am in such a sad and miserable state.*

When the bus arrived after what seemed like a very long time, she took a window seat, away from prying eyes. The rickety bus rode through fallow land on both sides. The ticket collector, a middle aged man with a pleasant smile, thick spectacles, and greying hair, looked at her as she handed over the bus fare. Handing her the ticket stub, he asked, 'Beti, are you alright?'

"I am fine."

He moved on, one eye on her. She had been crying since the time she stepped into the bus. He felt concerned but didn't pry.

From her window, she saw a man with a little girl on a cycle; the girl was in a school uniform, water bottle and bag in hand. The man had a prosthetic leg.

She started to cry bitterly, again.

The bus stopped in front of her house. As she walked through the gates she noticed the guards look at her and begin to talk in hushed tones.

*I don't care! Let them think whatever they want to.*

She walked past into the hall and momentarily paused to look at the guest room. In the bedroom she flung her bag and mobile phone on to the bed. She opened the drawer and took out a blade, the one she used to cut out interesting newspaper and magazine articles. She went to the bathroom and collapsed on the floor. Her hands trembled and she pulled at her own hair like a mad woman.

She made cuts on her forearms. Then she closed her eyes and leaned back against the wall, waiting for relief.

Even the cuts did not help. She felt the suffocation mount inside her.

She looked at the mirror inside the bathroom. Could she bang her head into it? Maybe that would pacify her head which was on fire.

That evening Shravan returned home and kept his suitcase on the hall table. He saw Radhemohan and asked him about Devika. Radhemohan had seen her walk into the bedroom but hadn't seen her come out since.

Shravan hurried into the bedroom.

Her mobile phone and bag were thrown carelessly on the bed but she was missing. He called out her name; no response. He sat on the bed wondering where she was when he saw the attached bathroom door ajar.

He pushed open the door. Devika was sitting in a corner of the bathroom, on the floor. Her hair fell over her face. Her eyes were red with tears. She had a blade in her hands and cuts on her forearms, clean cuts from which droplets of blood oozed out.

"My God, Devika! What did you do to yourself?" He snatched the blade out of her hands.

Devika grabbed her hair and said, "I am sorry. Please leave me alone. I am feeling very low."

"Not in this state, Devika. Come on, get up and come with me," he said.

Devika started to cry profusely. "I'm such a big failure, so wasted, Shravan." She began to slap herself recklessly till Shravan caught hold of her hands.

"Stop it, Devika! Tell me. What happened?"

"I hate myself, Shravan, I hate myself." Again she started to scratch claw her own face . Shravan caught both her hands and forced her to get up and go back to the bedroom.

"Papa is dying and I cannot do anything about it." She choked.

"Breathe! Breathe! Don't lose hope. He is doing well." Shravan led her to the bedroom.

"I need the pill, Shravan. Not bloody primrose, but Serta. Today more than any other day. Give it to me. Why did you take it away from me?"

"Are you out of your mind? You know that an anti-depressant pill is harmful for the baby. What's wrong with you? How much we have prayed for this child. Do you want it to be born deformed?" Shravan was furious.

"I want this baby, Shravan, I really do... but I am feeling awful inside. Tell me what to do."

"You can do whatever else you want to do Devika, but not the pill. You hear me?"

"Please save me."

"No, Devika! Anything but the pill."

"Shravan! I don't want our baby to be born deformed. Please understand me. I am just unable to take all this today."

"Relax! Everything will be fine. Look into my eyes." She looked at him.

"Drink this glass of water and take a deep breath."

Devika drank the glass of water and Shravan dabbed some antiseptic liquid on her scratches.

"Breathe! Breathe!" he told her repeatedly.

Shravan asked Radhemohan to make coffee for Devika and fetched a chocolate bar for her from the refrigerator.

"Shravan, I feel so much sorrow inside me. I feel lost in this world. I don't know what I am here for and what is expected of me."

"Everyone feels like that. Your's is not a special case. It's not an excuse for you to lose track. Just breathe!"

"I really don't know what matters. I am lost. Does it matter if I write this book? Does it matter if I have this child? Does anything matter for that matter?"

After an hour or so he talked her into narrating whatever had happened at Sarvanpur Central Jail that afternoon. He knew it was important for her to get the muck out of her system.

"Devika, I think you are taking way too much pressure given the situation we are in."

Devika replied, "Do you think I should stop working on the book?"

"A practical man would advise that." He said as he placed his hands on her shoulders.

"However, I think you should not let the situation defeat you like this."

Devika could not believe her ears.

"I am so glad you said that, Shravan. My father used to tell me the same thing when I was younger. Once a person tries to evade difficult situations in life, it will become a habit. Life will reach nowhere if we live by taking short cuts and living in our comfort zones."

"Devika! Did your father see you in this state?"

"I hope he did not see me when I was on the way to the bedroom."

"It will kill him to see you like this. It is important for us to maintain a smiling face at all times, even when we feel miserable inside."

"I know that, Shravan! Sometimes I just feel like shit and cannot control it. Anyway, like my father said, I will not take it easy. I started on a journey and I will not abandon it mid-way."

"Cautiously, but firmly towards the goal. Just when you think you have done your best comes the stage when you should hang on a little longer, focus a little more and work a bit more harder to realise that you had grossly under-estimated yourself previously." He put his palms on her palms.

Devika lifted her hands and placed her fingertips gently on Shravan's cheek as she looked into his eyes. "Just like Leonard Woolf."

"Who is that, Devika?"

Devika sighed. "A noble man who exists only in the pages of some old books. One who tried very hard to keep his wife happy."

# PART - III
# Cult Members

# September: Cold Walls of Solitary Confinement

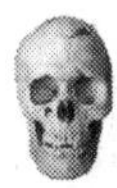

As usual, Alpesh came home for lunch. Since there was no electricity, he couldn't watch television and kept himself busy with the magazines he loved reading at such times along with the food his wife Monica served him. To her he seemed to be married to his work, TV and magazines, in that order.

Alpesh ate his roti, dal and palak paneer without uttering a word. Then suddenly he said, "One of my colleagues in office cracked a good one. Listen to this, you will like it."

*Here comes another one of those out-of-the-blue jokes. Shouldn't he be asking me how my day was or how I feel today? Does he care?* Monica thought.

"There was an accountant who developed a skin disease because of which his skin became very dark. He wanted to participate in the office fancy dress competition and told his wife to get him a dress.

She got him a snowman's suit and he became very angry. 'Foolish woman!' He screamed. Have you ever seen a dark faced snowman? So the wife went to market and this time returned with a Santa Claus suit. The accountant became angry again and screamed, 'Foolish woman!' Have you ever seen a dark faced Santa Claus? The third time she went to the market and got a bamboo stick. She asked him to go to the fancy dress naked with the bamboo stick up his rear side."

"And what would the accountant be?" asked Monica.

"A Chocobar!" chuckled Alpesh.

Monica was not amused.

His duty to converse with his wife over for the afternoon, Alpesh returned to his magazine before getting back to work.

It had been Monica's decision to be a home-maker since she was prone to vascular headaches every alternate day. When they did not have kids for years and Alpesh refused to adopt a child, Monica was left without work and without a child, and most of the time, without a husband either.

The phone rang, too loudly, she thought. "Hello. Oh, you! How many times have I told you not to call me?" She listened, distracted, an eye on the door through which her husband had just left. "No, please, it was not love, just momentary stupidity and I'm glad that all that talking on the phone did not lead to anything."

As she listened intently now, her face turned red with anger. "Forget about the past. I was just lonely and out of my mind. Keep the phone down and don't call me again, please." She put down the phone receiver.

Alpesh was off to Sarvanpur Central Jail. Since 1968, it had been taking in high security prisoners and was in need of urgent renovation but prisons rank low in the government's list of priorities at a time when even hospitals and schools were not allocated enough funds. Alpesh had once read a quote by a famous Russian writer, 'The degree of civilisation in a society can be judged by entering its prisons'. Alpesh wondered that going by that logic a lot was yet to be desired in both – our prisons and our society. Inside the prison, it was a regular day. The oldest inmate of this jail was Pranav Dhul. Today he would have to be disturbed during his afternoon nap.

"Is my father inside his prison cell, Pranav chacha?" Pranav who was sound asleep on his mat did not respond to the question.

"Pranav Uncle! Is my father in his prison cell?" This time Pranav yelled back, "Your father is not there; also, did I not mention that I don't like being called uncle or brother or bhai, or for that matter anything but my name."

"I am so tired of everything. Life has come to a standstill. There is no window in my cell. The whole day I stare at the metal bars of my door and the black stone wall in front of it. That's all I do," said the voice from the adjacent cell.

"Then go shoot yourself. What did you expect when you came here? Daily live musical performances along with tandoori meals?" Pranav shouted out sarcastically.

"I badly want to take a leak. The commode at the corner of my cell is revolting! I don't even feel like urinating into it."

"You should see the common lavatories they have for general prisoners; waterlogged, knee deep filthy water, urine with floating faeces. There are only a handful of inmates who do not vomit every time they go inside," said Pranav. "The poor guys go into the lavatory with a cloth tightly tied around their noses."

He waited for the expected grunt of disgust from the adjacent cell and continued, "Believe me! Having a personal toilet here is a privilege. You have earned it my friend, earned it by being a bigger nutcase than the lowly thieves and conmen in the general prison ward."

It was a relief for Pranav that one of the other troublemakers, this youth's father was not present. A fast track court was proceeding with the trial of the father and son duo. Pranav had heard the guards call out their names, Mrinal and Kunal. Since the day the father and son duo arrived in the jail, Pranav felt sandwiched in his cell, the father's cell on his right and the son's cell to the left. All prison cells in the High Security Ward - B had a metal door, uni-directionally facing a black stone wall. Everyday these men had long conversations with each other without seeing each other's faces.

While other general ward prisoners could cook, weave, make shoes, weave carpets and engage in carpentry, thus earn some money, this ward consisted of prisoners who were psychologically unstable and convicted for gruesome crimes and were therefore not allowed to stay outside their cells for more than an hour every evening. They were not allowed to work and earn money inside the prison as well. Kunal and Mrinal belonged to this category.

Pranav got no response from his neighbour. The only sound was that of the prison guard's portable radio from the other end of the corridor. After a while there was the creaking sound of metal doors opening. Some prison guards were heard speaking and then the guards opened the cell to the right of Pranav's cell.

"They just dragged your father into his prison cell and dropped him like a sack of rice," Pranav whispered to his neighbour.

"Father! Where were you? I was so worried for you in here."

When Mrinal replied, he sounded exhausted. *"Haraam ke Pille!* These bastards vented their frustration on me. The bloody new jail superintendent and his team."

"What the hell happened, father?"

From the father's cell, all they could hear was a loud sigh at first. And then he spoke, dragging the words. "I've had rashes on both my legs for the past few days so Girdhari, the guard outside our wing, escorted me to the chief medical officer's room. I was standing in the queue like the other patients waiting for my chance to meet the doctor. The door to the next room was wide open. Inside, there were discarded old wheelchairs, broken furniture, medical equipment and stretchers. There was a window in this room which overlooked the corridor outside."

His son Kunal was curious, "What did you see there?"

"On the other side of that window I saw the queue of people waiting for Mulakat. Poor miserable people!" said the father.

"What happened?" Kunal was excited.

His father now spoke in a hushed tone, "There was this woman in the queue. Clad in a dark red blouse and sari with floral patterns. She was very well endowed to say the least. The dark red of her blouse triggered me like a raging bull."

"Papa! Control yourself!"

"I miss those days! The Rainbow girls. You won't believe this but even your mother and I would get fidgety every now and then, years after she hit menopause. After they put me here, I am frustrated," added Mrinal.

Pranav who could overhear the conversation between father and son was surprised at the level of vulgarity. Stranded between the cells of these two maniacs, he felt sick. Meanwhile the father and son were giggling hysterically in their respective cells.

"So, I got triggered by her shiny red blouse. I pushed the guard who was holding my hand and he fell over a flower pot. I latched the door of the room behind me. Then from between the iron bars of the window, I tried to grab her red blouse. I got a grip on the sari and pulled it. The woman shrieked. The guards broke open the door and caught me," continued Mrinal.

"They must have given you a sound thrashing after that," Kunal said.

Mrinal sighed, "I was trampled under their boots, kicked like a football and assaulted like a punching bag. Yet, not for a moment did I regret what I had done. The look on that woman's face during the ordeal was priceless."

Pranav was furious with his lunatic neighbours,

"Can the two of you just shut your filthy mouths for ten minutes?"

The bell at the other end of the corridor rang. Pranav knew that today was the prison inspection day of the DIG-Prisons. All the inmates of the Sarvanpur Central Jail knew what should be done when senior officers visited. They took off their footwear and placed them near the concrete partition concealing their filthy commode from the rest of the prison cell. Their prison caps came off their heads and were placed between their armpits. They clasped their hands behind them and their heads bowed in respect to the visiting dignitary. The DIG-Prisons Alpesh Singhal was visiting. The smell coming from the ward – a mixture of urine, old rags, sweat, and rotting vegetables disgusted Alpesh and he wrinkled his nose before masking his expression in front of the inmates. It was still better than the godforsaken stench in the general ward near the common toilet.

Behind Alpesh, jail superintendent Jaykumar trailed like a halo.

He looked at all the prisoners in their ritual poses. "Do not perform these weird feudal rituals in front of me. I am not a zamindar. Everyone stand straight." Alpesh commanded as he entered the ward. As he passed each cell, he made a comment that was inaudible to other inmates. In front of the father's cell he said, "You are one lucky son of a bitch. That woman assumed you to be some insane inmate, which is partially true. Hailing from a poor family she thought it was useless to press charges of molestation against you. So you have escaped that misery. However, I am not happy with the thrashing you received today. So take rest my friend, before Jaykumar and his men resume tomorrow."

"Do as you please."

"Arrogant dog!" Alpesh spat out the words.

Alpesh paused in front of Pranav's cell. "I was reading your files. You have spent the longest time here."

"Twenty-two years." Pranav looked up at Alpesh.

"Considering that a life sentence is 14 years, that is an incredible amount of jail time."

"Sir, I had accidentally murdered a Mangalorean fellow. They sent me here on life term. I was a few months away from release when the Mangalorean fellow's brother, a known gangster, was also convicted and sent to our jail. When the prison riots broke out in 2004, we had a face-off. He was after my life. In self-defence I beat him to death with an iron rod and my jail term was extended."

"I am aware of the details of your case. What is strange is that in all these years you have not sent any postal mail to anyone. Also you have refused to meet anyone who tried to meet you."

"Sir, I am fine here and don't feel like meeting anyone."

"The records say that at the Government Shelter... Alpesh was not able to complete the sentence because Pranav interrupted.

"Sir! I have no one. I prefer to be left alone."

"Alright, Pranav! Let me know if you need to talk to a psychiatrist to ease your mind. I can arrange for the sessions even if it means a lot of approvals to be solicited from my side."

"Sir, I am at peace with myself."

The DIG-Prisons left after his inspection. Pranav tried to sleep but the voices coming from the adjoining cell disturbed him.

Kunal was whining, "Papa! These bed bugs and body lice are draining the blood out of me."

"Shut up and go to sleep, you wretched bastard," Mrinal yelled from his cell.

"Father! You have some hashish or ganja on you?"

"I wish it was home. I could have barged into your room and beaten you to pulp!"

Listening to the father and son chatter over trivial things, Pranav recollected his initial months in prison. Unlike the father and son, he had been silent and dazed at what had happened. He had been a normal young man – part-good, part-shrewd. This was before the people of law took control of his life.

*What wrong did I do to deserve this? Why me of all the people? Why is the world so unfair?*

The questions hounded him but he found no answers. Now after all these wasted years, he did not seek any answers.

# October: The Covert Group

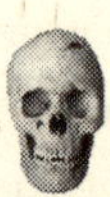

In a locked hostel room of Sarvanpur Engineering College, five friends, Ujjwal, Kaustubh, Sandesh, Kenny and Mandar were going through some design documents and models. The walls of the room were decorated with posters of Hollywood action films and scantily-clad models. The floor was a mess with scattered electronic parts, toothpaste, towels, chips packets, equipment and wires.

Ujjwal said, "Remove all the Chinese parts. It will fail us when we want it to work. Korean parts are better, or even local parts will do. That will be fine."

"It will be difficult to get those, you know how tough it was to get these," protested Kenny.

"I agree with Ujjwal! The Chinese parts have to be removed from this. We need to get more reach...." said Kaustubh.

"Reach is the key!" Ujjwal yelled.

Mandar, who had been silent until now, said, "I think there is scope for design modifications to achieve the required reach. I can work on that. We need to increase the capacity too."

"We need to test it and will have to go to some deserted place in the interiors between the hills of the Western Ghats to test both the carrier and the mix," said Kaustubh.

"I don't think this will work. Firstly, the carrier has a margin of error and limited reach. Secondly, the mix is still to be tested. Let's abandon this plan. We have no Shaman to guide us and we are making mistakes," said Kenny.

Ujjwal opened the drawer and took out the red envelope and letter, thrusting it at Kenny's face.

"Read this, asshole! Who sent this? They all thought that she was dead and destroyed. They were so wrong, but I knew it all along." Ujjwal laughed emphatically. Kenny looked at the words on the paper.

> Dear Team,
>
> Follow MY path and You will become like Me. An aberration of NATURE which gets carried forward
>
> \- MEHEK

The others who had already read the letter smiled at one another. "Like the religious heads of some ancient religions who are re-born time and time again at different places. Risen again and resurrected. Like a true messiah. Our Lady of Darkness!" Ujjwal proclaimed.

"Bullshit Dopehead! Someone is playing games with you all. I think someone within our group. You guys are such morons." He laughed self-deprecatingly.

Ujjwal took out his country made revolver fashioned like a *Beretta* and pointed it at Kenny.

"*Haramzaade!* Don't test my patience. Don't show me your fucking attitude. Shaman is not gone and she is there guiding and supporting us."

"Don't point the gun to my head, Ujjwal!" Kenny was petrified.

"Speak up bastard! Are you going to become a martyr of your belief?"

"Yes, Ujjwal!" Kenny trembled as he looked at the gun pointing towards him. He looked away, fear gnawing at his mind. Everyone else in the room sat motionless, they knew it would be counter-productive to pacify Ujjwal in this state.

"No. Say it!"

"I will become a martyr of my belief." Ujjwal tore down the buttons of Kenny's t-shirt, exposing his bare chest. On it there was a tattoo which everyone in the group had. The tattoo read 'I am a soldier of a bright future. I will kill and die for my belief like a soldier.'

"*Saala kamina*. Now keep your hands on your chest and say it!" Ujjwal was almost yelling.

"I will become a martyr of my belief," said Kenny, gulping his fear, petrified at having to stare up the dark muzzle of a gun.

Ujjwal was still in a rage. "Will you waste your life doing useless desk jobs to make some multinational company rich or will you be the pioneer who came ahead of his time and sacrificed his life to show others the right direction?"

Kenny shivered as he spoke, "I will make a difference with my life."

Ujjwal looked him in the eye. "Is this world a worthy place to live?"

"No. This world is a place full of shit and I want to bring it down."

This time Kenny spoke with genuine conviction.

Now Ujjwal started laughing hysterically. The others in the room were puzzled and looked at one another. They giggled along with him, more out of fear of his unpredictability than at Kenny.

"Look at this *Behen-Da-Taka!*" Ujjwal continued laughing, "I think his pants are wet. *Saala Haraamkhor!* Why do you try to act smart when you don't have the balls for confrontation?"

"Ujjwal, leave the poor boy. He is under stress nowadays. Not having much fun since Vijayanti Aunty has stopped being nice to us after Shaman left," Mandar tried to lighten the mood while trying not to enrage Ujjwal.

"The rainbow is not as colourful as it used to be," Kaustubh added with a smile. Meanwhile, Sandesh got a call on his cell phone but disconnected it. Kaustubh asked whom it was from.

"My folks from Singapore. They must have reached home after their week-long trip to Thailand and must have realised that they have not called me for a week. Why do they fucking care? They can shoot themselves and fucking go to hell!"

After they completed their work the boys smoked marijuana and filled up their glasses of whisky. On a CD player attached to mini speakers they played death metal songs. While Ujjwal and Kenny enjoyed the music, the others simply feigned pleasure. They raised their glasses for a toast, "On the path to becoming invincible! Led by our Shaman! Family sucks. Friends are all we have. Cheers!"

They topped up the spirit and weed with a sniff of cocaine.

# October: Escape Plan

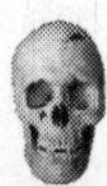

"One toothbrush and two soaps," said Pranav from across the solitary grilled window placed midway on the wall of the high security wing. This window faced a portion of the prison shop. The attendant of the shop placed the articles in front of Pranav. These articles belonged to brands from the outside world but were new to Pranav. Binaca and Ralak were now replaced by Pepsodent and Dettol. In less than a year he would be released from prison. He was petrified at the thought of facing the unknown outside.

Pranav tore a ten rupees coupon and a twenty rupees coupon and handed them across the window to the attendant of the prison store. The prisoners in the general ward got coupons of 650 rupees and above for their work which included carpentry, working in the jail kitchen, leather work, blacksmith's work and weaving. However, prisoners in the high security ward were not allowed to work and were given paltry coupons of 300 rupees at the end of the month. Nobody protested since most inmates of this ward were weirdos enough not to comprehend the injustice that was being done to them.

It was four thirty in the evening. For one hour every evening the inmates of the high security ward were let out for an evening walk. The only condition was that they had to be within the boundary wall of the wing at all times.

As he walked back to the stretch where the other prisoners were walking, Pranav saw a group of cleaners – prisoners from the general ward – behind the guards' toilet. They had caught a bandicoot while cleaning the sewers and were roasting it over a makeshift fireplace make of bricks and dry twigs. Prisoners in this prison made the most of whatever resources were available to them. During winters, Pranav had himself heated cold chapattis on old rubber footwear set on fire, but he would never eat a rat.

A slight movement behind the cleaners caught Pranav's eyes. Mrinal and his son Kunal were opening the lid of a sewage manhole behind this toilet. Stealthily they looked around to ensure that nobody had spotted them. They were trying to escape through the sewage line.

After they had jumped into the manhole some prison guards rushed to the spot. Laughing, they put the lid over the manhole. In his 23-year long prison tenure Pranav had not seen a more foolish escape plan than this one. It was so obvious an escape route that when the prison was first commissioned in 1968, they had put grills in the outer end of each sewage outlet line. Now the prison guards were having fun at the expense of these two wannabe fugitives. When they resurface from one of the sewage manholes on the side which was the general ward, the father and son would be received by the guards and beaten to pulp.

That night, as expected, Mrinal and Kunal did not return to their cell. Pranav heard the guards at the corridor chuckle while mentioning the kind of thrashing the pair was receiving.

"*Saala!*" One of them chuckled. "Both of them have proved themselves to be such *ghadyas* by trying to execute a plan like this."

"Girish, I am very scared of that *yeda* doctor."

The other guard said, "You know Bhaskar, one day I went to have a look at his cell. *Yeda* told me that I looked ill and asked me to open my mouth so that he could see my tongue. *Meri toh phat gayi.*"

The guard said he had refused the offer.

"*Bhau*, what was the harm in showing him? I agree he was running a kidney racket, but he would not have put his hand down your throat and pulled out your kidneys," the first guard replied in a bantering tone.

"*Ai shapat!* I will never allow that *panauti* to touch me. *Khali-peeli marwane ka nai.*"

Next day in the morning the guards dumped Mrinal and Kunal in their respective cells. The next few hours were filled with groans radiating from either side of Pranav's cell.

Finally, around afternoon, Mrinal called out from his cell, "Kunal! Are you alright?"

"I am in a lot of pain, father!"

"When we got out of the manhole on the other side in the general ward, guess whom I saw among the crowd of convicts?" Mrinal asked.

"Any ex-politician?"

"No, you idiot. I saw Doctor Carlton."

Kunal was inquisitive, "The bastard from Rachel's Maternity Home? Are you sure?"

"I saw that face so many times in the newspaper that I cannot be wrong. That son-of-a-whore ruined everything."

"Papa! We should destroy that asshole."

"It looks like yesterday that the beautiful girl came to our home along with your sisters from college," Mrinal was abruptly sounding nostalgic. In his cell, Pranav shook his head at the conversation.

"Nutcases."

"Our lives changed after that," added Kunal.

"You know what, Kunal, I had never had so much fun before or after that phase of our lives. I enjoyed all the pleasures that had evaded me for long. And I made you people join the party as well."

"All that changed because of that doctor. Papa, do something."

"Now we are in this dark prison cell looking forward to a dismal future. That bastard, he will pay the price for it," said Mrinal.

To distract himself from the chatter, Pranav sat on his mat and took out three books from a small wooden shelf in the corner of the room. The *Bible*, a book on Buddhism, and a self-help book by Deepak Chopra. These were gifted to him on his birthdays every year by the previous Jail Superintendent who was a cheerful old man hailing from Uttaranchal. He used to say, "Read these and they will help you clear your mind."

Once again, in the light of the flickering old bulb of his prison cell, Pranav opened the books, flipping the pages to the passages that held a special appeal for him.

# October: Curfew

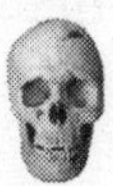

She had had the same kind of feeling when she visited Vaishno Devi temple in Jammu, the Lotus temple in Delhi, the Golden Temple in Amritsar, the Ajmer-e-Sharif in Rajasthan... as if the turbulent waves of the sea inside her had momentarily transformed into a placid lake and all her problems had come to a standstill, leaving behind only peace of mind and body. Today Jesus Christ was in front of her; nine feet tall, on a cross which had I.N.R.I inscribed on top. To his left side was a statue of Joseph holding the infant Christ and to his right, Mother Mary. Kneeling before him, Devika prayed for her father. At this juncture of her life, she required all her inner strength to help her sail through each day. The only sound in this place was of the old fans fixed to the walls of the church with its high ceiling and old rafters. She liked this place; she wanted to return soon.

She stepped out of the Holy Cross Church located at the centre of a large area owned by the Holy Cross Foundation. Towards the left of the church stood the Holy Cross School; towards the right was the orphanage and office of the foundation. Behind the church, beyond a hillock full of trees, was the cemetery. The hospital run by the foundation was two kilometres ahead on Annie Besant Road. Devika headed for the school, one of the oldest in Sarvanpur. The building was painted white but was now a shade of dull yellow and required maintenance. She went up the stairs, past the library, to the staff room. She had an appointment with Geeta Sakseria, one of the school's oldest teachers.

Geeta Sakseria was in her fifties. She had small sharp eyes, greying hair and a smile that immediately made Devika feel at ease, as though she had known her for years. "Come Devika! Let's sit in the canteen." She extended a hand to Devika, drawing her into her circle of trust and friendship.

Lunch time was two hours away and the school canteen was vacant at this time.

"I've had a persistent cold for the past three to four days. I was not planning to come today and then I remembered that I had asked you to come; I'll take an off tomorrow instead," said the teacher as they sat down.

"Ma'am, thank you for being so accommodating."

"To tell you the truth, I am also equally excited about this. In our profession we rarely get interviewed. So this will be a new experience." She smiled.

"Ma'am, you have served in this school for 25 years. There is not a single student who has passed out of this institution whom you have not taught or influenced."

"That's what we teachers should do. Influence the little ones so that they become responsible and capable grownups. That is our duty."

"Ma'am, I am here to research for my upcoming book about one student in particular."

"You mentioned that on the phone. Little Mahi or Mehek – the talk of the town. Well, she was one of the girls who used to come from the Government Shelter for Girls. They could not afford education for all the girls with their measly budgets. Our institution had offered to help since in the '90s we did not have too many children in the orphanage run by the church's foundation."

"How was she as a student?" asked Devika.

"Bright! She would rank among the top ten every year in her class. She was very pretty but very much an introvert. You know the problem with her hands, right?"

"She got a plastic surgeon to fix that later on."

"I think she had a massive inferiority complex; always lost in her own world. One aspect I particularly remember; she used to get hurt every now and then in the playground and would frequently be found in the school's medical room."

"Uh-huh! From what I know about her, she was eccentric and used to do that to get attention," commented Devika.

The teacher continued, "As she grew into a teenager, she gained in confidence and loved the attention from the boys. Her studies suffered during that phase. Yes, she was a bit eccentric, she was." The teacher seemed lost in her own thoughts.

Devika waited a while before asking, "Ma'am, any instance you particularly remember?"

The teacher thought for a moment and said. "Every year the public library of Sarvanpur dumped some old books in our school. We allowed the students to pick one or two books from the pile depending on their area of interest. I remember Mehek picking up a book on hypnotism and one written by a lady who was a pioneer in the field of Theosophy. She was 12 years old and I asked her why she had picked those books."

"What did she say?"

"That the unknown interested her. She wanted to venture into territory not explored by normal people."

Devika asked, "Anything else that you remember?"

"The children from the shelter used to make fun of Mehek's habit of getting up in the middle of the night and standing near the foot of her bed while having conversations with dark emptiness. I assumed back then that Mehek probably had a sleepwalking disorder. I am getting old, as of now I don't remember much more than this."

"Why did she choose the nursing profession in the later years?"

"Devika, students in our school are orphans or come from poor homes. They all come with dreams of becoming doctors or engineers; later, these dreams are crushed by reality so they opt for more practical career choices eventually."

Devika took out a piece of paper from her handbag and handed it to madam Geeta Sakseria. "This has the name of the school bus driver and his helper who were working here from inception of the school. Could I have their addresses, please, Ma'am?"

"You may need to go to the admin section. Loretta is in charge of the records. I will call her and inform her about your request. Any issues?"

"These two people are missing for more than a year now." "I am aware of that, Devika."

"Ma'am, the driver and the cleaner disappeared within two weeks of each other."

The teacher looked on more attentively as Devika continued, "Mehek had told her husband that she was sexually abused as a student. If there is any truth to that story and if these men were responsible, then in all probability they both are among the many dead bodies found in the cult's grave yard."

"You mean they were abducted and killed by her people?"

Devika nodded.

She was sure Mehek had used the cult's resources for personal vendetta as well. The meeting went on for another 15 minutes, after which she bid adieu to the teacher and went to the admin section to meet Loretta for the addresses.

When the lunch bell rang, children came out of the classroom like flood water breaching the banks. Standing among the children in uniform running helter-skelter, Devika remembered her childhood.

She touched her baby bump. *One day her child would be like them,* Devika thought and smiled.

At home she had a hearty lunch of *kulcha* and gram curry with her father, and then took an unusually long afternoon nap.

In the evening, Shravan returned from work grumbling about the unusually long day he would have the next day.

"Shravan, tomorrow is Gandhi Jayanti, it is a public holiday, so take the day off!"

"Independence Day, Republic Day and all other holidays are for the general public. Not for the police. You are reacting as if this is the first time."

"Why doesn't the department allow you any rest?"

"There is a prayer meet tomorrow at K. Jadhav Stadium to be attended by a consortium of religious leaders and intellectual groups operating around the state."

"Like?"

"Like Sanatan Dharma Parishad, Islam for Harmony, bishops and representatives of Churches around Sarvanpur."

Devika was curious. "That would be a peace meeting then why do the police need to be there?"

"Mathrubhumi Morcha!"

"Oh those right wing fascist bullies!"

"Devika, this time also they have issued a warning to all participating groups against being part of such an event. There was an article in a local newspaper yesterday where the Islamic Liberals Party also urged the people not to participate."

Devika understood the gravity of the situation. When the inaugural prayer meet had been conducted at K. Jadhav Stadium the previous year, Mathrubhumi Morcha, a right-wing political outfit which until then was famous for blackening the faces of couples in public parks and vandalising shopping malls on Valentines' Day, had issued a warning against the event. Their goons had gone on to physically assault members of the Sanatan Dharma Parishad on their way out of the venue. The Police Commissioner had promised extra security for the event for the coming year. This year with the municipal elections round the corner, the situation was more volatile. Even the Islamic Liberals Party had got involved to make a statement.

"Duty is duty," Shravan said as he took off his cap and placed it on Devika's head.

"You do what you want to, ACP."

Devika, Rameshwar and Shravan had a hearty dinner together. Rameshwar's appetite had improved and he had started putting on weight. After dinner, they sat together to watch the classic Hindi thriller, *Jewel Thief*. After the movie when Devika was going to lock the main door, she saw something in the lawn in front of her house. In the dark moonlit night the neighbourhood cat Zeenu was running all around Radhemohan's daughter Laali as she was sitting, murmuring something and looking at the moon. *I thought the cat was rabid and the girl was rather unlikeable. It is strange how this is working out!* Devika thought.

The next afternoon Devika started her online research on the activity of Devil worshipers in the country and was surprised to stumble upon an article on an international website.

## Satan Worshippers attack Churches in Mizoram

May 11, 2012 - Satan worship is rising as a disturbing trend in the Christian dominated state of Mizoram in India, its rising popularity is a cause for concern among parents, church leaders and followers. In three separate incidents in the last 10 days, vandals drew a pentagram on the altar of the church and burned papers and books inside the church. Yesterday, a similar attack took place in a Presbyterian church in Kolasib in Northern Mizoram.

It was a revelation for Devika that such attacks were taking place in the country. A related article on the same website described an attack on a renowned anti-superstition activist who was pushing for laws against black magic, witchcraft and superstition. A Hindi teacher by profession, the activist was shot and critically wounded by unidentified gunmen on a motorcycle. For years, this senior rationalist had campaigned against black magic and was pushing for an anti-superstition bill in the Goa state assembly. The bill was eventually passed as an ordinance three weeks later.

These may not be standalone incidents, she thought. Just out of curiosity Devika searched the Net for similar attacks around the country. When the search results appeared on screen Devika froze in her chair. It was unbelievable.

She took out the red envelope from her cupboard, the last letter she had received.

> Dear DeViKa,
>
> How is LIFE?
> Sharing my Happiness. 102 will make INDIA and its people
> Stand up and TAKE notice unlike 815 and 825
>
> – MEHEK

Devika now looked at the numbers again 815, 15th August. The link on the laptop screen read.

> Website – www.asianews.it
>
> August 15, 2011 - When the whole nation was celebrating Independence Day on 15th August, some miscreants suspected to be devil worshipers broke into Malankara Catholic Church at Warje Malwadi, Pune and desecrated the holy Church and defaced the premises, causing large scale damage to...

She looked at the other number in the letter 825, 25th August. Another link on the laptop screen read

> Website – news.catholicate.net
>
> August 25, 2011 – St Mary's Catholic Church, Secundrabad, Hyderabad, was attacked by some unidentified people believed to be devil worshippers. The head of the church, the bishops of other churches and the Archbishop of Hyderabad are constantly in communication with the parishioners and have asked them to remain peaceful in prayers...

Devika was now certain that the numbers indeed represented dates. All the pieces of the puzzle were falling into place. If that was the case then next attack would happen on 102, that is 2nd January or 2nd October, which was... Today! Devika rushed to the phone and without any further hesitation she rang up first Shravan, and later, Inspector Anshuman.

"An attack will happen today. You need to provide police protection to all the churches in and around town!"

From the adjacent room, Rameshwar heard Devika yelling on the phone.

Within the hour all churches in and around Sarvanpur had a posse of police constables deployed in their premises.

Devika felt an abnormal amount of anxiety. The panic had a valid reason but she had to stay calm. She took the transparent yellow primrose oil tablet which was a natural remedy for mood swings.

*Where would the attack take place?*

Devika frantically turned the pages of the photocopy of Mehek's diary for clues. After a round of glancing around the sheets she gave up. *Damn! Nothing here!* She paced around the room restlessly before returning to Mehek's diary.

> Before the end of this year, we will show you a small demonstration of the infinite possibilities which are implementable if we use our mind. Infinite possibilities if we work together and channelise our resources. Religions of the world will automatically help us get to our objective.

If indeed the 'sleeper cell' of the cult was targeting a religious place, what was the significance of doing that today? It was not even a Sunday, so there would be very few people in most of the churches. So a church being the target of attack was ruled out. The last sentence of the paragraph was clearly indicating something pertaining to religions. Religions and not religion. K. Jadhav stadium! That was it! The attack would take place there.

Sarvanpur's only stadium, the K. Jadhav Stadium, was fairly big one, with stands on three sides and a tall wall along the fourth side. There were two towers with low intensity floodlights illuminating the venue. The stadium was packed with eight thousand people representing various faiths. Three women constables frisked Devika thoroughly at the entrance – a complete security check with a metal detector scan and sniffer dogs. Inside the venue, there was a group of musicians on a small stage who had just finished singing 'Vasihnav Janato'. Religious leaders of various groups were seated on the main podium. The speaker from Arya Samaj was currently on stage sharing their views on the current state of the nation and what they could foresee for the near future. After the speech the musicians started to sing 'Allah Tero Naam, Ishwar Tero Naam'.

Devika walked up to Shravan and Anshuman. "I was reading Mehek's diary, my feeling is that something will happen here, in this stadium, tonight."

"You must have seen the security arrangements when you entered this place. The stadium is a fortress," said Shravan confidently.

"What if they have already placed something here?"

"The sniffer dogs have been at work since morning. The place is clean," said Anshuman.

"What if they barge into the complex with an explosive laden van or something?"

"Devika Ji, the entrance of the complex is too small to drive something into the premises. Also, we have fully armoured *rakshak* vehicles outside." Anshuman said.

"The metal detectors and sniffer dogs will catch any suicide bomber in a second," added Shravan.

"I don't have any concrete proof but I am sure we are standing at the epicentre of trouble. What if they have implanted something inside their body?"

"Devika Ji, this is not Afghanistan or Iraq. Such things don't happen here, as per our knowledge," said Anshuman.

Shravan took Devika along with him, "Devika, please don't strain yourself. I think you are taking way too much of stress. It's not good for the baby. You should stay out of here." He led her to the armed police van outside the stadium.

Devika sat in the van and looked her watch. Six pm. The prayer meet was expected to conclude at 6.30 pm.

Devika started praying.

Time appeared to be moving slower than usual.

Fifteen minutes. Maybe it was just a silly hoax. Devika wondered if she had taken the letters too seriously and ended up making a fool out of herself in front of her husband and his colleagues..

Out of the blue, the crowd at the stadium heard a strange sound as though a swarm of bees was hovering above them. They looked around but could not spot anything. It was getting dark. Even the speaker on the podium paused to look around for the cause of the disturbance.

An object seemed to be moving into the stadium from across the high wall, from the direction of the mangroves beyond the wall. As the buzzing intensified, people began to panic.

An object crashed into the stadium and exploded on the ground.

What followed was pandemonium.

People ran in terror. Smoke filled the arena as a second object came crashing from the sky and exploded inside the stadium.

From a section near the entrance, Devika watched aghast as people tried to shove past one another, terrified, eager to be as far away from the stadium as quickly as possible. Devika's heart started to beat fast, started to sweat profusely as she turned her eyes away from the chaotic sight. It was too much for her to handle in the state of pregnancy.

A third object fell from the sky and exploded among the crowd, followed by two more explosions at opposite ends of the stadium. A cloud of smoke and dust engulfed everything. All around the stadium, pamphlets, flags, foot-wear and blood stained clothes littered the ground along with badly mangled bodies and spilled blood. Shrapnel from the explosion caught unsuspecting victims.

The injured were carried to Sushrut and Holy Cross hospitals.

As more and more TV channels rushed to the spot, live coverage from ground zero continued till the wee hours of the morning as the town woke up to the horror of what had happened.

The next day the national newspapers carried headlines about the terror attack in a stadium at Sarvanpur where a religious prayer meet had been organised. The casualties included seven dead, 36 injured, and 12 seriously injured. The attackers used Chinese made miniature radio planes which have been banned in India since 2009. Back then, after denying NOCs to several consignments at the Mumbai Port Trust, the customs had destroyed around 3,000 RC planes. Now they had to be smuggled into the country. The miniature plane could be flown from the palm of one's hands.

These radio controlled devices operated at frequencies of 400-500 MHz which interfered with the communication devices used by the Indian security agencies. These planes worked on FM and not AM as directed by the government. The battery strength had been substantially enhanced to increase their range and could deliver a payload of anywhere between10 and 20 kilos. The explosives mounted on these planes were a mixture of the usual ammonium nitrate, sulphur, potassium and fuel oil. A lot of research on the internet and multiple rounds of test runs were the key to getting the proportion right. The explosive mixture was detonated by integrated circuits and a timer. The shrapnel used were metallic rivets, bolts and pieces of metal. Once the explosion took place, these shrapnel flew off like a hundred bullets in all directions.

The forensics team was unable to gather any significant fingerprints or evidence from the crime scene. There was no warning issued by the IB (Intelligence Bureau), and in all probability, the terror attack was not the work of known terrorist networks.

The next morning some miscreants threw a petrol bomb at the Mathrubhumi Morcha office in Jaynagar in what looked like an act of retaliation. Some of the Mathrubhumi party members ransacked the Islamic Liberals Party office at Baba Amte Road.

Two weeks later, 16 young men were arrested from the slums around Baba Amte Road and Sarvanpur Railway Station in connection with the terror attack, only to be released on grounds of insufficient evidence.

The town continued to be tense and under curfew.

# November: Diwali Bash

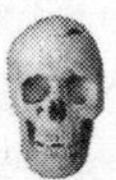

"We will be providing better food to our inmates in the coming year. For a start, there will be a paneer dish and jeera rice special dinner every week starting tonight," Alpesh announced on the microphone to all the assembled inmates of the jail.

As usual, he was the chief guest of the Diwali celebration conducted every year in the prison courtyard.

Pranav listened to him from behind a circle of policemen who separated the prisoners of the general ward from the prisoners of the high security ward.

"Also, from next month, we will have yoga and meditation classes twice every week," Alpesh announced.

The speech was to be followed by a play enacted by some inmates where they would depict an episode from the Ramayana, a one act play that would start with Lord Rama's killing of Ravana and his return to Ayodhya where his brother Bharat would receive him. It would end with Rama and Sita's coronation.

The police constables in the circle in front of them were slightly relaxed because all the inmates of the high security ward were in handcuffs. The more violent ones like Mrinal and Kunal had loose padlocks as well. These allowed only limited mobility. Pranav could see both father and son engaged in a lengthy conversation. When the play started and everyone started clapping and whistling, Mrinal and Kunal sneaked out from the assembled crowd.

*Yet another escape plan*, thought Pranav. He saw them going up the stairs to the gallery around the courtyard where a police constable stopped them. Mrinal said something to the constable and he allowed them to go the washroom at the other end of the gallery. It was a dead end with a flight of stairs coming down to the other side of the courtyard. Pranav wondered if they were really going to take a leak. The two walked towards the washroom but instead of going in they took the stairs down the other side after which they disappeared.

Pranav watched the play being performed with a rare smile illuminating his rugged face. The same cast, same play, same settings and same costume every year. The inmate playing Vibhishan's role had been released on parole so his role was taken up by a Sikh inmate who hailed from Ambala. The crown on his head had moved sideways, revealing his turban. He also had a thick Punjabi accent which made him a misfit among the performers but the audience was amused with this Sardarji from the Ramayana era. Some in the audience whistled while others made catcalls. A different atmosphere than the one some years back.

Pranav clearly remembered the eight-year-old episode. It was the day after the Diwali celebration. His release was due in three months. The Maharashtra Police nabbed an absconding gangster who had evaded the police for 15 years and put him in Sarvanpur Jail. Unfortunately, he turned out to be the elder brother of the person whom Pranav was accused of murdering. Prison riots between rival gangs erupted on Diwali day. Burning with vengeance, the gangster chased Pranav, who was then in the general ward, with an iron rod. That day for the first time Pranav killed someone in his full consciousness with the same iron rod that he was carrying. The only reason he evaded death sentence was because it was proven with reasonable doubt in court that it was in self defence.

A sharp cry of agony broke into Pranav's thoughts. He looked over a policeman's shoulder. There was mayhem among the inmates on the other side. Doctor Carlton, an inmate of the general ward, was screaming in agony, his neck bleeding; Mrinal was trying to strangle him even as his son punched Carlton repeatedly in the stomach. The father and son's handcuffs and padlocks had done nothing to tame them.

"You killed her. Why? Why?" Mrinal yelled repeatedly. "You bastard! This is from Mehek for you."

Furious, the two of them would not let go of their victim. The prison guards rushed to the spot and attacked the assaulters ruthlessly with their sticks, but it took their combined effort to finally free Doctor Carlton from their clutches.

The play had to be stopped abruptly and all the convicts were asked to go back to their respective cells. For Pranav, Mehek's name triggered old memories and made him sleepless through the night.

The cold walls which had initially been his enemies, had soon metamorphosed into inseparable companions for Pranav. He had assumed that his long period of imprisonment would slowly but steadily remove him from his previous life. Just when he had started believing that he was a liberated man, his illusion was shattered.

The unpleasant past again knocked on his door two days later when the assistant of the prison superintendent Jaykumar personally handed Pranav a letter in his prison cell.

"Sir, where is this from?"

"This is from someone important. I hope you give it a good thought before deciding," said Jaykumar's assistant as he left in a hurry.

Dear Mr Pranav,

My name is Devika Soni. I am a columnist with the *Konkan Times*. I am also a writer. Though my first book met with only limited success, I am very enthusiastic about the second one and need your help for the same.

My next book is about Mehek and the cult which had spread its tentacles around our small town. My journey in pursuing Mehek's story and my background research has led me to you. Your story is the crucial juncture, the point from where the chain of events brings us to the chaotic present. I would like to meet you just once so that I can have answers to the questions that have been baffling me for a while. I know you have never done this but I believe that my portrayal of Mehek will be incomplete without your story.

Thanks and Regards,

Devika Soni

After re-reading the letter, he stared for some time at the wall in front of him, lost in thought. Finally, he kept the letter aside.

*Your story is at the crucial juncture...my foot!* He grunted in disgust.

# November: The Illusion

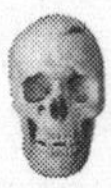

The walls of the living room were covered with the magician's photographs taken along with famous politicians, film and sports personalities. A tiger's head hung above the flat screen television. The room's decor was in grey.

Devika looked carefully at the tea table in front of her, the magazines below it, the wooden chairs and other furniture items next to it in the hall.

The magician finally entered the room followed by a bodyguard dressed in black. Six feet tall and clad in white kurta pyjama, the man wore a chain of rudraksh beads around his neck and loops of red sacred thread around his right forearm. He had long greying hair, a prominent moustache and a lush beard. He walked on crutches.

Devika tried to put together as much of the information as she had garnered about the man in front of her. Trilok Barua, born to an Assamese tea plantation trader and an accountant mother who was from Sarvanpur. The man himself had lived in Kolkata till his parents' divorce when his mother brought him along to Sarvanpur. The young fatherless boy dropped out of school where he fared poorly in studies and left home to look for a job in Mumbai. Young Trilok worked as junior artist in Hindi films at the Filmistan, Natraj and Chandivali studios. His life took a turn for the good when he was hired as a helper for a magic show troupe belonging to a famous magician and illusionist named Indrajit.

While working under Indrajit, young Trilok learned a lot of tricks. He also read books on magic performances and staged illusions which further improved his knowledge in this domain. The troupe performed all around India. Trilok even got a chance to meet some of the more famous contemporaries of his master.

One such chance encounter was with the legendary P.C. Sorcar, Junior. Trilok was amazed to hear that this man had made the Taj Mahal, Victoria Memorial and Indore-Amritsar express disappear in front of unsuspecting audiences. Equally surprising to him was the humility and down-to-earth nature of the man who'd performed such glorious feats.

Trilok aspired to be in the big league of illusionists and escape-artists. After working for five years with the troupe and honing his skills as an illusionist, Trilok decided to break free from his master. He started his own troupe and named himself Timur. After a humble start with small shows, his group and skills both gained momentum. He made famous landmarks disappear, floated in air, caught a fired bullet with his teeth, locked himself in an iron chest placed on a rail track in the path of an incoming train and locked himself in chains-n-padlocks inside a kerosene soaked wooden shed which was set on fire. The audience would be in a state of frenzy when he emerged out of these death traps, unscathed.

For the next 21 years he performed in India, UK, Thailand, Singapore and the Gulf countries. Along the way, he began to mint money by smuggling cocaine along with his paraphernalia of items used during the stage performances. More than two decades later, there was a freak accident during an escape stunt. Hanging upside down on a crane 30 feet above the ground, his hands slipped and he had a free fall before his staff could properly place the safety nets. True to the name he had borrowed, Timur became lame.

Timur was amused that this reporter who had come for an interview was wearing dark shades. When he asked her about it she attributed it to an eye infection. She pulled down the shades to the tip of her nose to reveal the reddening left eye. "I am surprised that the *Konkan Times* has suddenly got interested in my life. I have been out of the media light for close to eight years," he remarked as he playfully looked at the obviously pregnant reporter.

"We are doing a series of interviews on musicians, cartoonists, singers, writers and other famous personalities from this region who have had a significant impact in the national and international arena." Devika paused to have a sip from the glass of water placed in front of her and continued, "Your interview will be the first in the series."

"That's an honour, I must admit," said the magician.

Devika wondered whether it was a genuine remark or sarcastic. His narrowing eyes and sly smile always confused people talking to him.

"Mr Timur, if I may call you that, tell us about your childhood and youth."

As Timur narrated real and imaginary tales from his life, speaking as if at his own pre-funeral memorial service, Devika kept her eyes averted, choosing to stare at the tea table between them or at the sofa edges rather than at him.

"Mr Timur, what is the secret behind all the mind boggling tricks you have performed?"

Though he was slightly flattered Timur concealed it well. It was a long time since he had heard praise for his unique abilities.

"The core principle is the same. Make-believe. Influence your audience in such a way that they are open to take the ride with you. Once they suspend their inhibitions, you can play with their senses and manipulate them."

"You make it sound very simple but the answer still does not satisfy my curiosity, Mr Timur."

"It's simple. It starts with figuring out a trick where you are able to bend someone's perception of reality. Then you add layers and layers of complications to make it appear really big. Then practice it so many times and so well that it becomes natural. Actually, by today's standards, what we used to do in our times was no big deal," said the magician. As he spoke, he would occasionally scratch his beard with his little fingers.

"I think you were, and are, a legend!" said Devika.

"Not exactly true today! Do you watch cable TV? Those young chaps... Criss Angel, David Blaine and our own Ugesh Sarkar. They pick up random people on the street and perform unbelievable tricks. That's the level to which practice takes you."

"Do you have any students?"

"No! I concentrate fully on my business of antiques, coffee shops and shacks nowadays."

Time to switch gears. "Something about your business. What do you have to say about the police raid on one of your warehouses two years back when they recovered 900 grams of heroin there?"

Taken aback by the question, Timur tried to conceal his bewildered expression and replied,

"It was proven in court that the warehouse incharge was involved in the drug business. The court had clearly stated that there was no evidence of my involvement in those transactions and I was acquitted."

"We are told that there is a threat to your life at all times, Mr Timur." Devika looked at the bodyguard.

"Yes, I have enemies. It's like that in my business. Our region is a treasure chest of opportunity for businessmen with foreigners coming in from all around the world in such large numbers. I have a lot of rivals who want to gain a firm footing in my business domain. They get angry when I don't allow them to."

"What's that hanging on the wall?" Devika asked.

Timur asked his bodyguard to get that object, and while the two were momentarily distracted, Devika picked up a small black box from her file and stuck it under the tea table, concealing it in the design.

The bodyguard came back with the framed certificate which Timur proudly showed to Devika. A certificate of appreciation from the Ministry of Culture, Thailand.

"So Mr Timur, why is it necessary for illusionists and escape artists to undertake the risks they undertake? What is the primary reason for performances going wrong?"

"In our profession we have to constantly explore new boundaries, or else we will become redundant and boring. That's what takes us on the path of newer and greater risks. Three things can kill you. First, being unprepared like the great Harry Houdini, who was punched to his death when he was not ready. Second, being over-confident like me when I was doing the crane stunt. Third, being even slightly jittery like the base jumper who tried to fly over a bridge in Colorado."

"So even though you taught her a lot of your skills, Mehek could not save herself when she was under duress. To which category would she belong?"

Timur's expression changed visibly, "Who is Mehek?"

Devika smiled, "The whole town has been discussing her for the past six months. The same Mehek, Mr Timur. You've not been reading the newspaper, Sir. In her diary she had written that she was having an affair with you ever since her Sharada Nursing College days."

Devika was bluffing as there was no such entry in Mehek's diary, just indirect references to Timur and his residence at many places. However, his anxiety made it clear to her that she was on the right track.

"No, it is not true. If that was true then the cops would have grilled me by now. I don't know any Mehek. Also, I did not teach anything to any Mehek and I have never had an affair with anybody called Mehek." Timur was furious. "I think this interview is going nowhere."

"I am sorry, Mr Timur, if I have offended you. I only mentioned rumours floating around town. Nonetheless, let's leave that aside. Tell me about your experience of performing in front of audiences outside the country."

"Well, it was good. There is a difference between audiences in India and outside India. That is... actually... Ma'am, I am not in the mood today for this. I would appreciate if we can continue with this interview some other day."

"Aren't you well, Mr Timur?"

"Nothing much. Some other time, please."

"Alright, as you wish. It is important for the interviewee to be in a relaxed state. I am sorry if I upset you in any way."

"My bodyguard will escort you to the front gate. I will let you know when we can meet again."

Devika smiled, got up and left along with the bodyguard.

The bodyguard asked the guard at the gates to open the massive gate. Devika walked along the pavement towards the left, then she took the lane going right, to the Indian Ocean apartments behind Timur's house with a common wall between the two blocks. On the third floor of this building, the police department had occupied an apartment. Devika rang the bell of this apartment.

Anshuman opened the door, "I don't think it was worth going there."

"You people had no better ideas. If you had sent a lady police constable acting as a press reporter, Timur would have spotted the fake reporter in five minutes. I wanted answers to some questions face to face with him before you arrest him. Also, I am pregnant, hence assumed to be harmless."

Anshuman looked at the officer seated behind him with headphones connected to a laptop, "Clear?"

"Yes Sir, clear. I can hear what he is talking to the bodyguard."

"Devika Ji, where did you plant the audio-bug?" asked Anshuman.

"Below his tea table. When his henchmen and peddlers come there for the meeting this evening, I am sure they will be seated in the hall, at least in the beginning," she said.

After a gap of three months Timur would be having a meeting with his accomplices involved in the drug racket. He was likely to make an important announcement and possibly the arrival of a major consignment. The police had collected enough evidence to nail him this time and the audio-bug could be the final nail in Timur's coffin.

A week ago, a red envelope had reached the *Konkan Times* office addressed to Devika with a cryptic message.

*'I pleaded for help but no one came* – MEHEK'.

Along with it was a photograph from the *Konkan Times* of a deserted MG Road during the October curfew. A café called Rainbow Ice-cream Parlour was marked in bright red.

Devika read and re-read the message multiple times to make sense of it. When the meaning dawned upon her, it was a revelation, the most startling she had come across in the case till then.

In February, when Mehek was trying to escape Doctor Carlton, she had locked herself in the nurses' room on the first floor of Rachel's Maternity Home. While Carlton banged the door frantically from outside, Mehek had used the phone extension in the room to connect to the board line to call her trusted friends residing nearby for help. By only searching through her mobile records, the police had missed a vital clue. With Shravan's help, Devika had managed to trace the numbers from the telecom company.

The first number belonged to Jaffer, a country-made arms dealer. An ATS team tracked him to his workshop and shanty in Mohammed Rafi Road. During the police interrogation he admitted to have supplied two country made guns styled like a Beretta to Mehek. He also confessed that Mehek had called him in distress from the maternity home on that fateful night and that he had flatly refused to help.

The second number Mehek had dialled was the landline of Timur's house. From what Devika could make out, Mehek was two timing Aftab and Timur. The old magician must have introduced the young nursing student to the world of illusion, magic, practical hypnotism and drug sources. In return he must have got the one thing which he wanted, a romantic fling and physical intimacy with the young beautiful girl. Mehek, it was evident used the tricks she learned from the illusionist to impress her cult followers by seemingly floating in air, pulling random objects out of thin air and making articles disappear.

The third number belonged to Rainbow Ice-cream Parlour. Under Shravan's instructions, Inspector Karim of MG Road took over this mission. Plain clothes policemen snooped around. Initially they did not find anything suspicious. After keeping a close watch on the people going in and coming out they figured out that the numbers did not match. Eventually, when they raided the parlour's premises they uncovered a booming prostitution racket in the large basement which had been converted into numerous small cabins. In the process, the police rescued underage girls between 15 and 17 years of age hailing from calamity-hit regions from across India. The owner of the parlour, a middle aged woman called Vijayanthi, was arrested by the police. When police raided Vijayanthi's house across the street, they found among other things a framed photograph of Vijayanthi standing with her arms around Mehek in front of the towering Duke's nose at Khandala. They were close friends. During police interrogation Vijayanthi admitted that Mehek called her in distress from the maternity home on that fateful night and that she had refused to help. She had been fully aware of Mehek's crimes of infanticide and wanted to stay out of trouble with the law.

The police department had earlier tried to nab Timur; this time, it had pulled up all its resources to catch the elusive magician red-handed. With the audio bug that Devika planted in his house, it was just a matter of time before he would be apprehended. A search warrant and arrest warrant was to follow.

Devika left the Indian Ocean apartments after some time and spent the rest of the afternoon meeting up with nurses who had worked with Mehek at Rachel's Maternity Home. When she reached home by evening, Shravan and Alpesh were already at their daily tea ritual.

"How are you Alpesh Ji? You and Monica will not ditch us this Saturday, right?"

Alpesh replied, "When you are hosting a dinner, will we dare ditch you? By the way, I met Rameshwar Uncle inside; his health is improving day by day."

"God has shown mercy! The Ayurveda medicines from Umbergaon have helped after the chemotherapy," said Devika.

Alpesh put his hands inside his pocket and handed Devika an envelope. "This is for you. Jail Superintendent Jaykumar gave it to me."

"Thanks! You both enjoy while I freshen up and join you."

As she walked into the house she was unable to stifle her curiosity and opened the envelope.

Dear Ms. Soni,

I am in receipt of your letter and am glad to see your enthusiasm to meet me. However, I must decline the proposal. When I had yelled and screamed out in courts and during interrogations, nobody heard my story. They dismissed me as an unstable and insane man cooking up improbable stories as per his convenience. Nobody took my version seriously and I resigned to my fate. I am sorry to disappoint you but I have not met anyone from outside in the two decades of my captivity. I would like to continue with that.

Regards,

Pranav Dhul

# November: The Young Blood

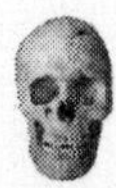

Devika switched on the tv to watch a re-run of the show, *Highway on my Plate*. The energy levels of the two hosts were infectious and every episode had something new. Other than shows on National Geographic pertaining to crime stories and mafia, this was the only show she watched. As she switched on the tv, the channel which started by default was the local news channel which Shravan must have watched before leaving for work.

A tv news reporter was screaming into the mike as the camera zoomed towards the third floor of a hostel building in Sarvanpur.

"The boy who shot the dean and security guard has been identified as Ujjwal Rawat, a final year student of the Electronics and Electrical stream. The boy was in a state of uncontrolled rage after he was handed the expulsion order by the dean." The reporter then turned to a middle-aged, plump, balding man with spectacles and said, "We have Professor Bakshi here with us who has been associated with the Sarvanpur Engineering College for 11 years. Professor Bakshi, why did the college management expel this particular student?"

The professor who was basking in the glory of his ten minutes on television replied, "Last morning, the hostel warden caught him smoking weed in the hostel room. He had got suspension and warning letters twice before and this time the college decided to expel him."

"Professor, why was he given warning letters before?"

"In the second year, he got his first warning when he was caught cheating in the examination hall with an audio reception-transmission device inside his shirt collar. He had generally fared poorly only in management subjects. In the third year he got a warning letter for ragging three of the freshers so badly that one of them had an emotional breakdown and opted out of the college."

"Thank you, Professor Bakshi."

The reporter turned towards another person, a frail dark uniformed guard,

"This is Bhola Ram, the college security guard. He was with his colleague Maan Singh when Maan was shot through his leg by this student. Tell us Bhola Ram, what was going on?"

"*Sahab Ji*, he was yelling inside the Dean's office and then we heard a shot fired inside. We tried to subdue him on his way out and he fired at Maan Singh. Then he fled to the hostel room in the commotion and took some other boys as hostages."

"Where do you think he got the gun from?" Bhola Ram looked at the reporter with a blank look. The reporter continued unperturbed, "Was it a country made rifle?"

"No Saheb! It was a small gun, like the ones we see in English films."

Devika had been sitting hunched before the television set. She sat up straight, her attention riveted on the screen, at the information that had just filtered through. There were three types of guns illegally available in the dark underbelly of areas around Sarvanpur. One was the Katta, a crude country made pistol with six rounds. Another was a variant of the Colt, the fakes of which were frequently shown in B-grade commercial Hindi films. The third, and the rarer variant, was modelled on the Beretta, which was showcased in many commercial Hollywood films, especially of the late 80s and early 90s.

The reporter looked intensely into the camera, "Where did this student get this gun from? Why has he held four of his best friends as hostages? All this remains to be seen. Stay with us."

Devika quickly changed into her kurta and jeans, picked up her bag and left home. She took a rickshaw from outside her house. At the main gate of the Sarvanpur Engineering College, she saw the TV reporters and crowds trying to get past the police circle. Devika could also see that a group of officers in plain clothes were preparing their bullet proof vests and guns to break in. They were the encounter specialists of the police force. On the way she had called up Anshuman on his mobile phone intimating him about her visit. He was at the main gate, clad in his uniform, looking concerned.

"Devika Ji, I was surprised by your call. Why here in between all this chaos?"

"Anshuman, the arms supplier Jaffar, whom the circle inspector and his team had arrested from his workshop, had sold two pistols to Mehek. One was recovered from Mehek's house. Where is the other one?"

"We had thought of that possibility but there could be many such pistols all around town with the local criminals."

"Anshuman, this boy belongs to the sleeper cell which bombed the stadium. With their educational background and some research they are capable of pulling off something like that. Don't think of them as harmless and impulsive young men. These are brainwashed trained minds."

Anshuman looked at her surprised. How could she be so confident?

"Alright, come with me," said Anshuman as he led Devika through the crowd inside the college gate. Since the explosions at the stadium, the police took Devika's suggestions seriously.

The college was a fairly large complex with the main college buildings, hostel, playgrounds and canteens. Once inside they took a left towards the hostel. It was a yellow three storeyed structure which had been evacuated by the cops. Each hostel room had a small balcony with two big balconies in the middle of the structure. In the small annexe next to the hostel building there was a snack counter, a meeting area and discussion rooms. The police had set up their makeshift control room in this area.

As Anshuman walked over to a desk, the man sitting there looked up at him from his landline phone and stick-it notepads.

"This is our negotiator Shailesh Karnik. Shailesh Ji was previously in our training academy for close to sixteen years. He managed to talk to this boy Ujjwal twenty minutes back... Shailesh Ji, this is Devika Soni, an expert on the cult groups," Anshuman lied convincingly.

"Hello! And she is here for?"

"What we strongly believe is that the boy holding the hostages belongs to the group which was responsible for the mass graveyard on Vasco Road and the bombing at K. Jadhav Stadium," said Devika.

The negotiator looked confused as he tried to link all the events together.

"What were his demands?" asked Devika.

"I talked to him at 11. He said that he wanted three staff members of the college, Professor Neelam Choudhary, Professor Biplab Goenka and hostel warden Agnello Fernandez, in exchange for the four boys he's holding hostage."

"These three people I am told were the people who had implicated him for his misconduct every time he received a warning letter and suspension from the college management," Anshuman added.

"The four boys who are now held hostage were always seen with this boy Ujjwal and they are believed to have been good friends," said Shailesh.

"Shailesh Ji, has he given a deadline?"

"Yes! Ujjwal has said that if his demands are not met, he will shoot one boy every hour and drop the dead body from the third floor hostel window," Shailesh looked straight at Devika.

"Oh crap!"

Anshuman was surprised to hear Devika use the cuss word but she was in a state of shock.

"From what he has done already, shooting the dean in the chest and badly wounding the guard by shooting his leg, I don't doubt his ability to carry out his threat." Shailesh added.

"Ujjwal's parents?" asked Devika.

"From the college records and testimony of his classmates, we can make out some facts. His mother died when he was two years old. His father is in Bahrain where he married again and has a daughter. Ujjwal did his schooling and college from Sarvanpur while he stayed at the house of his mother's cousin," said Shailesh.

"As usual, the great family story!" sighed Devika.

"The professors here swear that the boy was a genius in all major streams of science and technology. He headed the robotics club of the college and they won the second prize at the Robotics competition at IIT, Mumbai. However, he had a major attitude problem," said Shailesh.

Shailesh thought for some time. He scribbled some notes on one of the stick-it pads and said, "Let me see if I can buy some more time from this boy."

He dialled a number on his mobile phone which was connected to a speaker.

There was a group of eight policemen around the phone now.

They could hear the phone ring at the other end. Meanwhile, the breaking news that the bombers of the K. Jadhav Stadium had been traced and were holed up in their hostel room at Sarvanpur Engineering College was all over the new channels. Within minutes a commando unit rushed to the spot. The encounter specialists were at this time using the fire exit to reach the terrace.

When the phone went unanswered, Shailesh dialled Ujjwal's number again. This time he picked up the call.

"Listen Ujjwal. I have a suggestion, if you don't mind."

The voice on the other side said, "Speak up, *Haraamkhor!*"

"Ujjwal, my friend, your demands are very difficult to fulfil. I think you need to give us some more time....."

"I want the professors and the hostel warden to be sent to my floor now! Or else I will shoot these bastards one by one."

Devika now picked up the pad on the desk, scribbled something on it, and showed it to Shailesh.

He read it and said, "These are your friends. Why do you want to hurt them?"

"These wretched scumbags! We were a great gang. They were there along with me in every adventure, encouraging me to go as wild as I could for their amusement. Now when my career and life are at stake, all they give me are words of consolation while they prepare for the good life ahead of them. No way will I allow that! They will rot in hell with me."

This time Devika quickly scribbled something which Shailesh did not understand but spoke on the phone, "That woman, Mehek, she brainwashed all of you."

"So you people know about her. Of course not! She showed us the path, we were bubbling with anger against the system. She channelised it. Then she left us; but we promised her that we will never become slaves of the system but martyrs to our belief."

Shailesh spoke in a compassionate tone, "Your mind has been corrupted, son. It's not too late. Drop your weapon and get back on the right path."

"Mine is the right path! You people are the ones who have lost your souls."

"Life is waiting for you and your friends on this side," said Shailesh.

"You will say this now and then, later, when I comply with you, you will send me to the hangman's noose. My true lord is Satan and he has given me a good life till now. Even henceforth he will take care of me. *Shemhamforash!*"

He disconnected the phone.

"Please ask the encounter guys to stop. These are misguided youth who just made some big mistakes," said Devika.

"Madam, you need to talk to Shravan sir. He may be able to do something," Anshuman remarked.

"I really don't think we need to employ any drastic measures," Devika insisted.

Ten minutes later while everybody was debating on a plan of action, a gunshot was heard. Five minutes later a bloodied dead body was flung out from the third floor window; it landed on the second floor parapet.

Kenny Pinto, Ujjawal's friend, was the first hostage to be killed.

The encounter specialists had been waiting for further orders; the killing gave them their go-ahead. They barged into the third floor from the stairway at the other end of the corridor. Ujjwal saw the team charge towards them and started to fire at random. In the mayhem that followed, he took three bullets and collapsed.

The other three students, Kaustubh, Sandesh and Mandar were rescued and later arrested by the police. In Ujjwal's room the team found a mini spade, a shovel, bullets, sachets of cocaine and four bright red envelopes with letters supposedly from Mehek. One letter had a cutout of Devika Soni's column from the *Konkan Times*. The letters were made of words cut from newspapers -

*'They tried to destroy me but I am around. Devika Soni is not following instructions. Intervene Sternly.'*

*'I didn't want you to harm Devika Soni. Drop the Job. Get me out of the pit to my destination. Focus on the 2 OCT mission.'*

The next letter was whiskey-smeared.

*'Follow my path and you will become like me. An aberration of nature which gets carried forward.'*

The last letter read,

*'Best of Luck. You are the face of change. We are just having fun with no consequences.'*

The letters were sent to the State Forensic Laboratory at Kalina. Five weeks later, the consolidated report was sent to the local police. The legible finger prints on the envelopes belonged to the five boys. All envelopes had stamps amounting to six rupees. It was fairly evident that the letters were made from words cut out of the sixth page of *Konkan Times* from the 1st to the 6th calendar day of each month. Nothing special was discovered about the paper, glue or envelope used. Nothing in the report was substantial enough to help in the investigation. The trail was a dead end.

# December: Inside the Devil's Lair Again

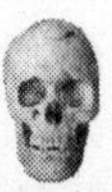

The arena and the fear were familiar. She was in the predator's lair again, self-invited. The special meeting room next to the Mulakat room smelt damp. A plumbing leak in the ceiling caused drops of water to fall one by one in a corner of the room, setting up an unlikely rhythm for their conversation. The cobwebs on the ceiling were detached at some points and partially floating in the air like silk curtains. She looked across the glass barrier and the metal railings and waited for the man to arrive though less a man, more a demon. When the iron door opened and the devil in handcuffs and padlocks shuffled forward, Devika felt the familiar rush of blood as if in front of a charging predator.

"Look who is here! Our lovely tragedy queen," said Mrinal with a sly smile on his face. "I wonder why you gave me the privilege of another meeting. What did I do to deserve this honour?"

"The pleasure is all mine, Doctor."

"Wait a minute! I understand you a little better now," the doctor said, his smile wider, "Is this like a therapy session for you? You come here, cry and get the muck out of your system. Calms down all the noises in your mind. Makes you feel better. Tell me the truth, Devika, you like all this, don't you?" He leaned forward menacingly.

"I am not sure whether I like it. Let's just say that you are brutally honest and don't hesitate to tell people what you really feel about them. It's a rare quality. Nonetheless, I stumbled upon something and wanted to discuss it with you," replied Devika.

"Sure Devika, my dear. I am all ears."

"Let's starts with a small background on what this is all about. My native town is Sagar in Madhya Pradesh. Most of my mother's siblings and their families are settled there. This includes my cousin Satish who works for the local newspaper *Dainik Ujala,*" Devika looked at him directly, the expression on her face revealed precious little, "I know all this may not be of interest to you but we will get to how this is related to you. I asked Satish to find out some details about somebody who was of personal interest to me.

"My cousin stumbled upon an article published in his newspaper in 1962, according to which, on Diwali night some high ranking officials having a liquor party at home attacked and raped two women." As she spoke, Devika watched Mrinal. His eyes darted around the enclosed space. "The victims, a mother and her daughter, used to work as maids in the house of the person hosting the party. They filed a complaint at the local police station the next morning."

"Sad story!"

"What is interesting is that from the next day onwards, the story disappeared from the papers. What is even more interesting is that the victims and their family also disappeared. Vanished from the face of earth!" Devika continued her narration after a pause. "My cousin tried to do some research from the police records of that time – a tedious exercise among hundreds of files lying under layers of dust. The page of the FIR was torn, but he managed to figure out the name of the young constable who was on duty that day."

"Can you please write this crime fiction of yours and give it to me so that I can read it in my free time inside the prison?"

"My cousin took a month to track down the now retired constable. The old man admitted that back then it was commonplace for people in powerful positions to easily manage such accusations against them. He also mentioned to my cousin that the host of that night's Diwali Party of 1962 and the prime accused of the rapes was a senior officer called..."

"Called what?" Mrinal sounded frustrated and bored.

"Ashok Tenmala." The only sound in the room was that of the water droplets from the ceiling.

Mrinal Tenmala stared at Devika with his brown piercing eyes.

Devika continued, "So I thought about all this and came up with an idea. Something I am planning to implement shortly. In my book along with the details of your criminal antics, I will have a chapter dedicated to your family crime history. I strongly believe that this may not be the only criminal case against your father. And I am sure, with some effort we will be able to dig out more stories."

She smiled as she continued. "The saga of a family of criminals and the depraved. Also, I will make your father more famous than he already is by personally distributing copies of my book in your native place, Arvinwadi. I am sure they will lap it up like your story! Let's see what those angry people do to the Ashok Tenmala Road and his small frugal memorial."

Like a wild animal Mrinal sprang up from his chair and leaned towards the iron railings,

*"You will not write anything derogatory about Ashok Tenmala!"*

"You cannot do anything about it, dear Doctor. You are a caged bird, after all." The interviewee and interviewer stared at each other, tables turned. Devika was not going to back off again and feel intimidated.

Mrinal gave Devika a fleeting stare as he pondered over a thought, "Alright! Let me calm down. Okay! Go ahead and ask your stupid questions."

Devika had not anticipated such an easy turnaround. She had a more elaborate plan to try the breakdown but she had hit the spot sooner than she had expected. Though a bit ruffled for the moment, she regained her composure pretty fast.

"I am not interested in knowing anything about you. My questions are related to Mehek..." Devika said as she picked up her writing pad.

"I am glad to hear that. Now, let's skip to the questions and get over with them."

"I hope you understand that brief and shallow answers will not satisfy me. We will end up spending more time with each other than either of us would like. So please be comprehensive enough with your responses."

"I will do anything to see the last of you lady."

"Alright! With all the money and resources she was mobilising, what was Mehek's ultimate objective?"

"Mehek wanted to be the new-age Crowley."

"Excuse me, Doctor, what was that?"

Mrinal looked around as if he was going through an ordeal he did not deserve. "I think everyone in town knows the answer to this one. She was a woman in one mad rush. Mehek had set some big goals to be achieved before she turned 25. Her life changed after she read a book by the 20th century occult leader Aleister Crowley. Have you heard of him?"

"A little. A figure revered by some artists and intellectuals worldwide; appeared on the album cover of *The Beatles*; was a beacon of interest for some famous people like Somerset Maugham, Jimmy Page, Jim Morrison and Ozzy Osbourne."

"If you would have read more about him you would also know that Crowley had conducted a social experiment in the 1920s. He made all his followers stay together in a place and called it Abbey of Thelema. Mehek wanted to start an equivalent organisation in this town."

"In your opinion, was there any particular reason as to why she was so impressed by Crowley?"

"I think Crowley was the only one who was able to demonstrate the power of black magic in real life. The level of pains and effort he took for his rituals was what probably impressed Mehek," Mrinal looked deep into Devika's eyes. "Do you know that at one point of time, Crowley propagated the sacrifice of babies for occult rituals? I think Mehek took the message seriously. She sacrificed some babies in the process." Dramatically, he clapped his mouth with his handcuffed hands, as if trying to stifle hysterical laughter.

Devika kept a straight face, swallowing the disgust that rose to her throat in a wild rush.

Devika had heard that by advocating the 'sacrifice of babies' Crowley had probably meant copulation without conception rather than actual killing. She did not want to correct Mrinal and lose the flow, especially since Mrinal was now getting comfortable. Maybe it had something to do with solitary confinement. People suddenly started talking too much when given the opportunity. This man had been holed up in a dark cell for close to a year. He may not like to admit it but he was actually enjoying the conversations, now more than ever.

"Where did she plan to start this institution of hers?"

"She was on the verge of finalising the purchase of a place outside town called the Portuguese Mansion along with the three acres of land surrounding that place. She had even registered the organisation as a non-profit spiritual organisation which she named the Shrine of Neo-Thelema."

"Any particular reason why she was fascinated with the Portuguese Mansion?"

"I don't know for sure. She had once remarked that the location, coupled with the directional alignment of the mansion, was ideal for the flow of energy. She loved the place." Mrinal's expression bordered between bliss and nostalgia. "Her temple was supposed to be a fun dwelling where followers of the occult would come together to live in bliss, conduct rituals, relax and enjoy their life with alcohol, drugs and free sex."

"Did she believe that people would subscribe to her bizarre concept?"

"Do you know how many people used to read her blog on the internet every month? When we ran a website analytic tool we found out that out of the total of 8,400 people, more than half belonged to western countries," Mrinal paused to clear his throat.

"She had major followers, around 26,000, on a micro-blogging website and the number of people she was connected to on a social-networking website saturated their quota of maximum contacts."

"So you people modelled an institution along the lines of some erstwhile semi-spiritual haven at the peak of the 1970s hippy era; institutions which attracted a large number of foreign followers. Is it a sustainable business model now?"

Mrinal's reaction to this was a stifled laugh. "Sustainable business model! Mehek asked her followers to contribute any amount as per their will towards the building of the complex." He lowered his voice, his eyes narrowed. "I was overwhelmed when the bank account mentioned by us got online transfers amounting to a total of around $ 31,000 and € 24,000 in a matter of days. That is more money than you will earn in your lifetime. Mehek was also investing the money I made from the hospital."

"That's not the truth, Doctor. She lost a lot of that money. Wasted your hard earned dirty money in illegal betting!"

Mrinal became silent for some time. He had suppressed his rage and Devika knew that for more information she had to stop irritating him. However, it was tempting for her to play with the maniac's ego and make him speechless.

"So this Shrine of Neo-Thelema. Did you people believe that it would have survived with the way law enforcement, activist groups and the general public view such hedonic ashrams?"

"You think there is law and order in this country? I disagree. Mehek had her honey-trap to handle that. Anyway, our plan was to run it in Sarvanpur only for five years. After this we would do what most organisations have done before us – re-locate outside the country."

"So Doctor, what was in it for you other than the money, sex and drugs?"

Mrinal smiled. Again, he looked at her through narrowed eyes. "What a person wants when he is young and what he wants after a certain age are very different. Unlike the younger generation which seems to be having a lot of fun, our lives were rather dull, boring and orthodox. At the age of 50 I realised what a futile life I had led until then." Mrinal paused. "The cult gave me that purpose. After spending years and years of my life as a 'nobody', I was finally part of something big. It felt great to be spearheading a revolution, or so we thought."

"You had everything going your way. What was the need to kill all those people? " Devika looked into his brown piercing eyes fearlessly.

The doctor laughed aloud shrilly, almost hysterically.

"Thrill! It's an addiction that you will not understand. I must admit that any son-of-a-bitch who killed someone and said that he is plagued by remorse or grief is a fucking liar."

The doctor raised one eyebrow; his white teeth glistened even in the dim light.

"On the contrary, when you strangle another person's life with your own hands, you feel unimaginably powerful. You feel the power to influence someone's destiny flowing in your grip....."

The doctor held out his handcuffed hands as if strangling someone. His long fingernails were dirty. Devika felt sick.

"Okay, enough of that! What were all those letters Mehek wrote to people all around the world?"

"Birds of a feather flock together!"

"What?"

"Isn't it obvious? A revolution, my dear, starts slowly, very slowly, with like-minded people and organisations coming together for a purpose. It has been like that from the very beginning. Nazis, the Taliban or Bakht. Mehek felt that all the followers of anti-establishment operating in isolation will not lead to anything substantial on the world stage until they unite. So she wrote to the Church of Satan, The Temple of Set, College of Thelema and numerous such organisations mushrooming around Europe to come under a consortium working in coordination and working towards a New World."

"Did these organisations respond to your communication?"

"No! They did not. You see, these organisations are yet to reach our level of maturity. Mehek believed that eventually they would come to us. All we needed to do was grab their attention."

"The bombing of the stadium. Why was that important?"

"I was not part of the plan; she kept all of us in the dark about it. However, I can think of many reasons why she would have initiated that. Firstly, Mehek was a firm believer that anarchy was the only way to clean the planet before rebuilding it. Secondly, the terror attack was to prove a point to all anti-establishment organisations that civil anarchy was easier to create than what is widely believed."

The doctor looked into Devika's eyes with his piercing brown eyes and brushed back the hair falling on his forehead.

"Also, by setting difficult targets she could test the loyalty of her team members. She must have assured the poor chaps that the low intensity blast will not kill anybody, just create panic. The boys could not fathom that the ensuing stampede would kill people even if the blasts did not."

"Took her followers down the crime pit, one level at a time till they could not come out of it. Shrewd, very shrewd indeed."

Devika picked up her notepad and bag; she got up from her chair and abruptly said, "I am done with my questions. You can go now!"

The dismissal was hurtful to his ego; Dr Mrinal Tenmala continued to sit in his chair and stare at her.

"By the way, Doctor, a comment on the pseudo-feminist bit from our last meeting."

"That was just one of the many words I used to describe you. I am happy that you were offended by it," said Mrinal.

"Just my response to that. I don't know which strange, ego-fuelled world you live in. In my world, you use all the contacts you can to get the job done. I just got my job done!"

She winked. Mrinal hated her confidence.

Devika turned and was about to leave when she turned back.

"By the way, if you reflect on the start of our conversation, I had not promised anything and even before I could make an offer, you jumped the gun to answer my questions."

"What the hell are you saying?"

Devika smiled, "Just that since we did not have any agreement prior to your spilling the beans, I am still going ahead and publishing all the details of your father's dark background in a chapter dedicated to you and your family history of crime."

As Devika left the room, Mrinal charged against the metal railing, threatening and abusing her in uncontrolled rage, butting his head against the railings like a madman.

When she got out of the room Devika had a smile on her face. She called up Shravan.

"So how did it go?"

"I made the sleazeball eat his tongue!"

Shravan had a hearty laugh. "I wish I was there to see all this," he said. "See! Trust your ability and you can tame any demon."

"Shravan Soni, I love you!"

"Devika Soni, I love you too."

# Part - IV

# The Source of Evil

# December:
# The Portuguese Mansion

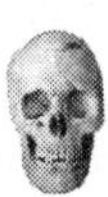

Devika returned with some books on criminal psychology from the Sarvanpur Public Library. When she entered the hall Radhemohan came out from the kitchen. Her father was in the hall sipping his tea and eating Marie biscuits.

"How was your day *beta*? I think you should stop all this travel and take some rest now onwards. Your final trimester is about to start."

Devika replied, "Another week and after that I will not step out of the house, Papa. Radhemohan, get me some tea please."

"Madam, here is a letter from the *Konkan Times* office. They called when you were away and I went to collect it," he said as he handed her the red envelope.

At once Devika tore open the envelope and took out the sheet of paper.

Her father stared at her, wondering why she was in such anxiety.

Dear DeViKa,

You are FINE?

So you did not get my GIFT. Alas! All the precautions necessary had been taken in front of law. Looks Futile now.

- MEHEK

Devika thought for a moment and said to her father,

"Papa, I will join you in 15 minutes. There is something urgent."

As she walked towards the bedroom, the old question sprang to her mind once again. After the shootout at the engineering college all the remaining cult members had also perished or were in jail. She had assumed that at least now the letters would stop. However, she was proved wrong and it was now evident that the college boys were not sending the mail.

*So who was sending these letters and why? What is this Gift that is mentioned in the letter? What precautions in front of law?* Then Devika recollected something from one of her research meetings.

She went into her bedroom, took out the diary and scanned through the pages until she reached a name and number.

She dialled the number from the landline in the bedroom.

"Am I talking to Nurse Mariam?"

The voice on the other side replied "Yes."

"Hi! I am Devika Soni. You remember we had met?"

Mariam used to work along with Mehek at Rachel's Maternity Home. Devika had previously met the nurse at her residence to get some insights into Mehek's behaviour at her workplace.

"You had mentioned during your meeting that you once met Mehek when you were shopping," Devika said. "She had told you that she was there to meet her lawyer."

"Yes! That was the only time I had met her outside the maternity home," said the voice on the other side.

"Mariam, which place was this exactly?"

"The market area on Baba Amte Road."

"Are you certain about that?"

"Yes. I remember it well."

In the evening, Devika searched for lawyers' offices on Baba Amte Road on the internet and in the telephone directory.

Unlike Mohammed Rafi Road, Baba Amte Road was broader, with fewer shops and a lesser crowd. The first office at the eastern most end of the road belonged to Rai & Rai, a large office with a photocopy shop and STD booth leased out in front of it. Their stream of expertise was industrial disputes and corporate litigation. Devika was pretty sure that Mehek had not approached them. Theirs was a totally different stream which would be of little interest to Mehek. She walked a little ahead. The next office belonged to Advocate Iqbal Sheikh, a tax lawyer. When Devika entered the premises and requested his assistant if they had a customer named Mehek, she said firmly that the firm did not divulge information about their clients. Nonetheless, Devika fixed up an appointment with advocate Iqbal Sheikh for the following Tuesday. As she returned to the road Devika spotted something on the opposite side. Almost petrified, she barged into the adjacent sari showroom and dashed straight to its rear end. On being asked about her requirement, she pointed towards the entrance. A group of eunuchs in bright saris were out for their morning collection. They sometimes harassed pregnant women for money, and no matter how much was given to them, they made a lot of fuss. The shop attendant pointed to the trial room and Devika hid inside it for close to 20 minutes.

At the end of a long row of shops selling plastic items, she saw another office. It belonged to the criminal lawyer Advocate Umesh Chouhan. This should be the one, she thought.

Inside, the office was neat, clean and vibrant. She asked the receptionist if she could meet Advocate Chouhan.

“He comes here in the afternoon, Madam. He has to coordinate the shifting of all the records and paper from our MG Road office.”

“Since when has this office been operational?”

“Since three days.”

Devika walked out dejected. This was not the place she was looking for. She continued to walk, her pregnancy obvious to everybody. Craving some food, she entered Nathubhai Halwai and ordered for a plate of kachoris and lemon juice. As she took a bite of her kachori, she noticed a board on a building to her left.

Revathy Pai – Divorce Lawyer.

Devika knew the 52-year old Revathy pretty well. She was an active member of the local chapter of 'India against Corruption'. Revathy had been out of India for close to a year now, visiting her daughter who had had an accident while skiing in Aspen. She thought of calling up Revathy but it would be night time in America. Instead, she approached Revathy's apprentice, Perizad.

"How are you Devika? My goodness, you are going to have a baby!" Perizad smiled.

Devika replied with a smile, "Decided to go the family way."

"Congratulations!"

"Listen, Perizad! I was here for a work related query. By any chance do you know of a client of Revathy called Mehek?"

"Let me check," said Perizad as she picked up a file from a numbered rack. As she flipped the pages, she said, "Voila! It seems she was our client for divorce proceedings with her husband. Also, we helped her by referring her to a lawyer to get an anticipatory bail from the Sessions Court. Mehek has also registered her will with the sub-registrar, something which was coordinated by our madam. There is a note here which says that there is a certain Document number 27 in the safe custody of our locker with instructions to be dispatched in the event of her death."

"Can I have a look at her will?" asked Devika.

In her excitement Devika caught the corner of the sheet Perizad was holding and tried to peep into it. Perizaad looked obviously annoyed. "I am not sure if we have a copy. Even if we had it, it wouldn't be right to share it with anyone. Let Madam come back and let her decide on that."

"I'll talk to your madam tonight. She will call you up tomorrow and give you the instructions."

"As you please," Perizad sounded distant.

"Can you at least check if there is a Document number 27 in your locker?"

Perizad looked at Devika for a fleeting moment and before saying "Okay."

Perizad opened a locked drawer, took out a key and went inside the adjacent room with its locker for safe custody of clients' documents. She pulled out a packet and placed it on the table. It was a document and a VCD.

Within seconds, Perizad's expression went from annoyed to appalled.

"This is addressed to you, Devika!"

She handed the document and VCD to Devika as if half-heartedly finishing her job.

"*Me!*" Devika was as bewildered as she looked at the sheet of paper.

To be couriered to in the event of death of the client to-

Devika Soni
*Konkan Times*
Sarvanpur – 01

Dear Ms Soni,

I read your columns regularly in the *Konkan Times*. I had also sent an anonymous fan mail to this address which I hope you would have received. Your bold stance on many issues especially concerning women's rights found an echo in my heart. You would be reading this letter if something were to happen to me. Along with this I am sending a VCD that will be of interest to you. This is a small gift from my side. You in your position and capacity are perfectly placed to take this to the right level. I cannot trust anyone else with this.

There are people who will try very hard to suppress this. You are linked to a newspaper and your husband is in law enforcement. That makes you my obvious choice. Thanks in advance for your help.

Regards,

Mehek

Devika left Revathy's office along with the letter and VCD, a bit flabbergasted at what was happening. Once home, she first had lunch, then went into her bedroom and switched on the DVD player.

As she watched the happenings on the screen Devika felt almost paralysed by the shocking visuals. These were strange sights and it was incredible what this woman Mehek had managed to prove. How hollow, vulnerable and fragile people were.

Still in shock, she shuddered when a message tinkled on her mobile. Anshuman.

'Madam, got the keys for Portuguese Mansion. Will be meeting you there as discussed at 5.30 in the evening today.'

Devika decided to take an evening shower before she left for the Portuguese Mansion. She changed her dress, took her notepad and leather bag before leaving for the mansion. She took a rickshaw to the main bus station. From there she took a state transport bus which dropped her at a makeshift bus stop 200 feet away from the mansion. She would soon step into the third trimester of her pregnancy and already felt tired from the long journey from her home to the Portuguese Mansion.

She was late. The sun was starting its descent into the western horizon when she opened the grand rusting gate of the mansion. From this distance it looked like a miniature version of a European castle with arched windows, tall pillars and the tiled roof. Surrounded by dense trees on all sides but one, this single-storied mansion had an abandoned yet regal feel about it.

As she walked on the path between the trees which led to the mansion she could see it more clearly. At multiple places the cracks on the wall, the green algal growth and the termite attack on the wooden panels revealed its true age. It was a five-minute walk between the trees to the main door. While walking towards the main door Devika felt a strange sensation inside her stomach. Was the baby kicking or was she imagining it? The movement inside her stomach seemed to intensify as she approached the mansion. A bad thought crossed Devika's mind but she tried to brush it aside. She paused for a moment to catch her breath. At the door of this magnificent, old structure stood Anshuman clad in his police uniform, a striking contrast to the setting.

"Hello, Devika Ji. How are you today?"

"Hello! I am fine."

"Come inside! It was a difficult job to get the keys from the main creditor who had taken possession of the mansion after the old lady died. They are about to sell it to the highest bidder," said Anshuman.

Inside the house, Devika found herself in the centre of a large, spacious hall with a set of stairs in the centre leading to a gallery which encircled the hall. As it was getting dark, Anshuman went to the electricity mains box on the wall behind the stairs to switch on the main power supply. The whole place lit up and the central grand chandelier hanging from the hall's ceiling sent slivers of light throughout the hall.

"Look at all these paintings, Devika Ji. Feels like a museum in here. Somebody staying here was a fan of counterfeits."

"I know a fan of counterfeits. Her name was Mehek," remarked Devika.

Devika looked at the various paintings on the wall. The biggest one was a portrait of Vasco da Gama and a counterfeit of Francisco's painting of King John III of Portugal. The place felt haunted yet royal.

Anshuman watched Devika as she looked around the hall. She was surprisingly more quiet than usual.

"I wanted to discuss something with you, Anshuman. Looks like the engineering college boys, especially Ujjwal, were helping Mehek with other things and not just explosives or radio planes," she said suddenly, "They were setting up miniature cameras and button speakers in hotel rooms."

"Why would they be doing that?"

"Today I stumbled upon a VCD which belonged to Mehek. It was a total revelation. It was supposed to reach me months back but the turn of events delayed it. The visuals were dirty. It started with sex tapes of Mrinal's daughters making love with the Anarchy boys inside the ritual shed. Evidently blackmail tapes targeting cult members. Then there were candid videos of powerful people talking to Mehek before and after availing the service of underage girls from the Rainbow Ice Cream parlour."

"And who were these people?" asked Anshuman.

Did she hear a catch in his voice?

Devika sighed, "First there was Mehek in bed with Satyaraj Kale followed by sexcapades of politicians including Manmohan Gaitonde and Ranvir Dave, businessmen like Pyarenath Kothari, print media veterans like Raghav Shinde. And the biggest surprise – it had police officers like you, Inspector Anshuman."

Anshuman stared at her, his eyes wide open.

Devika added, "Totally sloshed, you were admitting to how exhilarating it was to be with the young girls from the parlour. You were also bragging about your past flings with married women."

Anshuman was tongue tied and began sweating. Admitted into Sushrut Hospital for dengue some years back, he had befriended a nurse named Mehek. This was just before she had joined Rachel's Maternity Home. This friendship took him on a roller-coaster ride to places where he had never imagined he would go.

"Tell me something, Anshuman! In the tapes you spoke about being two steps away from taking the wife of a senior officer to bed. It seems like the senior officer manages the jails of the whole region."

Anshuman looked down.

Devika yelled. "Who was this woman? Monica Thapar?"

"Have you shown the VCD to anybody?"

"No! Why is that important? I won't allow you to continue cheating on Jyoti like that," said Devika.

"What do you want?" Anshuman yelled. His eyes were red; he looked desperate.

"Come out clean. Tell the truth to Jyoti! Admit to everything and come out clean. The prostitutes and the affairs. Everything!"

The Saint Francis church gong rang the late evening hour.

Anshuman began rambling like a lunatic.

"Dammit! I cannot allow you to do this. My job, my marriage, my son – he will hate me when he grows up."

His eyes opened wider and he felt something below his nose. Anshuman wiped it on his sleeves. A drop of blood. He pulled out his service revolver and aimed it at Devika.

"I will not allow you to ruin my life like this," he said.

His behaviour surprised Devika. He was no more her husband's subordinate officer, a pleasant neighbour and a friend but now he was a man who had everything to lose. During multiple occasions when Devika had tried to pursue leads like Mehek's contacts, Anshuman had tried to discourage her by saying that it was a futile effort or that there was nothing more to the case. Now she knew why. Since Shravan and other superiors were directly involved, he had tried to appear neutral and his efforts at concealing the truths were rendered ineffective. If the contents of the VCD went public he would be charged not only for availing services of a prostitute but also for having physical relations with underage girls, a crime tantamount to rape in the book of law. He would have to serve prison time. His job, his marriage and his family were all on the line now.

Devika placed her hand on her baby bump and said, "Using your service revolver to kill me? I can't believe it."

"Oh I forgot! They will trace it to me easily. Thanks for reminding. I guess then I have no choice but to strangle you to death." His eyes red and darting randomly like a lunatic.

Shravan returned from work and found Devika missing. He tried calling her on the mobile but realised that she had left her cellphone in the bedroom.

He checked the messages and saw Anshuman's SMS.

He tried calling on Anshuman's phone but it was not reachable. Shravan read the last SMS again. It was getting dark.

At the mansion Devika stepped behind the stairs as Anshuman moved towards her.

"Do you realise that I am carrying a child?"

"I don't care about you or your child. I want my life back," said Anshuman.

"Do you think it is that easy to kill me and get away with it?"

"Oh! That will be a walk in the park. I will strangle you here and dump you in the mangrove forest. I have a police jeep, nobody will check. I will take care of the VCD in your house later. I have absolutely no motive to kill you and in my position I can play around with the evidence."

"Back off, Anshuman!'

"I am sorry but you have left me with no choice. You know too much."

Devika slowly stepped backwards and looked around. She knew she was in a tight spot. In a godforsaken place, she was with a man who wanted to kill her and she could not even run because of the pregnancy.

*How foolish to put myself and my unborn child in such a spot. What was I thinking!* She could scream for help but who would hear her? The place was so secluded that even prayers would not help.

She continued to move away till she felt the electricity mains behind her back. As Anshuman readied to pounce upon her, she turned incredibly swiftly despite her condition and yanked down the electricity main lever. Behind her, she heard Anshuman stumble against an urn and fall to the floor.

Devika pulled out the metal piston and knob which made up the switch and took it along with her. The entire place plunged into darkness.

As quickly as she could, Devika walked away from the stairs to the other side. She could hear Anshuman fumbling with the main electricity board behind her. In the darkness she made her way to the main door guided by the faint light coming from outside. Before Anshuman could find her, she was out of the mansion. She decided not to walk towards the gate or the mud road. He would surely follow her. She needed to hide somewhere for the time being. Devika ran into the woods towards the direction where the wall faced the bus stop. She could call out for help from there.

In the dark, she ran randomly among the trees, not knowing what was underneath her feet. Behind her, stood the mansion shrouded in darkness.

*When I took up this work I didn't realise I would be putting myself at such risk. Now I am fighting for my life and my unborn child's life as well.*

The trees seemed never ending and the wall nowhere to be seen. Devika felt lost.

*How could I be so careless? I should have guessed that Anshuman would react violently after the revelation.*

Finally, as fatigue caught up with her, she hid behind a tree. Panting, she tried to catch her breath. The night was silent, the breeze cold. Devika wondered if the idea of chasing the story of the dead woman was a blunder to start with. Now she would end up being the dead woman writer.

In the distance, Anshuman came out of the mansion like a rabid dog. He looked around and ran towards the main gate; finding nobody, he fired into the air. Petrified, Devika clamped her hands on her mouth, barely managing to stifle a scream of fear. She could see the faint outline of the Saint Francis Church far away in the darkness. Closing her eyes, she murmured a prayer and clutched her bag tightly; her other hand she placed on her baby bump.

In the faint streetlight, Devika could make out the outline of a wall behind the row of trees to her right. A little ahead of her, the grass seemed less dense than in the surrounding areas. Some kind of a white object glistened in the dark grass. Very slowly, Devika leaned forward and looked at it. In the dull light coming from a street lamp on the other side of the wall, she could read the black text written on white tile.

'Here Lies Mehek'.

Devika stood still and the blood drained out of her face. It was a tombstone marking the final resting place of the dead woman. Devika withdrew at once as if hit by an electric current. She panicked. Visions of the public burial ground with the empty grave flashed across her mind. A sharp sliver of fear ran down her spine, her hair bristled. Her heart felt heavy and her hands trembled.

Suddenly she heard the sound of feet on dry leaves. Quickly, she stepped back into the shadows. Slowly but firmly the sound grew louder and seemed to be heading in her direction.

Devika stopped breathing. The steps were only a couple of feet behind her.

There was only the trunk of the tree between her and the beast.

On Vasco Road Shravan drove his jeep at top speed when he heard the sound of a gunshot from the Portuguese Mansion. He drove faster up the slope and past the main gate. Just as he crossed the main gate, he heard another gun shot.

*Is something terrible going on with Devika?* Shravan thought, evidently jittery after hearing the two gunshots and fearing the worst for his wife.

He left the headlights of the jeep on, pointing towards the main door of the mansion as he walked into the open door. It was dark inside, pitch dark. He was about to take the torch out of his pocket when something sticky stuck to his shoes. He put his fingers on it and smelled it. The coppery smell of blood.

Shravan switched on his torch and quietly stepped forward. The light from the torch revealed a person on his knees in front of the stairs. Anshuman! He was bleeding from his jaw and was in tears. He had tried to shoot himself in the head but his hands had trembled at the last minute and he had misfired. The bullet caught the end of his jawbone. The sound of the shot was reverberating in his ears, almost deafening him.

"What are you doing here, Anshuman?" asked Shravan.

He did not answer.

"Where is Devika?"

Anshuman wanted to say something but collapsed on the ground. A woman's loud scream shattered the silence. Shravan took his torch and rushed in the direction of the scream past the tamarind, kokum and sal trees. A stray dog came running towards his side and fled. A few feet ahead, he saw Devika running towards him.

They collapsed in each other's arms.

"Are you okay, Devika?"

"Yes! I am fine now."

"Why did you scream?"

"It was the stray dog. It scared the life out of me."

"Who shot Anshuman?"

"I will tell you about all that, Shravan. Just let me breathe for a moment."

They walked to the jeep and Shravan handed his wife a bottle of water. Devika drank the water and choked on it.

"Relax and breathe!" Shravan held her close.

The headlights of the car faced the door.

Devika narrated the evening's incident to an increasingly incredulous Shravan.

Shravan tucked Devika into the jeep, wrapped a shawl around her body and called in the police highway patrol.

The patrol reached the spot in ten minutes along with an ambulance and took the unconscious Anshuman along with them.

Shravan drove Devika home. Her ordeal was finally over; a long day had come to an end.

# December: The Notebook

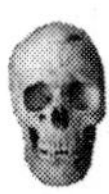

*The road in front of her looked endless in the dark. There was nothing but the black road, the yellow divider line and darkness on both sides. Devika was driving the car on Vasco Road at a good speed. She could see the full moon on her left. The only sounds that broke the silence of the night were the sound of birds from either side of the road. As she took a sharp turn she saw somebody walking along the sidewalk. It was a woman with grey hair wearing a gown. She seemed to be walking backwards. The headlights of the car lit her face and she paused for a moment. Devika's blood froze. The woman turned around and looked at the car. Her pale white skin was the colour of a candle. Hair more grey than black. The face so lean that it looked like a skull with a layer of translucent skin plastic wrapped around it and the eyes were sunk deep inside the sockets. Ghastly pale white hollow eyes. Devika stepped on the accelerator and the car zoomed ahead. Sweating in this cold night Devika prayed to reach home safely.*

*From the rear a voice said,*

*"You scared my mother, Devika! Poor thing died in grief when I jumped off the cliff. Then I got to dwell inside her lifeless body."*

*Devika turned around and saw Mehek on the back seat of her car clad in a black gown. Her hair was loose; she looked at her through piercing eyes.*

*"What are you doing here?"*

*"You were so hell bent on trying to find out everything about me. I thought of paying you a visit, my dear," said Mehek.*

*Petrified, Devika hit the brake pedal. In quick reaction she opened the door of the car and started to run out into the open. Mehek started to run behind her.*

*Devika was panting but she ran with all her might.*

*'Run! Save yourself!' Mehek screamed from behind.*

*Devika stumbled on a stone and fell down. Mehek pounced on her.*

Devika sprang out of her bed and looked around.

She had slept through the afternoon; it was evening now. *One wretched nightmare.* She sat on the bed till she got her breath back. Her hand slowly moved to her baby bump. There was again the same weird movement inside her stomach. Devika started to sweat. Her baby was getting uneasy. Devika wondered if all this was some strange coincidence or a creation of her mind. This happened at the Portuguese mansion and every time Devika was involved in something related to Mehek. *Are the dark energies after my child? Will they harm my little one?* The thought sent a shudder down Devika's spine.

She heard a faint laugh coming from outside. A woman's laugh. *Is that Laali?* she wondered.

Devika looked at the wall clock. It was 6 pm and time for her father's medicine.

One of Shravan's cousins worked in a bank at Umbergaon where there was a famous naturopathy physician who had successfully treated cancer. The cousin visited Sarvanpur every month and brought the medicines with him that helped Rameshwar deal with the after effects of chemotherapy. These included ayurvedic herbs to be boiled in water, ayurvedic tablets, herbal powder, aloe vera juice and gel. The chemotherapy sessions had substantially reduced the size of his cancerous growth. The ayurvedic medicines had had a positive effect on his health and immunity.

In his room, Rameshwar spent a lot of his time listening to music on his MP3 player or playing the VCD of Devika's ultrasound on the laptop. The movement of the tiny foetus across the screen filled him with joy and a sense of expectation that gave him the strength to live. As Devika prepared the evening dose of the medicine using the herbal powder, turmeric, honey and aloe vera gel, she wondered where Shravan was.

Shravan and Alpesh were at the upmarket Casablanca restaurant at MG Road. The ambience was classy with the regular Kenny G instrumental playing in the background. On their table were two beer mugs and a plate of French fries.

Alpesh looked haggard. His usual jovial self and corny jokes were a thing of the past.

"Jyoti leaving him and taking their child along was fair. That scoundrel Anshuman deserves to suffer alone in the hospital and later inside the prison. What I don't understand is why are you not going home and staying at the guest house instead? Go back home, Alpesh Ji," said Shravan.

Alpesh replied in a heavy tone, "What Anshuman did and Monica did deserve the same treatment. To tell you frankly, I don't want to see Monica's face again."

"No, Alpesh Ji, Anshuman cheated on his wife and availed the services of a prostitution racket. Monica just toyed with the idea of an extra-marital romance and abandoned it before it got out of hand. That's not even close," said Shravan

"It's the same thing. To think of committing a sin and doing so are very close."

"Very close, Alpesh Ji, not the same. At some point of time or the other, people reach a level of frustration with their spouses. It may be momentary but when it repeats itself, people start looking outside their marriage. It shows depth of character when a person is able to control himself or herself from going astray and destroying the marriage."

"Shravan, all I know is that after 15 years of marriage, I did not deserve this!"

"Monica is in our house since yesterday. She is in a very bad state. I think you should consider forgiving her."

"I need time, Shravan. I need time to clear up the mess inside my mind."

"One piece of advice from my side, Alpesh Ji, that is, if you don't mind... Spouses should not be treated like what people once did to black and white television sets – a delight once upon a time, dumped in some corner later."

"I don't get you."

Shravan thought over what he wanted to say.

"What I am saying is that, just because you married someone and she is yours, doesn't give you the right to take things lightly. As the years pass by, you should not neglect your spouse just because she is there and will be there with you forever. Instead, I think she should get extra respect and attention as years pass by for being loyal and caring."

"What you are saying is that even I am to blame for our marriage getting into muddy waters. However, I am in no mood for any advice now, Shravan. My family was all I had. Then some charming bastard walks in and walks over it, making me look like one big failure."

A brief silence followed as the waiter brought a pitcher of beer.

"As if I did not already have enough trouble. My reform scheme of providing good food in prison once a week has backfired. They served a contaminated dish this afternoon and many inmates have reported sick due to food poisoning."

"Anyone critical?"

"One young fellow is on drip and ORS. One prison guard is also critical. One of the oldest inmates of Sarvanpur Jail, a guy called Pranav who had just recovered from a month long bout of fever also ate the food. His condition is very critical... which reminds me..." he picked up his leather bag, opened it and handed over a notebook to Shravan.

"What is this?"

"This particular inmate Pranav, when he was being examined by the doctor, told one of the prison guards to go to his cell, take this notebook and give it to ACP Shravan Soni's wife. My colleague Jaykumar handed it to me at my office," said Alpesh. Shravan flipped the pages of the notebook with curiosity in his eyes before shutting it close.

"Thanks, Alpesh! I think Devika had written to him for an interview but this man had refused."

"Pranav's condition is critical. I am praying for him. If he dies, even I will have to face the brunt of departmental enquiry into the matter."

The two friends drank till it was dinner time.

On his way home, he looked at the empty deserted streets of Sarvanpur. At nine in the night, the city was never so asleep and afraid to step outside. At this time families used to go on walks after dinner and huddle near roadside balloon sellers and fruit juice vendors. College students would frequent ice-cream stalls, street food corners and pan shops, taking breaks from their study sessions. Then some people who wanted to create anarchy stepped in, defaced the town and altered its character. Fear and suspicion replaced the innocent youthful chirpiness and banter.

When Shravan returned home, he handed over the notebook to Devika. As if she had stumbled upon a hidden treasure, Devika started to read the notebook in the light of the table lamp in her bedroom. Shravan was sound asleep. Devika turned the pages of what looked like a memoir of events from Pranav's past. She turned the pages and read the words in disbelief. This was indeed a strange story of the events of a night, which happened more than two decades ago; the story Pranav tried to tell other people but they did not believe him.

# What happened 24 Years Ago

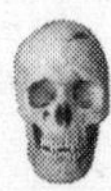

"The American accent made it very difficult for me to understand anything in the movie yesterday," commented Shipra.

"I think there was a problem with the Video cassette or the audio output of our VCR. But I think even without clearly understanding the dialogues, this movie was one of the better action films of recent times. This bodybuilder guy Arnold was menacing." Pranav said as he manoeuvred the steering wheel with one hand on a road empty except for two bicycle riders with tiffin carriers and jute bags hanging from their cycle bars.

"Once we are back in Bombay, you should take me out for a movie. The doctor has cautioned me against watching horror films, not all films." Shipra placed her hands on her five-month old baby bump.

It was evening and their car, a 1979 model Ambassador, was speeding along Vasco Road. The front windows were pulled down completely because of the heat.

Shipra was unusually bubbly, "I am so excited that we now have a vacation home. Is the villa big?"

"It may be a little less spacious than you would expect. Since there were no takers for the villa, it came in cheaper than the market rate.

People can make really profitable decisions in this country if they don't believe in superstitions. As you know, the purchase took away all the residual money from selling my firm and paying the creditors."

Pranav had just pulled down the shutters on his small firm that imported branded shoes and the couple were carrying 88,000 rupees with them in a leather bag. It was the consolidated fee for transportation of goods between Bombay and Bangalore that they had to hand over to one of their creditors after reaching the villa.

"Pranav, I think it was a bad idea to start with. In our country we don't care about big international brands. Buying shoes implies going to the nearest Bata store and getting good quality, value-for-money footwear."

"I think we would have done well had we just hung around for six months more, created a buzz around the brands and got the youngsters excited. Your brother could have bailed us out with his overflowing cash reserves. If you know what I mean."

"Was it mandatory for my brother to help us out? He may have a booming retail business, but remember, I am not even part of the family anymore," Shipra said.

"We don't have families. We are both orphans who will soon have a child who has no lineage as well," Pranav said.

"As a businessman my brother has the right to choose whatever he thinks makes business sense for him. The fact that he is still in contact with us is nice enough of him," Shipra retorted.

"Not just nice! It is a blessing bestowed upon poor souls like us by that angel who is sitting on top of a mountain of cash," Pranav replied sarcastically.

Why was he so jealous of her brother? She didn't like his attitude but decided not to comment on the matter.

Pranav and Shipra had grown up in the same neighbourhood in Rohtak. They belonged to the Jat community and were of the same gotra. When they fell in love, they had no option but to elope to Bombay to escape the ire of the Khap Panchayat – the community institution being strictly against marriages within the same gotra. In Bombay, they got married on the day of their arrival. Their families initially filed a police case of missing persons which was subsequently withdrawn upon news of their marriage. Their families disowned them but her wealthy elder brother was still secretly in touch with them.

"I don't think we have embarked on this trip to have fights," said Shipra.

They drove past the Saint Francis Church. Feeling hungry, Pranav stopped the vehicle near a makeshift roadside snack shop. There was only a Lambretta scooter parked outside the shop. Some locals were also standing there having their evening tea and the local snack *vada pao*. They were amused to find a well dressed couple from the city in these parts, especially a pregnant woman holding on tightly to a leather bag.

"*Two teas and two vada paos*," ordered Pranav.

The man preparing the tea at the counter asked, "Spicy or mild?"

"Mild," said Shipra.

"I read in the newspaper that a bus and oil tanker had a major accident about a week back. What happened?" asked Pranav.

"Saheb, these things happen regularly in these parts. It seems the bus driver was drunk," he said as he poured the tea from his aluminium kettle into two small glasses.

Oblivious of keen eyes watching them, the couple drank tea and asked for more snacks.

"I am taking three packets of Uncle Chips and two Campa Orange along with the bottles. Take the deposit money for the bottles and I will return them on my way back. What's the total?"

"Forty-two rupees."

Pranav looked at his purse and pulled out a hundred rupee note. The man preparing the tea returned the currency note saying that it was torn. Pranav checked his purse again and found one 10 rupee and one 20 rupees note.

"Give me a 100 rupee note from the bag," Pranav said to his wife.

Shipra opened the zip of the bag and pulled out a single currency note from the bundle, but the stapled bundle dropped out of the bag along with the note.

"This woman cannot do one thing properly!" Pranav muttered angrily as he stooped to pick up the bundle of notes.

Back in the car, Pranav did not speak a word. They took a detour from Vasco Road and went up a slope with numerous hair-pin bends. Gradually, the slope gave way to a mud road that snaked off into dense vegetation.

At last, Pranav parked his car next to a shed where a young village boy squatted in the sun. "Come Jagdish, help us with the luggage."

The boy jumped to his task but not without complaining. "I was waiting here for a long time, Saheb!"

Pranav looked at his HMT watch. 4.30 pm.

Shipra took the leather bag herself while Jagdish carried the rest of the luggage on his head along with the box of Nutan kitchen stove, holding only the can of kerosene in his free hand.

"Saheb, it was a good idea to bring this stove. The gas cylinder in the villa is empty and it is a long drive to get the new one from the agency; they don't deliver here." The boy walked ahead, the couple followed. Pranav held Shipra's hand tightly down the slope.

"Jagdish, did you clean up the villa?"

"Yes, Saheb. It is spotless." He grinned triumphantly at them and went down yet another slope.

"This mud road seems to be endless. Do you realise that I may need to climb up this slope also on our way back? That too with ..." Shipra looked at her tummy.

"I think it wasn't a bright idea to bring you along in this condition. Let's see if we can take long extended breaks with refreshments and do a slower climb on our way back."

"I am so glad we finally have a buyer for the villa. It's been quite some time since we have had people live here," said Jagdish.

"Jagdish! Do you know why people are worried about buying this house?" Shipra asked.

"Madam, is it because of what happened to the writer and his family?"

"That's a lousy rural myth. Look! The villa!" Pranav shouted.

The villa stood among dense vegetation on all sides. It was an old white structure with a tiled roof and a boundary wall of modest height. There were two pillars at the front and an embossed design of a big conch shell in the middle of the structure; above the post box on the wall was a fixed tile with the name 'Silent Villa' etched on it.

Some rare varieties of parrots with long tails flew around intermittently, camouflaged in the greenery. Shipra, who was expecting something bigger, was a little disappointed after all the toil of walking to the villa. Pranav opened the gate and main door as if it belonged to a grand Scottish castle and his wife was a queen on her annual visit.

'Silent Villa' was fully furnished with a hall and three bedrooms. The furniture in the hall included a cupboard, a dining table with four chairs, a flower vase, and a wooden double bed placed beyond the partition. There was an old Nelco television in the hall which did not work. The bedrooms had single beds. Jagdish had done a good job of cleaning the floor, walls and ceiling.

The electric switches were of the old style with external wiring; bulky Usha fans hung from the ceiling, their blades clean. The work area next to the kitchen was crowded with a black stone masala grinding unit, ropes, empty cans of kerosene, an empty gas cylinder, tool box, a sledgehammer, an axe, steel rods, old pickle jars and large containers to store grains. An old broken Tobu tricycle leaned against one side of the wall. The previous owners of the house had also left some of their stuff in the store room among old newspapers and magazines stacked in untidy piles. Among the empty audio cassette covers Pranav was amused to find Michael Jackson's *'Off the Wall'* and *'Lets Get It Started'* by MC Hammer. The previous owners of the villa seemed to have had relatives abroad who sent them these albums. There was also a damaged Singer sewing machine along with a cardboard box of blue inland letters and comic books for children including *Diamond Comics, Tinkle* and *Chandamama*. An old and damaged Remington typewriter stood forlorn among the rest of the discarded stuff.

Pranav connected his Sharp transistor and cassette player to the electricity socket and inserted a Sony audio cassette with its collection of popular songs.

The voices of Runa Laila and Bappi Lahiri wafted around the old house along with the fresh breeze from the windows Shipra had flung open. In the drawing room, she said, "Let's go for a walk."

"Yes, let's do that. Brisk walking and fresh air will be good for our little one."

Smiling happily, Pranav placed his hands on her baby bump.

The sun was inching closer to the western horizon when Pranav and Shipra left their house and stepped into its green surroundings. They carried the bag of cash with them, afraid to leave it unguarded in the house. Among the vegetation, sunlight was sparse, blocked by the tall trees. Other than the normal trees in the region, the couple also spotted some rare trees and the chirping of various birds echoed all around them. At a distance a tree looked different in its surroundings. As they walked towards it, they met with a peculiar sight, strange and rare which made their eyes widen.

"I wonder why all the crows are on top of that single tree?" Pranav exclaimed.

Shipra felt uneasy at the number of crows sitting on virtually each branch of the tree.

"It is kind of creepy, isn't it?"

The crows on the tree were silent as they stared westwards through glassy eyes. Pranav and Shipra were bewildered. "Why are they all so silent and motionless?" Shipra asked in a whisper.

"If we stand here any longer, we'll have a rain of droppings on us," Pranav joked, trying to lighten the mood.

The road curved steeply away from the trees. At a short distance, an object on the ground caught Shipra's attention. Curious, she stepped forward to take a closer look. One end of the shiny object was embedded in the ground and she had to yank it out.

In her hands she held an old Swiss Makers ladies watch. She wiped the dust off the dial. Its glass was cracked, the hands had stopped at half past four. Frozen time.

"Look what I've found!" She held out the soiled, old watch to Pranav.

As he looked closely at the watch, Pranav's expression changed; he snatched it away from his wife and threw it into the shrubs.

"What's wrong with you? It was such a pretty watch."

"Don't pick up abandoned stuff lying around such places. Not a good thing to do." He said and started walking ahead.

"Are you being superstitious? What harm can a watch do?"

"Shipra! Just leave that and let's walk."

Something in his voice washed over Shipra's anger. Quietly, she followed him through the trees and shrubs.

A pair of long-tailed parrots was circling over a tall tamarind tree on their left. "Look at them, they seem to be having a lot of fun!" Shipra said gleefully.

Pranav plucked a fruit off a cashew tree and bit into the nut. "I had this in my childhood on a trip to Goa. The fruit leaves a strange feeling on the tongue but it tastes exotic and smells even better," Pranav shouted out to Shipra.

Shipra looked at a house on the adjacent hill and said, "I am not eating that. That house on the hill, Pranav, nice one."

"It's called the Portuguese Mansion, not sure if anybody lives there. Don't ask me to buy it," her husband added with a smile. His speech seemed a little slurred from the nut he had tasted.

"Let's go, it's getting dark!" Shipra cautioned.

The couple were on their way back to the villa. Walking a little behind her husband, Shipra quietly opened the leather bag and dropped the watch she had retrieved quietly into it. A slight smile lit up her face. It was such a lovely looking watch.

Ahead of her, Pranav stepped into a small ditch. Intent on hiding her watch, Shipra heard him cry out before she saw him fall. They were close to the villa but Pranav had sprained his ankle and it would take more strength than Shipra possessed in her condition to help him limp back to the house.

"Why are you always so absent minded, Pranav? Now what will we do?"

"Don't panic. Just lend me a hand," Pranav said.

As the two made their way back to the villa as the darkness deepened around them. The birds had stopped chirping; the silence was broken intermittently by Pranav's groans.

Back in the villa, Shipra helped Pranav settle down into a chair. "Are you okay? Should I call a doctor?" asked Shipra.

"I am not exactly okay but the pain is kind of bearable."

"I am going to get some help!"

"Don't go out again, it's dark, and this place is full of snakes. I guess we have no choice but to wait for Jagdish to show up tomorrow morning," sighed Pranav.

"An isolated house such as this should at least have a telephone line," Shipra wailed.

"Relax, Shipra! We just need to get through the night. Believe me it's not as bad as it may appear to you."

Shipra went to the kitchen and boiled some water on the stove. She poured it into an aluminium bucket and put three spoons of salt in it. The warm compress would do him some good.

"Can you smell that, Shipra?" Pranav asked, one foot in the warm water, a puzzled expression on his face.

He looked around the room and inhaled deeply.

"What?" She looked at her husband; his eyes were closed.

"Why is the hall smelling of Jasmine flowers?" Pranav was puzzled.

"There must be a plant nearby," said Shipra.

"I did not see any jasmine shrub. Strange."

The Saint Francis church bell rang out loudly in the silent night.

No wonder the house was called 'Silent Villa'. It was isolated and tranquil, situated in one corner of the hillside. After chatting for some time, the couple decided to have an early dinner. Shipra retired to the kitchen to heat up the *paranthas* and cauliflower curry they had brought along with them. Pranav switched on the radio and tuned into Cibaca Geet Mala, the countdown show of Hindi film songs.

"Look at the swelling. It looks like I am in the initial stage of elephantiasis," he grinned through his pain.

"I am sure it is a hairline fracture. I am feeling so helpless stranded in this godforsaken villa," Shipra whined.

After dinner, the couple decided to sleep on the double bed in the hall rather than in the single beds in the bedrooms. It was a breezy night and the only sound that broke the silence of the night was the church gong.

A blue night lamp cast soft shadows around the hall.

The pain in his ankle made Pranav restless but Shipra slept well, oblivious to his discomfort. Through half open eyes, Pranav could see all the way across the hall to the kitchen and the large window there.

Was he asleep and dreaming? Did he really see the figure glide past? Pranav rubbed his eyes and jumped up from his bed and as he did so, the pain shot up from his ankle all along his leg, forcing him to sit still for a few seconds.

He was sure he had seen the shadow of a girl on the other side of the kitchen window, reading a book as she walked.

Pranav got up from his bed and limped slowly towards the window in disbelief.

*Who the hell was that?*

Before he could reach the kitchen, the shadow had passed. Pranav stood in the middle of the hall, bewildered.

*Was he hallucinating?*

As he turned around to return to bed, he saw the girl stroll past the bedroom window. Pranav limped into the bedroom. With trembling hands he opened the window. Nobody.

The night was still, the wilderness asleep.

Pranav could hear an irritating, metallic sound, faint but persistent, as if somebody was rubbing metal against wood. Following the sound, he limped past the hall into the passage. As he approached the closed door of the second bedroom, the noise intensified.

*Screech... Screech....Screech.*

His body turned cold, his knees trembled. Drops of perspiration appeared on his forehead as he tried to touch the door knob of the closed door with trembling hands. The sound was loud.

*Screech....Screech....Screech.*

He could not gather the courage to open the door. A heavy lump seemed to choke him, rendering him speechless.

As he turned the creaky door knob, the scratching stopped.

Silence. Silence more petrifying than the noise.

Pranav's heart beat so hard he felt it would rip apart everything around it. After the brief pause, the scratching started again, angrier now, more persistent.

*Screech....Screech....Screech.*

Pranav wiped the perspiration off his forehead and wondered what to do. He turned the door knob again with bated breath. Silence. This time there was the sound of metal falling on the floor, like a spoon or a fork dropped carelessly.

Pranav jerked open the door and switched on the light.

Nobody. Just the bed, the table and the wooden cupboard.

He stepped forward and looked around the room. Someone had scratched the table with a knife or a fork in rage but the instrument was not visible anywhere in the room.

Just my imagination, thought Pranav.

He breathed normally again.

Suddenly, two palms shot out from the darkness and came to rest against the window pane.

His eyes open wide, Pranav limped towards the window. The small hands of a girl. He could not see anything but a hazy image of someone standing behind the translucent glass. The palms pressed against the glass were pale and had no lines.

As he watched, the palms folded and the nails began to scratch along the glass in unexplainable rage. Like an enraged wild cat scratching endlessly against a tree trunk.

*God-damn-it! I am not opening this window.*

The wooden cupboard next to him started to shudder vigorously. Pranav stepped back, switched off the lights and left the bedroom. Drenched in sweat he slumped against his wife who slept impervious to the goings on in the house. For the first time in his life, Pranav Dhul's lips moved in a prayer.

The night was silent again, calm, and Pranav fell asleep. The sweet fragrance of jasmine engulfed the room again.

Pranav was half-awake. In the night-lamp's dull blue light he saw a woman with curly hair looking down at him from the foot of the bed. His blood froze. The face was not clearly visible. Pranav stopped breathing. With a trembling hand he nudged his wife.

"Shipra! There is someone in this room. Get up!"

Shipra jumped up from her sleep and looked around. No one. Woken unnecessarily from her sleep, she turned upon her husband. "Don't play funny tricks with me, not in my pregnancy."

"No Shipra! *There was a woman in this room.*"

"Go to sleep." She turned away.

Pranav lay awake and motionless in bed for some time till he finally fell asleep again.

The only sound in the dark night was of the blades of the heavy fan suspended from the high ceiling. For a moment it looked like it would be a peaceful night after all.

At midnight the church bell rang twelve times. Half asleep, Shipra got up from bed and walked slowly towards the kitchen. One by one she opened all the drawers of the kitchen, looking for something. Finally she got what she was looking for. The kitchen knife with an eight inch blade. Shipra used the knife to carefully scrape something on the kitchen wall. Still sleep-walking she returned to the hall and stood in front of Pranav, breathing heavily. As she raised the knife to stab her husband, Pranav woke up and turned towards her.

"What the hell is wrong with you?" Pranav yelled as he rolled away.

The knife plunged into the mattress.

Pranav rolled swiftly to the other corner of the bed and hobbled towards the switchboard. In the sudden light he saw his wife's face and the blood drained out of his own. Shipra's eyes were red, a droplet of blood dripped out of her nose. She charged at him with the knife, screaming in rage.

"Damn you, son-of-a-whore!" she grunted in a deep rustic tone. Her eyes narrowed and darted from side to side.

He moved sideways and grabbed her arm with the knife. She dug her teeth into his arms and it started to bleed. Pranav winced in pain but held on to her. With the other hand he slapped her face hard.

Shipra dropped to her knees. She threw the knife at her husband, but missed. Pranav limped towards her, grabbed both her hands tightly and dragged her to bed.

Shipra tried to break free, screaming hysterically all the while. Pranav had subdued her on the bed but she continued behaving maniacally. After a little while she fell unconscious.

Pranav took a moment to regain his breath. He then limped to the kitchen to drink water. As he entered the kitchen he saw something scribbled on the kitchen wall.

## Pranav – Money-minded bastard

At this moment Shipra woke up and called out his name. Pranav walked towards the hall and picked up the knife on the way. Shipra was puzzled to find her husband holding a knife, looking very angry.

"Come on! I am ready."

"What happened? You are freaking me out, what's wrong with you?"

It appeared to Pranav that Shipra was now petrified. "What do you mean by what's wrong with me? Why did you attack me, Shipra? Were you out of your mind?"

Shipra looked back at Pranav, aghast. He was very angry and dragged her to the kitchen.

"Come with me! Come on. You see this. What is this?"

In shock and tears, she fell to her knees, "I don't know Pranav. I did not do this."

"Of course you did this! Who else is there in the house and who else hates me so much?"

"Pranav! Not me, believe me."

"Tell me the truth. This is what you actually feel about me, don't you?"

"No Pranav, no!"

Pranav looked long and carefully at her. She seemed to be telling the truth. As bewildered as he was, he managed to calm down a little.

A loud thud came from one of the bedroom windows.

Pranav and Shipra jumped up in panic and hurried towards the bedroom and switched on the lights. A masked intruder stood in the bedroom wearing a black cloth mask which looked like an elongated skull cap that had dropped to his lips; his red eyes glared at the couple. The intruder had used the open bedroom window to sneak inside and held a ten-inch knife with a sharp blade.

"*Abey Behen ke!* Back off or I'll stab you both!" The intruder reeked of beer.

Pranav limped forward, positioned himself in front of his wife and said,

"Bhai! Whosoever you are, we don't want any trouble. Just go away and we will not report this to the police. Go away, please."

"Hand me the money!"

"What money?"

"Trying to be a hero *haraamkhor*, are you?" The man shouted. "The money in the leather bag. Hand it over or I will kill you both and cut you into tiny pieces."

Pranav looked at his wife; she was responsible for getting them into this mess. Shipra was petrified but stoic; she was anyway blamed for everything, all the time.

"Alright! It's in the cupboard in the hall under lock and key," said Pranav.

The intruder signalled them to move backwards.

"Get the keys. Open the cupboard and keep the bag on this chair. Now, *saale!* Now! "

At one o'clock in the night, the Saint Francis gong struck again.

Pranav froze for a moment.

"What's this smell?" The intruder looked around, surprised by the sudden fragrance.

Pranav's eyes turned red and a droplet of blood dripped down his nose; he looked as if he was trying hard to suppress himself.

He caught Shipra's neck and tried to strangle her screaming, "You useless bitch! I cannot live with your nuisance any longer."

The intruder stood motionless, utterly bewildered.

"I don't love you anymore. You failed me in every single way, you wretched whore. I will strangle you, dumb bitch." Pranav screamed, his voice a baritone, his eyes red with rage.

"Where are the keys? Give me the money now!" The intruder screamed.

Pranav who had been limping seemed to have forgotten his pain.

While Shipra struggled against her husband, the intruder pounced upon Pranav. They tumbled to the floor, rolling and punching each other. Shipra sat petrified on the bed, trying to get back her breath.

Pranav punched the intruder in his face and continued punching him mercilessly till his face turned into a bloody mess and he fell unconscious. Shipra slowly crawled towards the dining table but Pranav turned upon her with bloodshot eyes. He grabbed her neck again and tried to strangle her.

"Pranav! Leave me. Please," she could barely speak.

"Only after you stop breathing, my dear! Only after you drop dead!"

Desperate to save herself, Shipra grabbed the flower vase from the dining table and smashed it on the back of his neck. Pranav slumped to the ground, unconscious.

When the intruder regained his consciousness, he found himself gagged and tied to a sturdy steel chair with ropes; in front of him stood the wife with the knife in her hands.

"Shipra! Darling! I will never ever do anything to harm you or our child. Please believe me!" The intruder turned around to find the husband pleading with folded hands.

"To hell with you. You tried to kill me," said his wife, fighting her tears.

"Sweetheart, believe me. I am telling you that this villa is cursed. It is making us do strange things."

The intruder could sense expression of utter confusion in the wife's face.

"I told you the same thing, Pranav. I don't know what overcame me. You did not believe me then. I will never think of attacking you with a knife."

"Let's just get out of here, Shipra!"

"Where did you bring us, Pranav? It is past midnight now and we are in the middle of this wilderness. We can't escape. You with your injured leg and me with this baby bump." Shipra held on to the knife even as she fought back her tears.

Finally she said, "I want you to not hide anything from me now. Tell me what happened to the previous owners of this Villa? I want to know what happened."

Pranav sighed. Would he have to? "Alright. I only know a little bit from what some locals told me when I first came here to buy the villa. I dismissed it as superstition back then and did not tell you because I thought it would upset you."

Silent Villa was built a little more than five years back by a writer as a vacation home for his family. The writer's family was based out of Pune. Once the villa was ready, they came down to spend their summer vacations here. The writer intended to type his collection of short stories in the peaceful and tranquil atmosphere around the villa. For a week everything went fine, then one fine morning the writer's eight-year old son disappeared into the woods. The husband and wife took the help of some locals to locate their son. It turned out to be a tedious manhunt. They traced him by late afternoon from among the cashew trees down the slope. The boy did not speak a word. Staring into emptiness, he was lost in thoughts. All through the evening the boy was seen sketching weird drawings in his books and twisting and breaking his toys. After dinner the family went to bed as usual. The boy sneaked into the work area near the kitchen and returned with the axe and attacked his parents. The parents had to tie their son with ropes. Totally baffled, the family left that very night.

In Pune, the doctors, including general physicians and psychiatrists, were unable to figure out the young boy's problem. That was when, it seems, the writer's maternal uncle suggested that the family should dispose of all the articles they carried along with them to the villa including their dresses. The writer's wife was surprised to find a strange earring in the pocket of the shirt the boy had been wearing when he went missing. So the family dumped all the articles they had taken along with them to the villa including bags, books, the earring and clothes into the Moshi river. Only after this did the boy recover and the family's ordeal end.

The locals had told Pranav of the chain of events but they had no idea what happened to the family after they left for Pune.

Shipra went to the store room and started to ransack the whole place. Pranav followed her and saw her going through the comics which had belonged to the writer's son.

"Pranav," she called out form the store, "look at what this boy had done."

She handed him a comic. On the cover was written 'Nelson Periera, Class III – C'. Inside the comic, many of the illustrations were defaced by the boy. Using his father's white typewriter correction liquid he had painted the eyes of each character ghastly white. Using a red sketch pen he had sketched blood seeping out of the eyes, nostrils and mouths of many illustrations.

"An eight-year old boy made these? Can you believe it? I think we are in a really weird place," Shipra said, her voice trembling.

While they ransacked the store room, a dark figure peeped into the hall through one of the windows and saw his friend gagged and tied to a metal chair. The figure walked up the slope for fifteen minutes to return to his parked Lambretta scooter, wondering what to do next.

"Damn it! I am not running away!"

Shipra and Pranav heard a knock on their door. "I just pray to God it is Jagdish. I swear that once I am out of this devil's area, I will never come back."

"Hold your horses, let's see who it is." Pranav opened the door.

In front of them stood a man holding a knife and a black scarf tied across his face below the eyes.

"Let my friend go or else things will get very nasty down here," he said as he barged into the hall.

Pranav was in a dilemma. If he released the man tied to the chair there would be more repercussions. With an injured leg and a pregnant wife, he felt helpless. He loathed the moment when he decided to buy this wretched villa and put himself in such a horribly perilous situation.

It was two am. The Saint Francis Church gong struck again. The intruder's associate dropped his knife and stood motionless. Pranav and Shipra were puzzled.

"I loved her so much. I just loved her so much. Then why?" he whispered.

"What?" exclaimed Pranav.

"I loved her so much. Yet she was unfair." As he began to ramble, his face turned red. He went into the kitchen and locked it from inside. The couple stood bewildered. A cacophony ensued behind the locked door. What was the man up to?

Pranav spoke to the intruder tied to the chair, "What is this friend of yours up to?"

The frantic sounds coming from the kitchen ended with a loud thud. While Shipra curled up in one corner of the bed, Pranav limped to the dining table, took up a metal chair and rammed it repeatedly against the kitchen door. Finally, the latch fell off and the door flung open.

Pranav's heart stopped beating at the sight that awaited him on the other side. The intruder's associate had hanged himself from the ceiling fan hook using a rope from the work area attached to the kitchen.

Aghast, Pranav limped back to his wife.

"What happened?" asked Shipra trembling like a leaf in the wind.

Pranav was paralysed by fear. "That man just hanged himself." His voice shook.

Shipra's face turned a ghastly pale and her body trembled. The intruder tied to the chair started to get violent; gagged, he emitted stifled shrieks of desperation.

The couple looked at each other's face and wondered what to do next. Shipra took out the miniature copy of the *Shiv Puran* from her bag, closed her eyes and started to pray. Petrified by the events around him, Pranav tried to calm his wife. "Don't worry, my dear! All we need to do is get through this night."

"I don't think so Pranav. We will not get out of this alive." Drops of tears dropped one after the other down her cheek.

"I am sorry that I put you through all this. I am so sorry, Shipra."

At three am, the Saint Francis gong rang again.

Pranav, Shipra and the intruder looked at one another's faces suspiciously, wondering who would be next. Three lives stuck in a situation from which there seemed to be no escape.

Slowly, as Pranav and Shipra watched, the man's eyes turned red and he started foaming at the mouth. The chair jerked violently and his body jerked as though he was being electrocuted.

After twenty minutes of shaking vigorously, the intruder became calm again.

Pranav and Shipra prayed for some miracle to save them from the madness.

"I have a lot of questions and this man has the answers," said Pranav.

"No please, don't do that Pranav."

"Shipra! We need to know what is going on. Otherwise we will not get out of this alive."

He stepped forward and removed the man's gag.

"Why did your friend hang himself?" asked Pranav.

"*Haraamkhor!* You let me go or face consequences, you bastard. My elder brother is a famous gangster in these parts. I am sure he is looking around for me right now. If he finds you, God save you both!" the intruder growled in Hindi with a strong south-Indian accent.

"Answer my question, low-life! Why did your friend hang himself?"

The intruder remained silent.

"Go to hell!"

"Alright my friend. I don't think we have a conversation going between us. So I am going to gag you again," said Pranav.

"Wait a moment. Wait! Why did my friend hang himself? Isn't it evident, you brainless dog? "

Pranav stared at his face as he waited for an answer. The intruder's throat was dry.

Pranav took a bottle of water and poured it down his throat.

"So, we were talking about your friend."

"This godforsaken dreadful place drove him to end his life. Killed poor Fahad. Don't you get it? She is here between us and she will not stop until we all are dead."

To Shipra it appeared that this grown up man was on the verge of breaking down and sobbing.

"Don't speak in riddles. Who the hell is between us?" Pranav was also jittery.

"*Let me go!*" he yelled.

"I am not letting you go. You first tell me what is going on or I swear to God that I will leave you here stranded for the night!" said Pranav, his own throat dry.

"Okay! Catherine! Cathy! She is here between us, the one who smells of jasmine. Doing her dance of death as we speak. Run away if you want to live and let me also go. *Cathy of the Portuguese Mansion is after our lives*."

His eyes darted from one direction to another as he looked around in fear with the knowledge that he was trapped.

"I don't follow you. Tell the whole thing properly or I will gag you again and slash your face goddammit," said Pranav, pointing his knife at the intruder.

The intruder laughed nervously. "Alright! You want to listen to the legend. Then I will tell you all I have heard about it. Cathy's dark energy haunts this area. Once it gets into you, it finds out the darkest corner of your mind. Then it amplifies the dark thoughts till its spirals out of control."

"I did not get it."

"Anger into uncontrolled rage. Depression into suicidal tendency. Adventurousness into recklessness. Jealousy into the desire to kill the opponent. That's what Cathy does to you. She dwells inside the filth of one's mind and makes you do crazy things. Understood? *Now let me go, for God's sake.*"

Pranav gagged the intruder again with trembling hands.

Shipra was paralysed with fear. The intruder had mentioned a well-known incident, a story the people in these parts knew well.

The year was 1978. The first time Sarvanpur was splashed across newspapers and tabloids across the country. The famous case of Vasco Road. Born to a wealthy Anglo-Indian cashew plantation owner, Catherine had a childhood that was straight out of a fairytale. Loved by her doting parents she had only one rare deformity. She was born with one extra thumb on both her hands. Catherine, or Cathy as she was lovingly called, was her parents' centre of attention and affection. Catherine's father built the Portuguese Mansion in 1974, named so because of the architecture and because his own mother belonged to Portugal. His cousin had sold a large plot of land to Cathy's father. To fund this deal her father mortgaged all his land to the Indudurg Cooperative Bank. Later he figured out that the land had a dubious title of ownership and that many documents were forged. In rage, her father killed his own cousin in a property dispute outside his farm. He spent his days at Sarvanpur Central Jail until the Supreme Court upheld the order of the High Court and sentenced him to death. He was hanged. A few years later, plagued by loneliness, Catherine's mother married her second cousin, an army man who had two boys from a previous marriage. They all came along to stay in the Portuguese Mansion with the mother and daughter. Catherine's mother had issues with epilepsy and in the later years she was bedridden. For years Catherine was mistreated, physically abused and sexually molested by both her drunken stepfather and his teenage sons. Her only relief were the library books she used to get from the public library. These books took her on a flight of imagination to strange worlds. The author who particularly impressed young Cathy was Helena Blavatsky. On multiple occasions she had issued the two volumes of her book *Isis Unveiled* and the three volumes of her book *The Secret Doctrine* from the public library without her stepfather's knowledge. She was also impressed to know that Blavatsky's Theosophical Society had moved its headquarters from New York to India in 1878. Over a period of time she drifted away from the more positive philosophical domains to darker ones. She experimented by summoning spirits like her dead father with an OUIJA board and animal sacrifices for appeasement of dark forces. When she turned 17, during her weekly trips to the local public library, she fell in love with a Hindu boy who worked as an assistant to the librarian. When her stepfather came to know of it he turned furious, beat her up and locked her in her room for 12 days, after which he made her take an oath on her mother's name that she would never meet the boy again in her life.

This time Cathy lost her mind. On New Year's eve, as her stepfather and his sons lay dead drunk at the stroke of midnight, Catherine dressed up in her favourite dress, sprayed jasmine perfume, wore her favourite watch and some jewellery. She went to her mother's room to bid goodbye to her bedridden mother for one last time.

Then she barged into the party of the drunken trio and hacked her stepfather and his sons with a meat chopper. From 12 in the midnight till four in the morning she sat with the three dead corpses around her hurling abuses, cursing their corpses and stabbing them again at the stroke of every hour. Once she had vented her anger fully, she wrote a chilling note. In the note she confessed her responsibility for the crime and ended it with a wish for a second chance to live life afresh where time was not wasted on gods and faith. Then she walked into the woods.

On that cold morning, at half past four, she threw her bangles, earrings, rings and watch into the wilderness, and eventually ended her life by jumping off the cliff into the rocky patch below.

Shipra and Pranav had previously heard the legend of Cathy of the Portuguese Mansion. Considering the madness that was going around them since midnight, Shipra and Pranav knew that the entire locality was cursed. Maybe there was something inside the house that was cursed.

"I think we should not think about anything and just escape from this godforsaken place," suggested Shipra.

"Shipra, it is going to be four am and it is pitch dark outside. I cannot walk up that slope. Look at the swelling."

"Even I cannot climb the slope. I guess we have no other option. Even if it means crawling out of here on our all fours, I guess we will need to do that to save our lives." She walked to the bedroom, jerked the curtain violently to break the rivets and returned with a curtain rod.

"I think you can use this as support on your way up the slope. Let's take the torch and go. Please!"

Pranav took out their torch from the luggage and looked at the man tied to the chair. Looking at him struggling to break free and making muffled noises, Pranav wondered what to do.

Shipra asked, "Should we set him free?"

"Are you out of our mind? You see the vengeance in his eyes. Like he had said, he will cut us into tiny pieces in an instant. Let's leave him here and ask the cops to come and arrest him tomorrow morning," said Pranav.

"I am scared Pranav. He said his brother was some big gangster in this area," Shipra was in tears. Her knees trembled under her night dress.

"Shipra! Let's get out of this night alive. We will face whatever devils or gangsters come after us once this is over. Let's go!"

As the couple opened the main door and ventured out into the dark night, the man tied to the chair began to jerk violently.

It was difficult for Shipra and Pranav to walk but they had no other option. Their torch illuminated the path in front of them for only a few feet. Pranav held the torch with one hand while with the other he held the curtain rod as support. Shipra walked behind him carrying the leather bag with the money and the Swiss Makers watch inside it. At 4 am in the morning, the bell rang again. The couple started to walk faster.

Pranav stopped suddenly. Behind him, Shipra stood rooted to the spot. He had turned towards her; his face was ghastly, cold and expressionless.

Next evening papers at Sarvanpur described the gruesome murder that had taken place in an isolated Villa on Vasco Road. A man named Pranav Dhul was arrested from the premises. He was in a mentally unstable condition when captured by the police. A dead body was found hanging by a rope in the kitchen. The deceased was identified as a small-time crook Fahad. Another charred dead body was recovered tied to a chair from the hall of the villa apparently set on flames by Pranav. This victim was a serial offender called Anil Shetty, originally from Mangalore. His fugitive brother, an ace sharpshooter Roshan Shetty, was a top wanted man pursued by the Karnataka and Maharashtra police. Pranav's pregnant wife was found unconscious in the woods with a head injury caused by a curtain rod. She was in a state of extreme shock.

While Pranav was in jail, Shipra remained in a state of mental instability throughout her pregnancy. She stopped speaking and was insanely absent-minded.

On 9th February, she gave birth to a girl child at the Sarvanpur Government Hospital. Born premature, she had strange features and an extra thumb on either hand. The infant's mother was petrified when she saw the baby and even refused to breastfeed the child after which Shipra sank further into depression and eventually ended her life by jumping off the third floor of the hospital building. In the absence of any family members or immediate relatives coming forward to claim the girl child, the infant was placed in the Government Shelter for Girls. Her father refused to meet his daughter in prison throughout his tenure. This was after he saw her just once in the Shelter warden's arms through the grill in the Mulakat room. His eyes transfixed all along on the infant's extra thumbs during that brief meeting. At the Government Shelter, the warden gave the baby a name she thought sounded cute. Mehek.

# Devika's Book

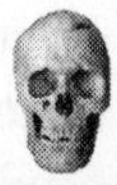

The stitches on her head still hurt, but not as much as the initial days. She hated the place but she had to hold on for some more hours. There were two rows of eight beds each on either side of the room, all occupied by children of her age. This was the children's section of the Sushrut Cancer Care Centre.

She took out a hand mirror from her mother's bag and looked at her face. Something she had done umpteen times, every morning since the surgical procedure. One side of her hair above the left ear was shaved off. This is where they had done the surgery. The bandage hiding the stitches which had not fully healed. Her mother had gone to the hospital cafeteria for her breakfast, leaving little Katie in her bed with her Barbie.

At the far end of the corridor Katie saw a doctor talking to a woman in a blue cotton sari with an infant in her arms. The lady looked familiar. The vibrant smile, the bright eyes and the strange choice of colours for dresses.

A sudden internal urge made Katie get up from her bed and walk across the rows of beds. Most of the other children in the ward were still asleep. Katie stood near the door listening to the conversation between the doctor and the woman she thought she knew.

"Devika, nothing to worry. It was just that your father's sugar level was abnormally low. His organs, pancreas and liver have started functioning slightly better now, so I think you can stop the insulin injections and take Amaryl tablets. Let him take some rest here till afternoon and we can start the discharge procedure," the doctor said.

"Dr Makhija! I was so worried. His general health was steadily improving. Me and Shravan along with the baby were out for a temple visit in the morning when this happened. It was my servant's daughter Laali who found him in the cold unresponsive state when she came in with the morning tea. She called the ambulance and along with her father admitted him to the hospital in nick of time. If it were not for her presence of mind and quick action, god knows what would have happened," said the woman called Devika.

Dr Makhija smiled. "He is doing well. Trust me! I had initially told that he had only a couple of months to live. Now it looks like he can pull on for a year at least if the cancerous growth does not spread."

The doctor looked carefully across the glass partition towards the other side and said, "I like his positive spirit, Devika. He is on a hospital bed but look at him reading a book with a smile on his face."

"He is reading a book written by me, Doctor. We had a weird bet, actually kind of embarrassing to mention. He challenged me that he would be able to find at least twenty-five mistakes in the book. This is his second reading and he has had only limited success."

"I did not know you write. Good to pursue what you like doing." The doctor looked at his watch, "I will see you in the afternoon during my rounds." Just before leaving the doctor looked at the infant in Devika's arms and asked, "What have you named your daughter?"

"Vaishnavi."

"Nice name. Vaishnavi!"

The doctor and Devika noticed the little girl looking at them from the adjacent room and smiled at her.

"Little Katie here had a tumour removed from her brain. The good news is that it was benign. So she will walk out of here like a brave girl and go to school like nothing happened. Isn't it, Katie?" Dr Makhija extended a hand towards Katie as he spoke.

Devika exclaimed, "Thank God! She has her whole life ahead of her. Children her age having cancer is depressing beyond words."

She stepped forward and touched Katie's cheek with her fingertips.

"How are you today, little Katie?"

Katie did not reply.

"Katie, sweetie pie, you should be in your bed; your mother will be looking out for you my dear," said the doctor.

Katie's eyes darted back-n-forth between the doctor and Devika. Her mouth slightly open as she looked dazed. Then, Katie turned and walked back to her bed rather reluctantly just as her mother Cynthia entered the ward with a glass of orange juice. Cynthia made her daughter drink the orange juice and said, "The discharge paperwork is over. We will now go to meet Papa and from there we will go home where Grandma is waiting for us."

Cynthia picked up the bag which she had packed overnight; Katie followed her, quietly.

Outside the hospital, Katie walked behind her mother to the parking lot where their car was parked. Cynthia drove the car to MG Road. They passed through a narrow road with shops on both sides. A six feet standee in front of the bookstore caught Cynthia's attention and she abruptly turned the car and parked it in front of the bookstore.

The display, promotional material and poster were advertisement for the new book, *The Dead Woman's Diary* by Devika Soni.

Cynthia asked Katie to be seated in the car while she went to the bookstore and bought a copy.

Once inside the car she quickly flipped through the pages, muttering all the while, "I hope this female has written something positive about Carlton."

She read some paragraphs, then turned the pages frantically, read again, then looked at the watch and started the car again.

They drove through Mohammed Rafi road, to a road leading to Puranwad. There was fallow land on both sides of the road along this stretch. After a long drive, they finally stopped in a vacant lot in front of Sarvanpur Central Jail.

Their lawyer was waiting at the gate for them. The mother and daughter entered the main gate along with their lawyer; after two rounds of security checks, they were at the line in front of the entry desk from where they were led towards the Mulakat room after another round of security check. In the dark cubicle with the double mesh wiring on the other side, they waited for Carlton to appear. Visibility was low across the mesh wiring and it was dark and dingy.

Carlton came in, clad in his prison clothes, a scar prominent along his neck. His eyes gleamed with happiness when he saw his wife and daughter.

"Katie, say hello to Papa," said Cynthia.

Katie came and stood next to her mother; she neither smiled nor spoke.

"What did the biopsy results say?" asked Carlton.

"All clear! The tumour was benign. Praise the lord!" said Cynthia.

"My prayers were heard, Cynthia! By the way, tell the advocate to come and meet me two days before the next hearing on 25th. He put up a pretty bad show last time. I will end up spending a long time in prison if it goes on like this. Two days back an inmate called Pranav, who had spent the longest sentence in this prison, was released. Everyone here was so happy for him. As I saw him take his belongings and papers to walk out of the gates of the jail, I wondered when my day would come."

Katie stared fixedly at Carlton. Even during the past many visits, her look would make Carlton feel uncomfortable.

"Your friend, Devika Soni, her book about the cult is out. I bought a copy on the way." Cynthia showed him the book.

"She had assured me that she would portray me in good light. Why can't people understand that my killing Mehek was in a state of momentary rage? Any father who had lost a child would lose his mind."

"Yes. I flipped through the pages; she has written along the same lines. Devika states that in rage you probably wanted to assault Mehek but her fall from the first floor was accidental."

"I am glad she wrote that. We met around five times here in the Mulakat room for the interviews. I have great respect for her and we became good friends. God bless her!"

Cynthia abruptly said, "I forgot to tell you. The sale of the hospital complex is over. As you had told, I am putting some of the money aside for day-to-day and legal expenses. Rest of it, I plan to invest by buying a shop on Mohammed Rafi Road, a small plot of land near Old Church road and a mansion on Vasco Road."

"Cynthia! Which mansion did you say you've bought?"

"Portuguese Mansion. After the old lady who owned it died, it was taken over by a creditor. We looked at many mansions and villas but Katie was adamant that we buy this one," said Cynthia.

"She is our princess. We should make her happy." Carlton dropped his voice. "Have you noticed how quiet and cold she has become of late?"

"Carlton! Your going to prison was a shock for her. It could also be because of the surgery. Brain surgery and medication can lead to behavioural changes. It's temporary, I'm sure. She has written a poem for you, read it."

Katie looked at Carlton, took out a piece of paper from her pocket and started to read in an impassive manner.

"Papa you are the best
We love you and we miss you
Come back to our life
For us boats in a stormy sea
You are like a lighthouse."

The last two lines made Carlton's eyes narrow. Strange words for her age. He had heard these lines somewhere before, but he could not remember where.

As his family left, Carlton looked at his daughter's piercing eyes. The bandaged scar above her left ear was exactly the same spot which Mehek had hurt on the staircase railing. Little Katie was there when Mehek crashed to her death.

She was different ever since that fateful night, complaining regularly of headaches till she collapsed one day and a CT scan revealed the growth in her brain. Carlton remembered the dreaded date, it was 25th April, a day before Carlton's birthday.

Later, Cynthia drove little Katie to their house on Old Church Road where she was welcomed by the little girl's grandma Rachel.

"I have to get up early tomorrow and clean up the house," Cynthia told Rachel after dinner that night.

"Why is that, mother?" interrupted Katie.

"Katie dear, tomorrow your Uncle Stephen, along with your cousins John and Joseph, will be here to spend their vacation with us."

Katie knew her mother's second cousin. He lived in Pune with his two children after his wife passed away two years ago. Stephen had supported Cynthia through all the turbulent times she had recently faced.

"Why can't they stay in their own house? Why are they coming here?" Katie asked.

"You should not speak like that, little one. It's very rude of you to do that!" Rachel intervened.

"I don't like people visiting us and bothering us like this," said Katie.

Cynthia looked at Katie and then Rachel with a puzzled expression on her face. They kept quiet. She had always been a different child, oscillating between moods of extreme joy and bitterness. The past few months had been worse. They had recently agreed to ignore Katie's sudden bursts of anger since she had been unwell.

After putting Katie to bed, Cynthia and Rachel retired to their own rooms. When the clock struck eleven in the dead of the night, Katie got up from her bed as if triggered by something inside her. She switched on the light and opened her wardrobe drawer, took out the gloves her father had bought for her during their Shimla trip, went to the hall, and switched on the computer.

She opened a notepad file saved on the desktop and clicked 'Print'.

> Devika Soni
> *Konkan Times*
> Sarvanpur – 01

She took the sheet, went to the bedroom and wore her gloves. She took out her paper crafts toolkit, glue, scissors and coloured paper. Among them there were specific pages cut out of the *Konkan Times* that she had kept below her bed. On the top of the pile was a newspaper with the headline, 'Sarvanpur's narcotics kingpin Timur nabbed near Indo-Nepal border after evading arrest for over 6 months'. There were stamps she had got from her father's cupboard which had among other things legal documents, stamp papers, seals, stamp pad, revenue stamps and postage stamps. Then she took out one of the fifteen bright red envelopes she had stolen from her mother's stationery and glued the address and stamp to the envelope.

She cut out random words from the pages of the *Konkan Times* and placed her letter along with two newspaper articles into the envelope.

Dear DeViKa,

Our paths diverge from here. My objectives accomplished. Sending something with this Letter. As you can See MANkind is moving towards no faith. We have a sizeable audience now. Maybe you disagree but I smell Victory.

- MEHEK

The first newspaper was a recent article published in 'The Times of India' supplement titled 'Rise of Occult'. The article states how popular musicians, artists, models and politicians around the world were believed by conspiracy theories to be believers of occult. Recently they have been bold enough to flash occult symbols like the Eye of Horus, Inverted Diamond, Horns of Satan and Baphomet in public. The second newspaper article was an older one.

Times Global, 27th May 2013
International News

## 'More and More Indians have stopped believing in God'

LONDON - *The latest Global Index of Religiosity and Atheism has found that the number of non-believers has taken a sharp upswing around the world. Atheism has risen by 3% with China (47%), Japan (31%), Czech republic (30%), France (29%) and Germany (15%) leading the survey in percentage of the population of convinced atheists. In India, the number of god-believers has reduced by 6% between 2005 and 2013.*

Katie glued the envelope close and put it inside her school bag. When she would resume school, she would post the letter in the letter box near her school bus stop opposite the Indudurg cooperative bank. Sometimes she dropped it in the letterbox near her swimming class in the club at Annie Besant Road opposite the police checkpost.

She walked across to the window and gazed into the star studded night. The night was beautiful, so silent, tranquil. Darkness was indeed the default state of the universe.

Little Katie remembered something.

She went to the hall and picked up the book from her mother's handbag. She looked at the cover.

*The Dead Woman's Diary* by Devika Soni.

The book started with a passage from the Bible describing a woman of low morals, a wild beast with many heads that she rode, her relationship with very powerful people and that she drank the blood of saints and martyrs of Jesus. The passage ended with the angel promising to reveal the full story of the evil woman and the beast who was her accomplice.

Katie flipped the pages and saw that one of the pages had the photograph of the Portuguese Mansion.

She smiled. After 34 long years it would be her home once again, her most coveted destination.

The movers and packers had been asked to start shifting their things after 25 days. Katie had selected her own room in the Portuguese Mansion, the room which used to be Cathy's bedroom. The room with a view of the trees and greenery and with a view to Mehek's final resting place prepared by Ujjwal. A room from where she could see the sun setting far away while a shadow was cast over the rock cliff from where Cathy had jumped to her death. Memories of the past and of sacrifices made.

That February night when she stood at the entrance to her father's hospital and saw a woman clad in nurse's uniform fall to her death, something inside little Katie changed forever. It was accidental, unintended and yet miraculous. Ancient religious texts speak of the soul being indestructible. The dark energies had accidentally achieved the same kind of invincibility. Cathy, Mehek, Katie. Nobody could destroy her, she was not a mortal. She would exist forever and follow her mission to enlighten the misguided world.

Katie flipped to the very last page of the book and started to read.

> *Some questions still remain. Is Mehek linked to Cathy in some strange mysterious way? Are their stories connected in a way which we don't understand? Is there a concealed world out there which we cannot see but has accidentally revealed itself to us in this one instance? These questions still seek answers, answers that may never come. There have been decade-old debates surrounding the elusive creatures inside the Loch Ness Lake or the strange Yetis of the Himalayas or the elusive Roland Doe and Taos Hum or even the Bermuda triangle. Elsewhere, cosmologists are constantly figuring out that basic laws and constants in the universe are so accurately optimum and highly precise that it looks extremely impossible that the universe or life could have been created just by chance. So is there an almighty creator or the universe was created by a highly unlikely string of coincidences? We don't know. The truth is, we don't even fully understand why some tissue in our human body starts behaving erratically, multiplying and destroying the same body in which it is growing. We should acknowledge that we don't have answers to all our questions. This world is a partially deciphered maze; we will never fully understand everything around and inside us. Let's leave it at that.*

*This episode in our small town gives us an idea of the turbulent times in which we live, of an era where one rotten mind, if coupled with communication skills and charisma, can contaminate thousands of others in a moment using technology-driven social networking. Like cancer it can spread quickly without a warning. The riots in Mumbai's Azad Maidan triggered by morphed photographs in the social media are chilling reminders of the fragile world in which we live. When religions, sects or nations clash nobody wins except for darkness. Darkness is indeed winning all around us. The shift towards greed, hate for others, hedonism and lack of emotions is remarkable in our generation. If this is the future, then we need to be worried. If more people adopt this, there is no hope. We are in an over-crowded world with very limited resources. Hate propagating all around us from one body to another, like a ghostly dark spirit. In the near future we face imminent struggles and conflicts. Each and every one of us will face a moral crisis sooner or later. A choice between wearing the Angel's mask or the Devil's mask. At the end of the day it will still be a mask, because the real human being is neither. Mankind's situation today can be better understood in Plato's words when he said – 'We can easily forgive a child who is afraid of the dark; the real tragedy of life is when grownup men are afraid of light'. We can see it all around us. The real tragedy of the world today is that grownup people around the globe are indeed afraid of light.*

Katie laughed hysterically. Wasn't the answer obvious?

"Let's see which direction mankind will go from here on. Be assured, to balance everything, the dark will always be around. This is not the end of the story of darkness, there is always more to come," she murmured to herself. She went to bed and it turned out to be a long dark night.